All the Broken Pieces

SANDY SINGER

WestBow Press books may be ordered through booksellers or by contacting:

WestBow Press
A Division of Thomas Nelson & Zondervan
1663 Liberty Drive
Bloomington, IN 47403
www.westbowpress.com
1 (866) 928-1240

ISBN: 978-1-5127-1472-2 (sc)
ISBN: 978-1-5127-1473-9 (hc)
ISBN: 978-1-5127-1471-5 (e)

Library of Congress Control Number: 2015916275

Print information available on the last page.

WestBow Press rev. date: 10/21/2015

Dedication

To Pete The Love of My Life

Forty-six years. Can you believe it? That's how long ago we said *I do*. We had no idea what our vows meant back then. We thought we understood love. How foolish and young we were.

But God has brought us to today. He has taught us. He has carried us through some difficult days. Along the way, I've felt our love grow deeper and wider. You are a godly man, Pete, filled with Jesus, his unconditional love, his faithfulness, and willingness to sacrifice for others.

Thank you for all you have done to encourage my love of writing. Without you, *All the Broken Pieces* would be nothing more than ideas floating around in my mind. You are my hero and the most gifted love letter author in all the world.

I love you all the way to eternity.

Of all the women on the face of the earth, I am among the most blessed because I am married to you.

To our children Tia and Peter and Our Amazing Daughter-in-Law, Chris

How fast the time has flown by. How can it be that you have children of your own, some who have already left the family nest?

I am so proud of the adults you are. You are loyal and strong. You are models of courage and sacrificial love, people who follow your dreams, even when it would be so much easier to turn your back on them.

I am among the most blessed of all women because you are my children.

To our Grandchildren—the Crowns of our lives—Joel, Andrew, Nathan, Jeremiah, Cassie, Sarah, and Emily

You have filled our lives with more joy than I thought was possible. Grandpa and I carry you in our hearts every hour of every day. We love you. We pray for you. We are proud of the people you are.

I am among the most blessed of all women because you are my grandchildren.

To the Unnamed Woman Who First Inspired This Book

It's been over thirty years since we met. You sat on your sofa in a dark living room, too burdened by the guilt inside you to make eye contact. You nodded in belief and agreement when I shared the message of salvation with you that evening. You believed it for everyone. Everyone but yourself. You told me your sin was too big, too disgraceful to be covered by Christ's death on the cross. Nothing could change your mind.

More than anything, I want you to know that Jesus loves you. He died for you. He stands ready to forgive and accept you as His own precious child.

This book is for you and all the other sin-burdened women. I pray as you read *All the Broken Pieces,* Grace's story will grip your heart. I pray you will receive Jesus and know he stands ready to forgive and give you the gift of abundant and eternal life.

To the Family of Chelsea Hanks

Chelsea Hanks made an amazing impact on the lives of so many. She was a woman of incredible faith and grace. Her deepest longing was for God's will, not her own. The astonishing words in Beth's letter—*If God takes me away, he has a better wife for my husband and a better mommy for my children*—are words Chelsea Hanks spoke shortly before she left this world.

I am among the most blessed of women because she was my friend.

To My Teachers and Writing Mentors

Mrs. Mc Naughton, my second grade teacher, who encouraged me, opened my eyes to the power and joy of words, and prayed for me. Never underestimate the power of a godly teacher.

Thanks to Jerry Jenkins' vision and dedication to train new authors, I was given the key to unlock my dream. Jerry B. Jenkins' Christian Writers' Guild, Sandra Byrd, John Perrodin, James Scott Bell, McNair Wilson, Dennis Hensley, Karen Kingsbury, Liz Curtis Higgs, and many more, including my fellow Craftsmen, sharpened my writing skills. This story would have never made it to paper without your wisdom and dedication to helping new authors.

To each member of All the Broken Pieces Prayer Team

Angela, Cassie, Chris, Connie, Dessa, Diane, Ellen, Gina, Ines, Joyce, Kellianne, Kelsey, Kristina, Laura, Marilyn, Nicki, Patti, Patty, Sammy, Sandy, Sarah, Shannon, Tia, Wendy—women whose prayers are more powerful than an entire library of books. Thank you for committing to pray for the readers of All the Broken Pieces. Because of your prayers, they are among the most blessed of all readers.

To My Lord and Savior Jesus Christ

Most of all, to my Lord and Savior Jesus Christ who forgave my sins and made me His own daughter. Without you, my life would be empty. In you, my life is full. Without You I wouldn't be able to fully forgive, love, and live in hope. In you, I am fully forgiven, loved, and filled with the hope of eternity.

I am among the most blessed of women because I am your daughter.

CHAPTER 1

Grace Will scooted to the middle of the taxi's back seat. If she pinched herself, would she wake up with no wedding ring? Would there be no Adam? No Kate or Sammy?

"Tesoro," Adam said as he took his place close to her. "Almost to the end of the island."

For a moment she considered giving Adam more room. What if he could feel her uneasiness? *Please, God,* she prayed. *I don't want to...* But before she could finish her plea, Adam covered her hand with his, causing almost every doubt to drift away.

The driver stretched the seatbelt over his belly and inched the taxi forward, merging into the flow of pastel resort vans. "About an hour to the bridge." The driver craned his neck, using the rearview mirror to glance into the backseat. His bloated face dripped in the Florida heat. "Honeymoon? Don't get so many honeymooners this time of year."

"Honeymoon's over." Adam stroked his thumb along the side of her hand. "We're heading home."

Heading home. She wanted to soak in his words. Tesoro was known as an island of escape, a postcard-perfect paradise of narrow palm-lined roads leading to soft sand beaches. Most people had a week, maybe two, before they headed back over the bridge, and home to real life.

But starting today, this was her real life. Tesoro, Adam, his daughters, Kate and Sammy. Life was going to be perfect.

More perfect than she deserved.

Since the day she met Adam, she'd filled her journals with each particular—how he liked his coffee strong and black and the creases in his slacks stiff enough to last an entire day. She'd drained more than one pen dry describing the amazing father he was—his down-on-the-floor tickle fights with Kate and Sammy, and how the tip of his chin always quivered when he listened to their bedtime prayers. She loved the way Adam mixed his southern drawl with her Minnesota jargon, a smile filling his voice whenever he said *uff-da* or *you betcha*, words he claimed he'd never heard before meeting her. *Uff-da, y'all can't be heading home, not when I'm fixin' to put on a pot of coffee.*

She especially loved the way Adam was always fixin' to do one thing or another.

Adam released her hand and reached for his phone. "I'll be quick," he promised.

Another particular, one she learned early, was that no matter where he was or what he was doing, a piece of Adam always stayed with his business. Even on their honeymoon, he'd look at her with his apologetic blue eyes. *"Just a quick call,"* he'd say before sitting at the desk with his planner and phone. He'd spend the next ten, sometimes thirty minutes, solving a problem with a building inspector, motivating a discouraged foreman, whatever it would take to keep construction on schedule.

It wasn't until the driver turned onto the toll bridge connecting Tesoro to the mainland that Adam finished his call. At first she thought his mind was still on work, but when he cupped her chin, turning her face toward his, there wasn't an inch of her body that didn't respond. "Sorry." His eyes appealed for understanding. "It's just that the guys—"

"Uff-da." She rested her head on his shoulder. "Sometimes I'm afraid your guys might be more important than your wife."

"Can't be." Adam wrapped a piece of her ponytail around his finger. "Not one of them has red hair."

They were on the island now, closer to home, closer to her new life. She couldn't wait to take on every responsibility, not just as Adam's wife, but as Kate and Sammy's mommy. She closed her eyes, willing her mind to silent every gnawing uncertainty. *Lord, show me how to build a new life surrounded by so many memories.*

Adam must have sensed her angst, because he kissed the top of her head. "Have I told you how much I love everything about you?"

Once again, his words pushed her doubts away. "What about my freckles?"

He touched the tip of her nose. "I'd travel around the world just to get a glimpse."

The road curved closer to the Gulf, so close she could smell the waves. They'd spent their honeymoon in the mountains where the air was crisp and light; but this was the air she loved—salty and often smelling like a grungy fish market. It didn't matter, not to her.

The taxi whizzed past ocean-front estates, pastel mansions peeking out from behind clumps of sea grapes and landscaped palms. Adam's home was different. Though it sat gulf-front, it was more like a cottage, a two-story whitewashed house with weathered verandas, windows as tall as the ceilings, and sunsets more beautiful than any place on earth.

"Adam," She traced the creases in his slacks. "I want you to know—"

"Let me guess." He brushed her cheek with the back of his hand. "You want me to know you love me." He took hold of her earring, giving it a gentle pull. "Don't go worrying. I kind of figured it out already."

"It's just…all of a sudden I have a family." She weaved her fingers between his. "It's almost too huge to be true."

"What's all this?" For the first time, his hand felt weighty on hers. "We already are a family, all four of us."

Adam was right, and by the time they rounded the corner where pink bougainvillea blossoms seemed to rise from the middle of the road, her heart was back where it should be. She closed her eyes, readying herself for the kiss she felt certain was perched on the edge of Adam's lips.

Instead, the taxi jolted to a stop. "You trying to kill someone," the driver yelled as he slammed the steering wheel. The car ahead of them sat half in the turning lane, half in their lane, waiting to turn into a beachfront parking space. "Forget how to use your turning signal?"

Adam squeezed her hand. "Are you okay?" She told him yes, but before she could ask about him, Adam drew her attention toward the parking lot. "Should have thought of flowers." She followed his point to a florist delivery van.

The island's service people frequently met in the shade of the roadside palms where they read the island paper and exchanged names of islanders looking to hire extra help. Flowers didn't matter. Everything was just as it should be.

Until she looked closer.

Without thinking, she grabbed Adam's arm. Derrick Dunn. It looked just like him, sitting right there behind the wheel of the flower van.

No, God. No. The words sprang from her heart, and she was amazed she was able to keep herself from screaming. *Not now. I haven't had time.* Without a blink, the Derrick man nodded and smiled, almost as if he was expecting her. Her face burned. She did her best to capture her fear. Even if it was him, what could he do to her? *Nothing*, she promised herself. *Nothing at all, not anymore.*

When the taxi inched forward, she wanted to look back. Maybe he was following them. She'd heard he'd moved away. If it actually was Derrick, had he come back just so he could tell Adam everything she should have told him months ago? Her mouth dried up and she could feel her skin dripping and shivering under her cotton sundress. She closed her eyes and tightened her grip on Adam's wrist until he pulled away.

"What?" he said. "You look like you've seen—"

"Nothing." She felt the inside of her throat tremble as she struggled to push out the lie. "Really nothing."

CHAPTER 2

Grace pressed her palm against her chest, trying to quiet the thumping of her crazy heart as she stood in the entrance of Adam's home. She was no longer a guest.

She was Adam's wife.

She imagined her hand in his as they walked up the stairs to his bedroom. When Kate and Sammy returned from their stay with Adam's parents they'd enjoy family times curled on the sofa with the girls scrunched between them, eating popcorn and watching silly movies.

On the backside of her imaginings, she heard the taxi crunch down the crushed shell drive, then Adam's footsteps, and just before his arms wrapped around her waist, she caught the aroma of wintergreen gum. "Even without flowers, I think I'm going to enjoy welcoming you home." He stood behind her, promising breakfast in bed, pushing away the power of Derrick's eyes.

Without leaving his arms, she turned to face him. "Let's walk on the beach first thing tomorrow."

"Before breakfast?" Adam took her hand and led her to the family room. Moments later she was dancing in his arms.

"Do you know your music is corny?" She rested her head on his chest. "I bet my dad would have traded his garage full of tools for just one of your albums."

"Smart man." He pulled her nearer, until his breath tickled her neck as he joined his voice with Sinatra's. "What are you doing the rest of your life?"

She'd heard the song a hundred times, but never like this. In front of doors that opened onto turquoise waves, she and Adam swayed in each other's arms, their legs touching, his chin resting on top of her head, assuring her that no matter what, the rest of her life was going to be glorious.

Adam pulled his fingers through her hair, lifting it off her neck, and letting it spill back into place. "I want to know all your plans," he said. She moved with him, deeper into his arms, deeper into her dream.

They might have danced forever if Adam's cell hadn't rung. As quickly as it started, the dance was over.

She spent the next half hour on the sofa, listening to music that was never meant to be enjoyed alone. When the music stopped, she waited in silence until she could wait no more. That's when she wrapped her hand around the knob on his office door. Maybe Adam wanted to be left alone; maybe he didn't. As quietly as she could, she opened the door.

To her relief, Adam waved her in. Seconds later she sat across the desk from him, listening as he tried to deal with a conversation that seemed out of control.

Adam massaged the side of his neck. "What do you mean they're demanding? Not the best time for me to go running off to Minnesota." Adam's forehead and cheeks grew red as he tapped the eraser tip of his pencil on his computer keys. "I don't give a horse's behind, Lane. I want y'all to understand; we don't challenge the city guys." She watched the sides of his neck bulge in ways she'd never seen before. "When they tell us to jump, we jump." He took a framed photo from its place on the corner of his desk. "You know, if I'm going to keep you guys working, we need the Stillwater contract. All of it." He released his pencil and let it roll to the edge of his desk before snatching it up. "I'm fixin' to… flight number?"

Grace leaned forward, folding her hands on the edge of his desk, willing Adam to remember she was there. But his eyes were duck-taped to the photo. She'd seen the picture before—the perfect family. In one arm, Adam held baby Sammy. With the other, he hugged cancer-bald Beth as Kate cuddled into her side.

For two weeks she hardly thought about Adam's first wife. But he had. At unexpected times, she'd sensed it and in those moments she was almost jealous, because she knew he was looking back at Beth and not ahead with her.

Adam returned the picture to his desk. Less than a minute later the call was over.

And that's when he told her he was leaving.

She couldn't believe Adam would do this. "When?" Not before the girls come home?"

"Tomorrow," he said. Even before the word sank in, he began dragging their luggage upstairs. "I'm sorry, Babe. I thought Stillwater was in my pocket."

Tears filled her throat as she followed him upstairs, so many that she felt like she might drown. She wanted to remind him about their unfinished dance and his promise to make breakfast and walk on the beach, but all she could say was, "You can't. This isn't fair."

"Hon, we'll talk about it after I shower. "Adam pulled his shirt over his head. "When things like this come up—I'm sorry—I don't get vacation."

"Vacation? Adam, it's our honeymoon."

Without turning to look at her, Adam closed the bathroom door. The next sound she heard was the shower.

She sat on the edge of the bed, her eyes fixed on the bathroom door. *Fair matters to me...promises do too.* Those were the words she wanted to say. But she was Adam's wife now. And so, like she suspected Beth would have done, she moved outside to the bedroom veranda, took a deep breath, and let the beauty of a perfect blue sky and the sound of lazy waves quiet her.

She was still standing there when Adam finished his shower. "I'm disappointed too." He stood next to her wrapped in a cotton robe, his blonde hair wet and smelling like a faraway forest. "You'll be fine. It's two days, three at the most." His hand cupped her chin, forcing her eyes to linger with his. "I'll be home before Mom and Dad bring the girls."

She followed Adam inside and sat on the bed while he pulled a pair of khaki slacks from a wooden hanger. Before he slipped his billfold into his pocket he removed a card. "I was fixin' to do this before our wedding," he said as he sat on the bed next to her. "Just didn't get to it. Give Island Interiors a call. Have them put together a bed, dressers, whatever you need."

"Uff-dah, Adam, this is fine. I don't need—"

"I'll leave the card here." He placed it on the corner of the nightstand. "Have them put a rush on it." He took her hand. "You're going to be okay."

"I know."

"Know something else?" His voice held a tease. "You never answered my question."

"Question?"

"What are your plans?"

"You're leaving. How could I have any plans?"

A smile raised the corners of Adam's mouth. "Plans for the rest of your life."

CHAPTER 3

Grace sat on the edge of the bed. It was their first night home, and she didn't know how long Adam would remain downstairs. The last time she checked he was in front of his computer. She pulled her journal from her unpacked bag, but before she could write more than two sentences, the floor behind her creaked.

"Still awake?" he said. "Why didn't you come down?"

Even when she felt the dip and sway of Adam moving into bed, she didn't turn toward him. "You were busy."

"I'm never too busy." He moved closer, until his chin rested on her shoulder. "What do you write in that planner of yours?"

"Journal." She did her best to make her voice sound firm, but the pleasure of his presence quickly worked its way into her voice. "I've told you a hundred times."

"Ninety-eight." He ran his finger along the edge of her pages. "I've been counting. When may I read it?"

"Never."

"Even if I tell you how sorry I am?"

She fought the impulse to turn toward him. "Trust me; it's boring."

"You could never be boring."

"I was, before I met you." She turned toward him. When she looked into his eyes she felt Adam didn't need a journal to know all there was to know about her.

"Then I deserve…" He reached for her book.

She couldn't let him read it. Not yet. She snapped it shut and tossed it on the floor, safely out of his reach. "Uff-dah. You've already discovered pretty much everything about me."

"Storms frighten you." He slid between the sheets. "What else?"

Her first thought was to tell Adam being alone frightened her more than anything, but that wouldn't be fair, so she simply shrugged her shoulders.

"How about those tiny lizards that hang around the house?"

Adam's eyes were like magnets. "Love them." She could feel the heaviness of the afternoon evaporate.

"Great, because Kate and Sammy are known to run through the house with the little things dangling from their ears, kind of like wiggly earrings. You should hear them, 'Daddy, Daddy,' expecting me to rescue them." He kissed her again. "I'm good at rescuing girls, ought to give me a try sometime."

Adam was right; there were many things he didn't know about her. He had no idea he'd already rescued her, no idea how his story about the girls calling his name fed the dream in her heart that one day Kate and Sammy would run through the house calling her name. Not Grace. They already called her that.

Mommy. The name she gave away.

She ran her thumb along the top of Adam's hand. "What frightens you?"

"Losing this," he said, reaching for his planner.

"No, something that would stop your heart, like...if I lost you, Adam…don't you know, I couldn't—"

"You could." Adam rolled onto his back, and for a split second she wondered if he actually felt it would be that easy to live without her.

Adam sat across the room watching Grace sleep. More than he could understand, that's how much he loved her.

He was still trying to figure out her nightmares. Once again, her cries had shaken him out of sleep. Of course he did his best to comfort her, wrapping her tremulous body in his arms and drying her tears with the corner of the sheet. As always, she refused to say what monster had terrified her. He hoped it wasn't because he was leaving in the morning. Even more, he hoped she didn't sense the thoughts that had been nagging him. Months ago, that's when he should have purchased a new bed, one without memories, and a dresser with drawers that didn't smell like Beth's powder.

It wasn't that he'd kept his love for Beth a secret, but he'd never told Grace about the sky-window. All Beth had to do was swing the window open, and she could hear every word—all Kate and Sammy's cute sayings and how he was keeping up with their prayers, just like he'd promised. She could see how Kate was still walking around in the old flip-flops her mommy once wore, and how Sammy loves feeding crusts of bread to sandpipers as they peck their way up and down the beach.

Truth was, since falling in love with Grace, the window that once gave comfort now supplied him with more guilt than he knew how to handle.

He dropped his head against the back of the chair and closed his eyes, massaging his temples. He could only pray that Grace knew nothing of his thoughts. Not a day went by that he didn't ask God why Beth had to die so young. His mind traveled back to that last week when it was clear Beth was not going to beat the cancer. That one week was baked into his soul. It was as if God wrapped her in a blanket of irrational peace. She stopped talking about how impossible it was for her to leave the girls. When she hugged them her arms didn't lock. Her eyes no longer clung to Kate and Sammy.

She was choosing to leave. And that made him angry.

Her words still resonated across his heart, "You're young and Kate and Sammy, they're just babies. They'll need a mommy." For some reason her frail whisper grew stronger those last few days. "Adam, I want you to let yourself fall in love again."

Of course, he argued, but two years later he did fall in love with Grace. Beautiful. Sweet. Grace.

He yanked his thoughts out of the past and landed them on his planner, open in his lap to the day that was just beginning. This little business trip was best for both of them. A few days away, and he'd come home a better man.

The type of man Grace deserved.

Chapter 4

Grace rested her head against the headboard. It was late, and all she could focus on was the one question that had been perking inside her head all day.

Was Adam's trip something more than business?

That morning, when they should have been celebrating with a walk on the beach, Adam walked out the door, his suitcase in one hand, tablet and planner in the other. She'd stood in the middle of the drive with a fake smile, waving, watching as he stopped to greet old Fisher Johnson who was carrying a sack of groceries home from the Island Mart.

All through the afternoon she hung onto the promise that he'd call as soon as his plane landed, but he didn't. Worse than that, he was in her home state and he hadn't even thought to invite her to join him.

He's not disappointed. The inside knowing weighed heavy. That's the way she'd always been; she had these whispers of knowing—or discernments, as her Mom had called them. Whatever they were, one thing was sure; her thoughts almost always worked their way into reality. *He's not disappointed, because tonight, instead of sleeping with me, he'll sleep in the arms of his memories.*

The memories pictured in the photo on his desk.

When at last the phone rang, she pressed it tight against her ear. She'd waited all day just to hear the sound of Adam's voice, but now all she heard was a tied-in-a-knot tone. She wasn't sure what disturbed her more, his voice or how long it had taken him to make the call.

"I'm glad I got a hold of you," he said.

"I've been here all day."

"I thought you might be out by the pool."

"It's been raining since early afternoon." She did her best to ignore the apprehension growing inside her. "Everything okay?"

"Look, I have a lot to do before I'm able to make it home." Adam's announcement broke into the tense tap of his pencil.

She wanted to ask him what he meant. Was this his way of telling her he'd be coming home later than promised? She pulled a pillow onto her lap and wrapped her arm around it, hoping the familiar aroma of Adam's shampoo would quiet her heart. All she wanted to do was hide between the sheets. But the bedding didn't even feel like it belonged to her. "Adam, you said—"

"Hon, don't do this. Being away from the job has caused some problems that I need to deal with."

"What about the girls?" She shucked the pillow to the other side of the bed. "You'll be home before your parents come with them, right?"

"I'll do my best to be home by Wednesday. That's all I can do," he said.

The call lasted only a few minutes more. Then, alone in the quiet of an empty house, she propped herself against a bundle of bed pillows and pointed the television remote.

"Rain ending sometime around midnight," the weatherman announced. "Sunshine tomorrow with highs in the..." As the announcer babbled on, Grace pulled the sheets to her chin.

It didn't take long before her mind was too tired to focus on the doubts of a day that had been much too drawn out and lonely. Within minutes her shoulders relaxed and she felt herself slowly give into sleep. She was almost there when the doorbell rang. She drew the sheets tight as an unexpected fist of fear thumped deep into her stomach. *Who knows I'm here...alone?*

When the bell rang a second time, she pulled her phone out from under the pillow and pressed Adam's number. But her call went straight to voicemail. "Adam, please." She tried her best not to sound frantic. "Someone's at the door. What should I do?" The phone trembled against her ear as she tiptoed to the bedroom door and locked it. If only Adam paid attention to his texts, then she wouldn't have to leave voice messages. She wouldn't feel this way if more people lived on the island during the summer. She leaned against the door, trying to convince herself that it was nothing more than a fisherman trying to sell his catch out of the back of his truck. Sure it was late, but most islanders didn't pay any more attention to clocks than they did to calendars.

As softly as she could, she made her way across the room to the doors that led out to the veranda. They were locked. How many people had keys? Adam's cleaning lady and pool people, they were probably just the beginning. Once again she pressed his number, and once again it went straight to voice mail. Why wasn't he returning her call? Why wasn't he home?

This wasn't the way it should be.

At last the doorbell went silent. *Gone,* she promised herself. She sat on the edge of the bed and gathered her hair onto the top of her head, allowing her neck to breathe until, out of the silence, the doorbell rang again. This time it was followed by pounding that seemed to shake the house.

For the first time since the racket began she realized the possibility that the pounding could be due to an emergency. She should have thought of it sooner. With all the rain, the roads had to be slick. The island had no street lights. What if someone needed help? She pulled her robe from the foot of the bed and, on legs that felt as flimsy as tissue, moved toward the bedroom door.

At first she couldn't take more than two steps into the hall. She leaned against the wall, trying to work up the courage she needed to go downstairs. As soon as her legs were strong enough, she moved to the banister, and stood there, looking down, waiting for the bell to ring again.

Two more rings. Three more fist-whacks.

Many more shadows.

"Who's there?" The rain pinged harsher on the metal roof. "Do you need me to call for help?"

She had no choice. Step-by-step, she edged her way down the stairs, until she stood face-to-face with the door. Her heart thrashed. "What do you need?"

It wasn't her imagination; she heard creaks, like someone tip-toeing across the porch's wood floor. She thought about making a run for the safe room. Instead, she flicked on the outside light and slowly, just wide enough to steal a peek, she opened the slats of the plantation shutter that covered the window closest to the door.

And that's when she saw the magnificent thing Adam had done.

The tip of a white rose peeked from its wrapping. At first she thought she'd leave the bouquet on the bench until morning. But she couldn't. White roses were her favorite. She wanted to smell the flowers, wanted to sleep with them next to her. She forced herself to turn the lock. It would only take a second, barely enough time to get wet.

What could happen in a second?

She tightened the knot on her robe and pushed herself outside, all the way to the bench. Bringing the bouquet close enough to rest the side of her face against the paper, she opened the package. What the roses didn't say, the paper they were wrapped in did. Adam hadn't settled for ordinary floral paper; he'd somehow managed to have her roses wrapped in week old newspaper. She stood under the porch light and read. *Gulf Shore Gossip*...Tenderly, she pulled the paper away from the bouquet. *In a private sunset celebration at Will's oceanfront home, island residents Adam Will and Grace Andrews tied the knot.*

For the first time since Adam said he was leaving, she felt the warmth of being treasured. The shadows, the rain, even Adam's sudden trip to Minnesota, none of those things mattered. Her roses were proof of God's promise, and that's why it made no difference that her robe was rain-soaked and clinging to her legs. God really was creating a new family. She played the promise over in her mind, looking ahead to the way it was going to be when Adam came home. Gently, she touched the delicate petals. Her insides throbbed, but not because of fear.

Because of love.

She didn't know what made her take her eyes off her roses, but when she did, she saw lights shining from behind the bougainvillea hedge.

Headlights. Just beyond the gates she'd forgotten to close.

In one heartbeat, she knew exactly who had delivered her flowers.

With the roses cradled in her arms, she ran barefoot toward the lights. She would stand up to him, refuse to let him ruin Adam's gift of roses. She'd insist he go away. Through warm puddles and chilly shadows, she scuttled holding her breath as crumbled shells dug into her bare feet.

"Derrick." Her frantic cry pierced the night air. The florist van moved forward, inch-by-inch until, for the first time in years, Derrick's hands and face were close enough to touch. "You can't sit out here and watch me like this." The resolve of a minute ago vanished in the soggy air. She felt ugly. Low. Trapped. "It's called stalking, don't you know."

"Evening, Grace." Derrick leaned out the window. "Getting wet, aren't you?"

She pulled the collar of her robe tight around her neck. "Leave us—"

"Congratulations on the marriage." He tossed his cigarette into the bushes. "Been a while, but you're looking good." As if to tease her down the road, he allowed the van to roll forward. Not even for a second did his eyes leave her. Slowly, he raised the window until it was open just a crack. "Be seeing you," he said. "Enjoy the roses."

And then he drove away, his brake lights flashing every few feet, until he rounded the corner.

That night Adam's roses rested on her pillow, close enough to smell, the wedding announcement close enough to read.

But nearer and truer was the knowing that her past would always be there, just over her shoulder. From this day forward, her future depended on one thing.

Keeping Derrick away from Adam.

CHAPTER 5

Be seeing you. Derrick's words were nothing short of a threat. They'd kept Grace awake most of the night, and when morning came, they cast a cloud over an otherwise beautiful day. She could think of only one way to block his words.

Pray.

At first she felt awkward walking around the house, talking out loud to God as if he was following her around with his god-sized journal. "There's nothing I won't do." She stood in front of the French doors that led to the patio and pool. "Just show me how to keep my past with Derrick hidden."

This was only her second day without Adam. It felt more like two weeks. She bit the last of the honeymoon polish off her thumb nail. Even in a room meant for ordinary things, she felt out of place. After all these years, Beth's cookbooks were still propped on a shelf between shiny copper gelatin molds and hand painted ceramic bowls. *Turn Up The Flame, Simply Spectacular, Cooking French.* All she had to add to Beth's collection were two gravy and chocolate stained books, the ones her mother had kept hidden in the pot holder drawer. "Lord Jesus, help me belong here," she prayed. She moved to the kitchen table and gripped the back of a chair as she tried to picture herself eating breakfast with Adam and the girls. Still, she could not forget Derrick.

As she walked through the house, her prayers came easier. She opened closets and drawers, touching, smelling, not being snoopy, but taking in every piece of her new life—praying over the home, almost every inch of the first floor, all the way upstairs to the bedrooms. With every step, it felt like God was leading her toward an answer.

An answer that would make everything right.

She stood in the quiet center of Kate's room, imagining what was to come. What would it be like to keep up with happy footsteps as they bounced from one room to the next, down the steps, and out to the pool or beach? Would she be able to answer their questions? Would she pick out the right clothes? When she opened Kate's closet, the strawberry scent of little girl perfume seemed to penetrate every perfectly hung blouse, every dress. She told herself to remember to buy shampoo and soap that smelled like strawberries.

Before she left the room, she sat on Kate's bed and held the picture from her night table. There Kate stood, clinging to her mommy's hand. They both wore pink beanies with Mickey Mouse ears. The same smile that stretched Beth's face stretched Kate's; the same long blonde hair fell to both their shoulders.

Two peas in a pod, that's the way Adam described them. And that's exactly the way they'd been all those years ago when Beth brought Kate to swimming lessons.

"Jesus, I'm just a swimming teacher," she whispered as she returned Kate's picture to where it belonged. "Two daughters, Lord? You know I don't deserve..." Her prayer swam around the room; and she doubted that her words made it any higher than Kate's butterfly stenciled ceiling, but that didn't stop her. Maybe God would hear; and he'd know how sorry she was and how much she wanted to do everything right, right for Adam, and right for Kate and Sammy.

If he knew, he'd understand why she'd decided to keep her past where it belonged—as far away from Adam as time could take it. And if God understood, he'd make a way for this to be her family, just like he promised.

Nothing could have prepared her for what happened when she stepped through Sammy's door. At first her shoulders stiffened. *If only I hadn't...*She tip-toed around a naked Barbie and a half-full box of crayons. "God, help," she said as she picked up the scattered toys. "Help me see her as Sammy and not..." She sat on Sammy's blue bedspread and examined the menagerie of puppies and bears that made their home there.

Thoughts of the other child who might have shared this room filled her heart.

Just when she thought she might drown in regret, the promise returned like a warm hand laid gently across her heart. *I am creating a new family, a family that will not look back in sorrow.* She didn't know if her heart saw the words or heard them. They were just there, as sure and powerful as they'd been on their wedding day.

The sun was already setting by the time she walked downstairs. She'd spent a good portion of the day going through the house, talking to God, laying every piece of her heart before him, and yet she felt God had something more.

As she opened the safe room's heavy door, she told herself to keep an open mind. Maybe in this windowless room God would give her the answers that would quiet every fear and shed light on each doubt.

Stocked with bottled water, canned food, first aid supplies, and enough flashlights to last through ten hurricane seasons, the room was a shrine to Adam's ability to plan. According to him, the entire house could blow away and this one room would be left standing.

But the room was also a reminder that part of Adam, and part of this house, would always belong to Beth. Clear plastic bins of Beth's photos and books posed like living memorials on the floor to ceiling shelves.

Despite an unexplainable urge to open a flowered hatbox marked, *For Later*, she left it sealed. It was different than the other boxes. More private or special, she couldn't explain, but whatever the box contained was none of her business. She was just about to leave the room when her eyes landed on two boxes stacked in the corner. The top box was marked *Kate's Memory Quilt,* the other, *Sammy's.* She carried the boxes into the family room and sat on the floor with them in front of her, telling herself it was ridiculous to entertain the thoughts going through her mind. She held up the first piece of cloth. Who did she think she was? She didn't even know how to sew on a button, let alone make a quilt. She couldn't stop her hands from trembling as she pulled perfectly folded squares of material from the boxes and held them against the side of her face, breathing in the sweet aroma of baby powder. If she tried, she could sew the quilts. It couldn't be all that hard. All she needed was online directions. Beth's patterns were tucked inside each box—butterflies for Kate and angels for Sammy.

Who'd think of such a thing? The question taunted her as she handled the tiny bundles of sacred cloth, each with two word labels attached by tiny gold pins. *First Easter,* yellow bunnies and tiny purple flowers…*First Christmas,* snow bunnies on red…*First Birthday,* embroidered balloons and butterflies…*First Steps,* rainbow seersucker and pink denim. No wonder Adam still loved Beth. She treasured her daughters' firsts. She would never have thrown even one away.

She draped the last two pieces of fabric over her hand, precious pieces of crispy white linen. *Baby Dedication.*

Kate to Jesus.

Sammy to Jesus.

She couldn't stop herself. She had to ask God why, why Beth had to die so young and why he chose someone like her to take Beth's place.

Forgiven, that was the word she had to remember. God had given her the gift of forgiveness. She was a new person now, maybe not as good as Beth, but the person God had chosen to be part of the family he was creating. She'd finish the quilts because God had not only chosen her for the promise of a new family.

He'd chosen her for the job.

CHAPTER 6

Adam sat on the edge of the bed, his planner open on his lap and hands cupped around his head. He'd felt like this before. How could he explain these attacks to Grace? The voices in the hall, the doors opening, slamming—he didn't need any of it.

He needed Grace.

But their call hadn't gone well. He searched his mind for ways he could have made things better. At first she seemed happy, talking about quilts and how she'd prayed over the entire house, every room except their bedroom. He could still hear how full of hope her voice had been when she said, "I saved our room for when you get home, because don't you think we should pray together?"

There were so many things he should have said, but hadn't. Instead, the truth spilled out, "I can't make it home before Thursday. I've done my best, but there's no way."

"The girls come home on Wednesday and your parents…" Her panicky voice still troubled him.

His shoulders weighed heavy as he moved to the window and pulled the drapes open. Ten floors below, the city beamed a greenish glow into the night sky. He tried to imagine the noises and smells that didn't quite make it to his senses, horns honking, people laughing, making deals and breaking them, car exhaust, crumpled bags of cold French fries and half-eaten burgers.

But up here, he was insulated from it all.

Insulated. That's the way he'd spent most of his life. It wasn't until Beth's cancer that the insulation began to crumble. Even then, he couldn't force himself to believe she wouldn't be healed. Bad things didn't happen to the Will family. God was on their side, always on their side.

He could go back all the way to before there was a bridge to the island, to the stories of how his grandfather bartered for a piece of property located almost at the tip of Tesoro. At that time the island was known for little more than swampy clumps of mangrove trees, secluded shell laden beaches, bountiful fishing, and a year-round crop of mosquitoes. His grandfather had built a cottage for his family, a place of escape when they needed to be insulated from the rush of city life or the dismal Georgia winters. In the years that followed, children and grandchildren were added to the family and a second story to the cottage, followed by a pool, fence, and gates to insulate them further. Then, on his and Beth's wedding day, the cottage had been turned over to them. Free and clear.

And that's where he and Beth planned to spend a lifetime. Soon Kate came along, as beautiful as her mother and perfect in every way. While he built his company, Beth volunteered at church and served on the board of the pregnancy center. But her heart and real joy was in taking care of their home and daughter. When Sammy was born they didn't think life could get better. And they were right. Worse was on its way. Less than a month after Sammy's birth, Beth found the lump in her breast. Twenty-one months later she was gone. And, even though he'd told no one, so was his simple trust.

He turned away from the window, stunned by the warm tears running down his cheeks.

There was one more flight tonight. If he left now he could make it; and he could fix the way he'd hurt Grace. But she'd hurt him too. Just what did she mean when she accused him of not having room in his life for her? The facts spoke loud and clear. Love didn't mean he'd let his business go and it didn't mean he would forget his past. Beth was part of him, always would be, and Grace would have to come to grips with that.

He reached for his phone. Four rings, then the voice mail. *Hello, you've reached the Will's. Adam, Kate, and Sammy.*

"Hon, if you're there, pick up." He fanned through the pages of the red hotel Bible that had been left open on the desk. "I'm fixin to try your cell. Anyway, call as soon as you get this. Love you." He pulled open the drawer to return the Bible to its place, but just as the book left his hands, he sensed a whisper, not an outside whisper, an inside one. He wasn't sure where it came from but he knew where it landed.

In the center of his heart.

Adam, why do you look back in sorrow? Trust Me. I've turned your weeping into dancing.

Grace couldn't sit still, not even on the veranda where the slow steady roll of waves and the swish-swash of palm branches should have been enough to lull her into cozied sleep. She'd tried journaling, but all her thoughts crawled backwards.

It wasn't just the house phone, now her cell was ringing. She moved inside and sat on the bed, stuffing the phone under the pillows. She didn't have the energy to talk to Adam, didn't even want to.

She wanted to talk to her mom.

She'd give anything to go back, back to when every wrong in the world could be explained away by her parents. Even in high school, when all her friends thought their parents didn't have a grip on life, she was convinced hers walked on water.

She still couldn't believe God took them. The roads were icy; that's what Dean Parker told her. And there was a drunk driver.

Don't question, Grace. The scolding words of her roommate came back, as harsh as the day they were spoken. *Never question God.* She could still feel the pain as the words were slung like stones at her wounded teenage soul.

But who wouldn't question? She'd been in the middle of her first year at Northern Bible College when her family—father, mother, even Grady, her little brother—were killed as they headed home after a weekend visit.

When she returned to school after the funeral, Dean Parker and his wife took her to see what was left of her family's van. She could still feel the penetrating cold as she stood in the middle of the muddy salvage lot. The van's roof, the windows, her family—gone.

If she had known before her family drove away she would have tried to stop them; and if that hadn't worked she would have climbed inside the van. One more time she would have touched her Mom's soft hair and listened to her Dad join his deep voice with those on his favorite C.D. She would have teased Grady. And let him tease her.

She tried to sit through her classes. But she couldn't concentrate, except in chapel where the songs and prayers scraped like sandpaper. How could she sing *Great Is Thy Faithfulness* or *More Than Enough* when her entire body ached for just one more hug from her dad and mom, when she no longer saw God as faithful or as being enough to fill her emptiness? She was wiser. And just like now, she was alone.

No one was there to stop her from dropping out. Her Dad's attorney took care of the bills for the house. She gave her pastor the keys and told him to use it for a homeless family or missionaries home on furlough. She didn't care. And she headed south to Tesoro Island where she took a job teaching swimming.

But even on an island called paradise, nothing could fill the empty places in her heart. She tried to keep busy; but when she wasn't in the pool, she was falling, falling into things she shouldn't, into the arms of someone who didn't know how to love her back, into the blackest pit of her life, a pit she didn't believe the light of God's forgiveness would ever reach.

But it did.

After all she'd done, after all the places she'd gone that she shouldn't have gone, and all the times she didn't say no when she knew she should, God simply gathered her into his arms and brought her back to him.

And that's when he carried her into this lifetime. If she wanted to stay here, if she didn't want to go back to the pit, she had to make some changes in her thinking.

Her phone rang another time. This time she pulled it out from under the pillows and walked back to the veranda where she sat alone on the lounge meant for two. She pushed talk and held the phone to her ear, waiting to hear Adam's voice.

"Hon, I've been trying to get a hold of you."

"I must not have heard. I don't know."

She had no idea how long they talked, long enough for Adam to say how sorry he was and promise that everything would be different once he had things under control. By the time he was saying good night, promising he missed her as much as she missed him, she no longer felt on edge and alone. She placed her feet on the small table and rested her head against the cushions. The sound of the waves mixed with Adam's voice, the familiar dank smell of the summer night lulled her eyes almost closed.

Peace belonged to her once again.

But then, without warning, a beam of light slithered out of the darkness.

Deliberately, as if it was slowly climbing the steps to the veranda, the light moved up, all the way to where she sat. *Adam. Help.* Her mind screamed, but the words never left her mouth. Adam kept talking as the light scanned her face and drifted to her chest. She had no idea how she scooped her body off the lounge or how she made it into the bedroom. "Adam, uff-da, listen to me." Her hand trembled on the lock. "Someone's out there. He has a light."

"Probably just—"

"He shined it right on—"

"Are the doors locked?" Adam sounded as if he were rationalizing with Kate or Sammy.

"This one." She was pacing now, from the door to the bed, back and forth. "I can't be here alone. You know I hate to be—"

"I know, Babe. But listen. Downstairs, did you lock the doors?"

"I think."

What if this was Derrick playing some kind of prank? She had no idea; all she knew was if she opened the bedroom door, there'd be creaks blasting from inside every wall. If she was really alone there wouldn't be so many sounds. "Adam, you have to come home."

"Grace, don't do this." Irritation dripped from each word. She was disappointing him, just like she was afraid she'd do. "I want you to go downstairs. Check the locks."

She pressed the phone against the side of her face. "Who has keys?" She closed her eyes to fight the dizziness. "I can't go down there." A surge of tears blinded her. "Please, Adam. Please come home."

CHAPTER 7

Adam stared out the window, marveling at how quickly the skyscrapers of Minneapolis gave way to farmland, little rectangles of earth divided by roads and rivers.

He needed to figure out what had made Grace so irrational. Maybe she didn't feel at home in Florida. Everything about Minnesota was different. Even though he'd never been here during winter, the stories about how lakes freeze so solid that people actually drive across them absolutely flabbergasted him. She hadn't told him much about growing up in a place so unlike his own; but the things she said were good, and he suspected a part of her might still call Minnesota home. For a minute he allowed himself to speculate if he could be happy calling a place so far away from the Gulf's warm water home.

The inviting aroma of coffee trailed the flight attendants as they made their way down the aisle. He accepted a cup and asked for a second. "It will save y'all a trip," he said as he lowered his tray.

And then he opened his planner. Other men used little handheld electronic devices to manage their schedules. He needed to see his commitments written inside boxes, and feel the pencil between his fingers each time he drew a thick line through an obligation met.

The last couple days he'd done little crossing out. Life was pushing in on him. But how could he stay in Minnesota when Grace was so terrified?

Thankfully, he'd had the sense to contact Joel last night. Joel not only agreed to check on Grace, he offered a solution. "A lot of club employees take odd jobs during the slow season," he'd said. "I know of one guy who may be interested in watching your house, especially if it gives him a place to stay. Last I heard, he's living on his boat."

As the plane started its slow descent, Adam handed his empty coffee cups to the flight attendant. Even if the threat was nothing more than Grace's imagination, or one of those nature lovers on a mission to protect sea turtle eggs, why take chances? He was actually glad to be heading home, and grateful he'd set up an interview with the guy Joel had told him about. The arrangement might be perfect. After all, the man was willing to live on property. Besides, now that he thought back, not even Beth liked being alone this time of year.

Grace swam to the side of the pool and pulled herself onto the edge as Adam walked toward her, his anxious smile like a kid hunting treasure, his tanned arms sticking out of a pale blue polo shirt. Before she could wrap herself in a towel he was there, pulling her up, into his arms. "Be careful," she said. "I don't want to get your clothes wet."

Adam didn't seem to care. "I should have been here," he said as he brushed her hair behind her ears.

Despite Adam's assurances, part of her felt guilty for calling him home. But once they were together in their bedroom, she felt as if the threat and panic of the previous night had all been swept away. Before she sat on the bed Island Interiors had delivered that morning, she covered a place with a folded dry beach towel. "I hope it's okay," she said as she smoothed her hand across the buttercream cotton spread.

"Can't say for sure." In one miraculous moment, he was next to her. "Not yet." He moved his hands across her shoulders and down her arms; and then he pulled her close, until there was no space between them.

If only she could make the moment to last forever, if only she could push the rest of life far away, but Adam looked at his watch and she knew it was over. "Interview shouldn't take long," he said.

She watched him take a fresh shirt from his closet.

"Do you want my help? It's not a problem," she offered.

"I got it." Adam placed the tube of sunscreen in her hand. "Finish your swim. If I decide to hire him, I'll come get you for the final okay."

She understood that Adam had been making decisions on his own for a long time, but that was one of the things she needed to talk to him about. She wasn't a sideline kind of person. Just the opposite, she liked to have a say in decisions, just the way her mom had. For now, she'd play along.

And that's what she did for close to an hour, floating around in warm water and wondering what the guy sitting in Adam's office looked like. Could she feel comfortable with some stranger living just feet away? Every few minutes she checked to see if Adam was at the door. When she could wait no longer, she wrapped her cover-up around her swim suit and headed inside.

"Move in tomorrow if you don't mind cleaning the apartment yourself." She was just on the other side of Adam's door when she heard him extend the offer. "Otherwise I can have the cleaning lady…" She wrapped her hand around the door knob.

"Sir, whatever works best for you and the woman." As soon as she heard the voice her stomach knotted. All the way to the tips of her fingers, she felt her blood pumping.

There was no mistaking that voice.

Her hand froze on the knob. God couldn't allow this. And there was no way Adam could. She had to stop him now. But the moment she turned the knob, she remembered she was bare all the way up to her knees, the rest of her covered only by a wet swim suit and flimsy cover-up. She pulled her hand away, but it wasn't a quiet release, more like a loud click. In that moment Adam realized she was there.

"Grace, perfect." He waved her in. "I was fixin to get you."

She felt her face turn hot red. "Let me go up…" She pulled on the hem of her cover-up.

Adam placed his hand on her back. "It will just take a minute."

She wanted to push him away. "I'm in my—"

"Honey, I want you to meet..." He wrapped his arm around her waist and led her through his office until she stood alongside him behind his desk. "Grace, this is Derrick…" Adam shuffled through a small stack of note cards. "Derrick Dunn. He'll be moving into the garage apartment."

Adam kept talking, but his words were nothing more than a swarm of mosquitoes buzzing around her head. Her stomach rolled and so did the room. She felt as if a fire had been lit under her skin. How much had he already told Adam? If she looked at Derrick, if he touched even her hand, she'd get deathly sick right in the middle of Adam's perfect office.

"Adam." Without taking her eyes off the top of his desk, she forced out the words. "We need to talk."

Adam took two bottles of water from his office refrigerator and as he opened the door, handed one to Derrick. "It will just be a minute." As if he was an old tennis buddy, he gave Derrick's back a friendly slap.

"Grace, what is this?" Adam motioned to the sofa. They sat there, Adam's knee touching hers. "You have to help me understand. I've never seen you like this."

"Adam, don't you think I should have a say in this? You can't—"

"He's willing to live here twenty-four-seven when I'm gone." Adam pinched the bridge of his nose. "I'll feel safer. Listen, you'll feel safer knowing someone is—"

"I don't need a security guard." Adam was too close. How could she make him understand when all she wanted to do was fall into his arms and tell him everything she should have told him months ago? She stood and faced him. "I suppose you've called references."

"He comes highly recommended."

"You have no idea what you are doing. Adam, I know him. That's all I'm going to say." Even though her back was toward the door, she could feel Derrick's eyes. "We worked together at the club and I don't like him. In fact, I'm very uncomfortable with this plan of yours."

"And here I thought this would make you more comfortable. Give me a reason, I'll send him packing."

"Reason?"

"Grace, are you saying there's something I should know about Derrick?" Adam took the cap off his water bottle and took a long drink before he reached for her hand. "There wasn't anything...not you and..."

His eyes were fixed on hers, waiting for an answer. This was her chance to tell him the truth. All she had to do was finish his sentence. *Yes, Adam, let me tell you about Derrick and me*—that's all it would take. But she couldn't. Not now.

And so, with her hand wrapped in his, she looked her husband square in his soft blue eyes. "Adam, there's nothing you should know."

Her insides shuddered as she pulled her hand away. "Uff-da. Go ahead, do what you want."

Once the lie was out, it was too late to take it back, and so she told another. "I don't really care."

CHAPTER 8

Grace opened a can of ginger ale and headed outside where she could see Adam walking along the beach with Kate and Sammy, their little plastic bags flapping in the breeze as they collected their sandy shell treasures.

Just three days ago, Adam's folks had dropped the girls off, and it hadn't surprised her that there'd been tension. To begin with, instead of staying in their own condo, his parents stayed with them. At first, she thought it was a wonderful idea, but that didn't last long. She could still hear his mother. "We'll bunk in Adam's guestroom while our men paint our condo."

She was certain Marjory had never "bunked" a day in her life. But the absolute worse—*our men?* She'd never heard anyone refer to another human in terms of ownership. A day later Marjory was at it again. "My girl's been sick for over a week; I might have to contact the service for a new one."

Haughty. It was the only word Grace could think of.

She took a sip of ginger ale and dropped into the hammock that was strung between two towering palms. From here she could see every corner of her world, the side yard where Adam had built the girls' playhouse, the pool, and beach. It was the perfect resting spot, a place where she could wrap her mind around her new life. This was her family. She was now responsible, right alongside Adam. And as soon as she worked up the courage, changes would be on the way.

It wasn't that she was naïve. Ever since Beth's death, Marjory had been the only woman in the girls' lives. She was prepared for the transition to bring its share of struggles.

What she wasn't prepared for was Derrick. He'd already moved his fishing rods and tackle boxes into the garage apartment. Every time she saw him, Pastor Karl's words flashed through her mind. *Satan's going to do whatever he can to remind you of your past.*

That had to be why her stomach constantly churned. It wasn't only the guilt she still felt each time she saw Derrick, it was the fear. *What if he tells Adam?* She woke with the thought and went to sleep by it. And the hours in between, she did everything she could to keep the two men apart.

She closed her eyes and ran her thumb back and forth across her ring. Who would have guessed little more than a year ago when she walked into Tesoro Island Church that her life would turn out this way?

But God knew. *No eye has seen…* The Bible verse she'd memorized when she was not much older than Kate flickered inside her. *Nor ear has heard, no mind has conceived what God has prepared for those who love him.* The promise brought her back to her first Sunday at the little island church.

It was the day she met Adam.

She'd never been in a church quite like it. The building was nothing more than a small wood structure. Like so many buildings on the island, it was painted cotton-candy pink. She had stood there in the crowded back row surrounded by people dressed in walking shorts and flip-flops. There was no question about it, her below-the-knee skirt and long-sleeved blouse announced her visitor status. The singing seemed to last forever. Almost everyone raised their hands or clapped as they sang words projected on a screen at the front of the sunlit room.

Around the third song, that's when she first saw Adam. From that point on, she couldn't help it, her eyes were glued. He was tan and well-built with immaculately cut blond hair. She counted the rows between them. Twelve. And yet she could see the creases in his navy slacks. He lifted his hands in worship, but she sensed his heart was someplace else. When it was time to greet, he turned and moved down the crowded center aisle, shaking hands with some, hugging others. As he came closer, she saw that his eyes were blue and his mouth didn't quite make it to a full smile. Everyone seemed to know him, to have some word of greeting and because of that, he never made it back to shake her hand.

For the rest of worship she wondered where his heart was.

When Pastor Karl stood to preach the anticipation she'd felt earlier that week when she visited his office returned. She forgot about the handsome man and how uncomfortable she felt in her long skirt. "If you brought your Bible with you this morning, turn to Psalm fifty-one," he said. She pulled the Bible from her purse.

Pages rustled and Pastor Karl waited for the room to grow silent before he stepped away from the pulpit, his thin Bible spread across the palm of his hand. He read the words as if they were a prayer. "Cleanse me with hyssop, and I will be clean." When he paused, she sat taller. Maybe he was checking to see if she'd kept her promise to give church another try. "Wash me and I will be whiter than snow." These were the same words he'd asked her to read when she met with him earlier that week. "Create in me a pure heart, O God, and renew a steadfast spirit within me." He put his Bible on the pulpit and spoke the rest of that morning's Scripture from his heart.

Every word reminded her of what he'd said when she met with him in his office. "I think you're tired of bearing the guilt. You long for peace, and that's why God had you stop by today."

He was right because before she left his office she prayed, asking God to create a new and clean heart within her.

Again that morning when Pastor Karl talked about King David, he came to life. He had a face and emotions, doubt, sin, and fear. He was every bit as human as she. And God was just as big and merciful in the tiny church as he'd been on the day David journaled his prayer.

When the service was over, she picked up her Bible and walked out, stopping only to shake Pastor Karl's hand and assure him she'd be back another Sunday.

She was unlocking her car when she saw the man walk out of church holding hands with two little girls. *Married.* She couldn't understand why the realization dropped such a large ball of disappointment into her morning.

But then the older girl ran toward her. The next thing she felt were arms around her waist. "Miss Grace, remember me?" It was Kate, one of the little girls who had been in her swimming class the first time she taught on the island.

The rest of the morning passed in a blur. Half an hour after leaving church she sat across the table from Adam, eating breakfast with his daughters at the Lighthouse Café. He was alone with his girls now. His wife Beth had been diagnosed with breast cancer shortly after his youngest, Sammy, was born. "Were you here then?" he said.

She told him no, she knew Beth, but she'd gone home to Minnesota shortly after Beth learned she was pregnant. She didn't tell him why. And he didn't ask.

"Minnesota, I'm working on a bid there, just outside Minneapolis," he said. He later talked about his construction business and asked about places to eat and things to do. And when she told him about Swanson's Supermarket, he almost choked on his coffee. "Only in Minnesota could a grocery be a tourist destination."

"It is. Uff-da, you have to try their wild rice soup. And the bakery—"

"No. Y'all can't be serious."

She was, but apparently he thought it was hilarious that she would include a grocery in a list of tourist attractions. Before long she was choking on laughter too.

When they were done wiping coffee from their mouths and tears from their eyes, she asked if he was interested in outdoor activities.

"Never been there in the winter when it snows, but I'd love to learn how to ski."

Sammy stopped the conversation right there. She sat on her knees and clasped her little hands in front of her. "Is snow really real, Daddy?"

She was the cutest child Grace had ever seen. She had her dad's tan skin and a head full of tight blonde curls. But it was the little girl's eyes that gripped her heart. Their anticipation never faded until she laid her head on her daddy's lap and fell asleep.

A few Sundays later he told her that Beth hadn't made it to Sammy's second birthday.

"Grace." Sammy's voice pulled her away from remembering. "Look at my shell." She waved her arms, calling Grace toward the beach. "It's a real Shark Eye. I'm going to give it to you, Grace."

Sammy placed the shell in her hand. "You sure you want to give this to me? It's beautiful, honey." With swirls of pinkish tan and a black dot right in the middle, the shell looked exactly like an eye.

All the time she was praising Sammy's shell, she felt Adam staring at her; and for the first time since the girls came home, she felt that maybe he was starting to see her as their new mommy.

"Walk with us?" Adam took her hand. "There are a lot more shells to be found, don't you know."

"Are you making fun of me?"

"Uff-da, I'm not."

"But you're fixin' to." She stepped out of her flip flops and tossed them onto the sand. "I can always tell, don't you know."

And then she walked along the beach with Adam and the girls, searching for shells.

Believing.

The sun's rays seemed hotter than usual and she wondered if it might be one of those rare island days when the temperature made it close to a hundred. There was only a slight breeze, one just strong enough to blow Sammy's hat from her head.

"Sammy, girl." Adam scooped the hat up just before a wave washed it away. "What's Daddy going to do with you?"

"I don't know." She shrugged her little shoulders. "I think, maybe buy me a new hat?"

"Want mine?" Grace pulled the hat from her head.

"Sure." Sammy spun and faced her. "It's pretty," she said as Grace slipped it on.

"Maybe we should put some sunscreen on that nose," Grace said. "It's getting as pink as your sunglasses."

"Your sunscreen. Okay, Grace?"

Her hat…her sunscreen…they might have been little things, but Adam had warned her that's what it would take. Lots of little things. And before she knew it, the girls would welcome her all the way into their hearts. She pulled the hat snug until the brim met Sammy's tiny shoulders. Then she dotted her shoulders and the tip of her nose and chin with sun block, rubbing it in, being careful not to scratch her soft skin. She couldn't remember ever feeling so completely full of joy. "Kate, how about you?" She held the tube toward Kate.

"No thanks." Kate took Adam's hand and pulled him forward. "I've got my own."

They walked further down the beach, Kate with Adam, and Sammy sometimes with her, but most times alone, in the middle. Without her hat, there was no protection from the sun. It wasn't long before she felt besieged by the rays. She bent down and splashed water on her arms and neck, but the water was as warm as a bath. "Adam," she called, hoping her voice would stop him. "I better—"

"Go in." Adam turned around. "We should too. I have to start the grill."

Even in the air-conditioning, Grace felt queasy. When Adam came in to the kitchen from the patio, she forced a smile. "Charcoal ready?"

"Sizzling, just like you." In one swift swoop, he scooped her ponytail to the top of her head and kissed her neck. "You okay? You look a little red." He laid the palm of his hand on her forehead as if he were checking for a fever.

"I'll be fine."

Ever since Adam rushed home to hire Derrick, they'd planned this meal, a poolside barbeque, just the four of them, the night before he returned to Minnesota. It didn't matter how sick she felt, nothing would keep her from enjoying the evening.

She stood at the breakfast bar slicing strawberries, watching Adam through the French doors as he brushed barbeque sauce across hamburger patties. *If only you could see this, Mom. It's like you and Daddy.* She thought of her family more often now, not in a grieving way, but in a warm, grateful way. That morning she'd opened her mom's old cookbook and taken her white Pyrex mixing bowl out of its hiding place at the back of the cupboard. She'd boiled potatoes and eggs, chopped celery and onions, and mixed the dressing just as she'd seen her mom do for a thousand summer picnics.

When she finished slicing the strawberries she set the cake on the counter and pulled the whipped cream from the refrigerator. That's when Sammy clicked into the kitchen wearing her little girl high heels. "What ya'll mixin' up?" She climbed up on the stool. "Looks yummy."

"Strawberries and whip cream. Want to lick the bowl when I'm done?" She handed Sammy a spoon. "Don't tell. I'm hiding the cream and strawberries inside the angel food."

"Angel food? My Mommy lives with Jesus and the angels. Does she eat angel food, Grace?" Creamy strawberries framed her little mouth. And her eyes looked like they'd arrived at an extravagant party.

"I'm sure she does." With all that was in her, she wanted to take Sammy in her arms. Sammy's heart was ready for that kind of love, almost ready to call her Mommy. But she had to wait. She had to make sure she could love Sammy all the way for who she was.

She was just about to swipe a damp paper towel across Sammy's lips when Kate walked into the kitchen and brushed by her. "Does Daddy have dinner ready, Sammy?"

"Kate, look. Grace made the kind of cake Mommy eats."

"Wipe your face." Kate pulled a napkin from the holder and handed it to her sister. "Mommy eats better stuff."

She couldn't figure Kate out, not when their relationship had started out so happy. She wasn't sure if it was the stress over Kate or if she was coming down with something, but by the time they were ready to eat she could barely sit at the table. Even Adam's laugh shook her stomach.

Adam had made everything perfect, lighting the oil lamps around the pool and filling the evening air with his music. "It's wonderful," she said as she set her fork on her plate. "I'm just not very hungry. Sorry."

"Are you sure you're feeling okay?" He placed his hand on top of hers.

"I'm a little dizzy. Too much sun, that's all."

He wiped the corners of his mouth with a napkin. "Did I mention I invited Derrick to join us for dessert?" His voice sounded apologetic. "I need to make certain we're on the same page with this arrangement."

Before she could respond, Derrick appeared. He was barefoot and dressed in what looked like freshly ironed hand-me-downs from Adam's closet. To her surprise, he'd taken the time to comb his hair into a neat ponytail. When he dropped into the chair next to Adam, his foot brushed hers and a fresh wave of nausea rumbled through her.

Adam passed a slice of cake to Derrick. Minutes later, when the last crumb was cleaned from his plate, Derrick sat back, locking his hands behind his neck. "How about some magic tricks, girls? Ever seen genuine magic tricks up close?"

Derrick spent the next half hour making coins disappear and cards change suite. Kate loved it. Before he was done, she was calling him by his nickname. "Please, Trick, do another trick." It was a joke Kate and Adam wrapped their laughter around.

When the magic tricks were over, Adam passed the dessert to Derrick. "Have another piece," he said. "Grace, scoop some extra whipped cream on it."

"No, I got it." A pleased look covered Derrick's face as he reached across the table for the bowl of cream.

She hated the way Adam was acting so interested in Derrick's life, as if he was a friend or part of their family. "You fixing to go back to the club come season?"

"Might be, or could take a run to Jamaica."

"Your boat can make it to Jamaica?"

"They don't make the 26X anymore." It was just like Derrick to turn a polite question into an opportunity to brag about his precious boat. "I can control the waves in that little lady. I'll take you and the missus out some time."

"Excuse me." Grace stood, gripping her empty can of ginger-ale in front of her. "I need to get another."

Adam wrapped his arm around her waist. "Let's just call it a night."

"I wouldn't worry about her." She hated the way Derrick could hide his face behind a mask of innocence. "I've seen you sick like this before, haven't I, Grace?"

Derrick angled himself so he looked straight into her eyes.

The three of them this close and connected made her insides quiver. She pulled away and began stacking plates, struggling to find a way to push Derrick out of her life.

After she placed the last handful of dirty silverware on top of the stacked plates, she stood back. Even though she ached to go in, there was no way she could leave Derrick alone with Adam. She had to stay close, ready to stop Derrick if he tried to say something. Kate stood next to Derrick, staring up at him as if she was trying to decide if the things he did were real. She wanted to pull Kate's eyes off him, tell her nothing he did or said was anything more than a trick, a mean and deceitful trick.

"If you have any questions…" Adam reached into his pocket. "Any problems with anyone prowling around, here's my card. I want to know the minute it happens."

"Sure thing." He stuffed the card into his back pocket. "Don't worry, Mr. Will." Derrick walked slowly past her, his arm brushing hers just as she lifted the stack of dishes from the table. "I've got everything under control."

Chapter 9

Adam's voice was little above a whisper as he tiptoed toward the bed. "Feeling better?" He sat next to her, his hand reaching for hers.

"Too much sun." She wove her fingers together with his. "And…" She knew it would do no good to bring up her concerns about Derrick again; but after the way he'd made her feel, sitting across the table, eating the dessert she'd made for Adam, she had to say something. "It's Derrick."

"Kate and Sammy enjoyed tonight." He kissed her forehead. "This time tomorrow night you'll be glad he's here."

When Adam headed off to the girls' rooms, she stayed in bed allowing the girls' happy squeals to wash over her worries. There was no question about it, Adam adored his daughters and they loved him back. She hated to think about the emotions that were sure to take over in the morning when he pulled out of their driveway.

It wasn't long before Adam padded back into the room. "Sammy's still praying for snow. You know she has since you told her it was real." He sat on the edge of the bed, his bare back toward her. She loved the way his muscles stretched and moved across his shoulders and down his arms.

"Sorry about not feeling well."

"Don't worry. Need anything? Another ginger ale?"

"A miracle would be nice." She slid to his side of the bed and wrapped her arms around his waist. "One that would make it possible for you to stay home."

"If you find that miracle," he moved into bed alongside her, "let me know."

No one had ever made her feel the way Adam did. It was almost midnight when he cupped her chin in his hand. "You're going to be fine." He folded the sheet back, almost to the foot of their bed. "I know it's late; but grab your robe. I owe you a walk on the beach."

Adam's suggestion surprised her. "What about the girls?"

"They'll be okay."

Adam led the way to the veranda and down the wooden steps. With arms around each other, they meandered along the crooked path to the beach. She loved the yowl of waves and the Christmas-bell chinkling of sea shells being thrust like holiday confetti onto the sand.

As wonderful as it was, she couldn't force away the dread of morning. Every foot print they left brought them a step closer to tomorrow, closer to the time Adam's car would back out of the drive. Unless God gave her that miracle, he'd be gone for one, maybe two weeks.

When it was time to turn back he stroked the side of her face. "Now I've seen you in the moonlight." He wrapped his arm around her and drew her close.

"Disappointed?"

"Mrs. Will, you could never disappoint me."

They were almost to the house when Adam stopped and pointed down the beach. "You're right. Derrick's everywhere, even—"

"I'll never be out of his sight, Adam. That's why this is a mistake."

"That's why it's anything but a mistake, Babe."

Just short of the house, Adam veered toward the hammock. Moments later they were side-by-side under a full-moon sky. "I want you to understand," he said as she snuggled against his shoulder, "this is hard for me too."

There in the safety of Adam's arms she pled with God. *Don't let tonight end. I can't be here alone with Derrick.* She swiped the backs of her hands over the tears that trickled down her cheeks. *God, just send Derrick out of our lives. What do you want me to do? I'll do anything.*

Even if she could turn back the clock to that day in Adam's office when he asked about her relationship with Derrick, she wasn't sure she'd be brave enough to confess. After all, just like Pastor Karl said, God had taken care of her past, thrown it so deep into the sea that no wave could ever find it. But Derrick was back, and with him, a daily reminder of all that was. Not only their sin, but the tiny spark of light God had shined into their darkness.

It was the light they had snuffed out.

CHAPTER 10

All through breakfast Grace wanted to stop the clock, not just for herself, for all of them. But she had as much chance of stopping time as she had of ridding herself of the lump of dread that had been growing inside her stomach all morning.

As soon as breakfast was over, Adam cleared the table, scraping their uneaten eggs into the trash while she loaded the dishwasher. "Girls," Adam folded the towel and hung it over the side of the sink. "Upstairs. Get dressed. Daddy's fixin' to leave."

Minutes later, she followed Adam and the girls to the car, standing back while the three of them went through their good-bye routine. After tossing his suitcase in the back seat, Adam drew Kate into a hug. Then he lifted Sammy into his arms, placing his planner in her little hands. Together, the three of them turned pages.

"See that day." Adam took Sammy's hand and touched his planner. "Unless something really big happens, that's the day Daddy will be home." He bent down until Sammy's feet could touch the ground.

She couldn't get over how tiny Kate and Sammy looked standing next to each other in front of Adam, their little faces turned down. Adam cupped one hand under Kate's chin, the other under Sammy's. "Know what would make Daddy happy?" Without lifting their eyes, the girls shrugged their shoulders. For the first time she realized how scary this must be. They'd never stayed with anyone other than Adam's parents. "Daddy will be happy if Grace tells me y'all are having fun, the three of you together."

"Daddy." Kate's voice was abnormally whiney. "But I need to ask you a question. It's important."

"What do you want to ask Daddy?"

"I want to take sailing lessons. Mister Derrick told me I can start tomorrow."

Kate alone…out in the Gulf with Derrick—Grace couldn't believe Derrick had the nerve to suggest such a thing. She was trying to figure out a way to smash the plan when Adam shook his head. "Kate, I want y'all to understand, a lot can happen out there. You're just not old enough. Trust Daddy on this."

Kate crossed her arms and Grace could tell she was on the verge of pleading her case when Sammy pulled on Adam's belt. "Daddy, that's very smart of you. Mr. Derrick gives me creepy feelings in my tummy. I saw him. He was standing there in the dark looking at my house."

"Sammy girl, that's what I'm paying him to do." He laid his hand on top of Kate's head. "Got that, kiddo, he's paid to look after you, not teach you how to sail away from your Daddy."

And then, it was her turn to be taken into Adam's arms. He held her close. "Being away is going to drive me crazy."

"Me too," she said. "More than you know."

As soon as Adam's car was out of sight, Kate took Sammy's hand and led her inside. Grace followed, listening to Kate promise Sammy she could use her big box of crayons if she wanted to draw a picture.

Half way up the stairs, Sammy peeked through the wood railing. "Can I put a stamp on my picture and mail it to Daddy? The stamps are in Mommy's desk."

As innocent as her words were, they pointed to the truth. In Kate and Sammy's minds, they had a Mommy. She could pray over their house and their hearts a million times, and they, this house, even a part of Adam would still belonged to Beth.

For the next few minutes, she sat alone at the table with her eyes closed, listening to Kate and Sammy's chatter drift down the stairs. *Give me something, God, something that says I can do this.* It was only after her prayer that she had the courage to climb the stairs. She stood in the doorway to the girls' playroom listening, waiting for God to answer.

Since the first time she saw this room, with ceilings that followed the steep roof line and window seats cushioned with worn pink and green pillows, she knew it was the perfect place for childish imaginations. But today, as she looked at Kate sitting on the window bench, staring out the window, a tablet and pencil forgotten on her lap, she wondered if she would ever find a way to break through the sadness stamped across her little girl face.

She turned her attention to Sammy who had strewn crayons everywhere, on the table, the floor, and chairs. Her curly head bobbed back and forth as she stood at the table coloring and talking to herself in whispers.

She was just about to move into the room when Sammy walked her picture over to Kate. "I'm going to send this one to Daddy." She pointed to her paper. "See, that's Daddy…you… me…Grace. Our family."

Our family. Joy danced across Grace's heart.

"You can put your name on it too if you want."

Kate turned and for a moment her eyes met Grace's. "Nice, Sammy. But you shouldn't forget mommy."

Sammy's proud shoulders slumped. "Kate, remember when Daddy told us he was going to marry Grace?"

"So?"

"Well, I remember you told Daddy that you prayed and prayed that Jesus would give us a new—'"

Kate stood and pointed a big-sister finger at Sammy. "Stop talking about that."

But Sammy didn't back away. She stood holding her picture, her voice stronger than Grace had ever heard. "I can talk if I want because I prayed and prayed too. And when you act this way I think you want to throw away a present Jesus gived us."

She was amazed at the spunk hidden inside Sammy. If Sammy wouldn't back down, neither would she. It didn't matter that the pounding in her chest felt as if it might crush her heart.

Sammy believed she belonged.

Kate turned back to the window. "Maybe God didn't answer our prayer. Did you ever think of that? Maybe Grace just wants Daddy to forget all about Mommy."

"What's up, girls?" She pushed herself into the room. "Sammy, may I see?"

Sammy looked at her sister and then Grace. "Sure."

Grace sat on one of the undersized chairs. "See that's my Daddy." Sammy's little finger pointed to the tallest figure, a man with two blue circle eyes and apple-red smile that reached from one side of his baseball shaped head to the other. "You can tell that's Daddy because he's the very tallest and he's wearing slacks."

"I see." A smile found its way into Grace's voice as joy and sorrow played tug-of-war inside her heart.

"And this is Kate." She pointed to a girl with long crayon-yellow hair. "Kate loves red dresses and butterflies. And this is me." Sammy patted her arm. "Know how you can tell it's me?"

Sammy was almost in her lap, her little elbow digging painfully into her leg. But she didn't pull away. "Because you're the smallest?"

"And I'm wearing a pink swim suit. Remember, you promised to teach me how to swim. And that's you." Sammy's hand rested on top of a figure with red hair and a purple dress. "You're standing next to Daddy and that's why he has a big, big smile. I heard him tell Grandma he really likes red hair so I used the reddest crayon."

"Beautiful. We'll—"

"Where are they?" Grace had been so caught up in Sammy's picture that she'd barely noticed Kate leave the room. But now she was back, standing in the doorway, wiping her eyes and nose with the side of her hand. "I said, where are they?"

"Kate, what are you talking about? I have no idea."

"You should. You took my quilt pieces, didn't you? Where did you..."

She could see it written across Kate's face, fear and fury so intense that she couldn't think long enough to finish a sentence. Kate was right; she'd taken them. Now all she had to do was convince her that she'd meant no harm.

Sammy hugged her big sister. "It's okay because Grace put them in her closet. It's a surprise. Daddy already told me." Her voice spilled anticipation. "Grace is going to sew up our quilts."

"You can't do that." She pushed her little sister's arms away. "I won't let you." Then she turned toward Sammy and in the most pathetic voice, she aimed cruel words. "Don't you love Mommy?"

"That's enough." She stepped between the girls. "I'm sorry, Kate. I'll—"

"My Mommy makes our quilts. Grandma told me you'd try stuff like this."

Grace took Sammy by the hand and walked toward the door. At the last minute she turned. "I didn't mean…I'm not trying to do anything except…"

But Kate pushed past them. "It's all your fault that I can't take sailing lessons. Just because you hate Derrick. Well, I hate swimming. From now on I hate swimming."

No, you don't. The knowing tightened the shadow that had already begun to strangle her heart. *You hate me.*

With her journal laid open across her lap, Grace curled up on the family room sofa. She loved the way the room flowed into the kitchen and how when the doors were open, it was a natural extension of the outdoors. White washed wood plank ceilings and floors gave the room its cottage feel. This was where the family gathered to play games, read, or unwind after a stressful day.

A day like today.

But tonight she was not unwinding. She was celebrating. It had been two nights since the Light Stalker—that was the name she'd given him—had showed up. If he stayed away, maybe Adam would agree to getting rid of Derrick.

But the greatest event to celebrate was the miracle of a happy ending.

Eight hours earlier if someone had told her she would end the day in one piece, she would have called them crazy.

Her pen couldn't keep up with all that was on her heart. *Thank you, Lord Jesus,* she wrote the words in big letters at the top of her journal page. *Just when I thought Kate's anger would bring down the house, you opened my eyes and allowed me to see into her broken heart.*

She grabbed the throw from the back of the sofa and draped it over her bare feet. Adam would call soon; and she would tell him everything.

Almost two days of cold silence, that's how long she'd waited for the slightest hint that Kate was willing to talk about the quilts or whatever it was that had her acting so hateful. But when Grace could take no more, she did as Adam suggested.

She stopped waiting and confronted Kate.

Lord, help. She'd approached Kate's room turning the prayer over in her mind. *Give me the words I need.* When she opened the door, she found Kate sprawled on her bedspread, arms wrapped around her box of fabric.

Grace made her way to the bed and placed her hand on Kate's back. "Are you asleep?" Kate writhed away. "Listen, I'm sorry." She sat on the edge of her bed. "But you've spent enough time being sad. Your Daddy says we need to talk."

"Maybe I don't want to." Kate propped herself against her headboard. "Where's Sammy? You're supposed to be watching Sammy."

"I put a movie in for her."

With half her heart she wanted to pull Kate into her arms and tell her everything would be okay. With the other half she wanted to lay down the law, tell her she wasn't going to get by with disrespect before handing out some kind of consequence like the ones her parents would have imposed if she or her brother had ever talked that way. She took the box of tissue from Kate's bedside table and placed it between them.

And that was when the miracle started.

God gave her a glimpse inside Kate's heart. Like jagged pieces of broken glass, fear and loneliness, anger and doubt, tumbled around, slashing her spirit. It was a faultless picture of what her friend Abby used to say. "It's amazing what God can do with a broken heart—if you give Him all the pieces."

How long since she'd heard from Abby? She was probably up north attending college, or in some foreign country working in an orphanage, dispensing Bibles and advice, over-doses of advice.

She took a deep breath and leaned closer to Kate. "With all my heart I wish that your mommy could finish your quilt. But she can't. There's nothing I can do about that. Do you understand?"

Kate grabbed a tissue. Those little gasps that take over after someone has cried too long erupted from her chest. "I, I kno-ow-ow."

Grace inched closer until her knees touched Kate's. And this time Kate did not writhe away. "I was wrong to take your quilt box without asking." At least Kate was looking at her. "I found the boxes and I knew the quilt was something your mommy wanted you to have. I guess I just got carried away thinking I could finish it for—"

"Mommy and I liked butterflies." Kate's eyes traveled to her window. "We planted a butterfly garden, but when mommy got sick it died."

She brushed her fingers across Kate's red cheeks. "I'm sorry." And that was when she knew that even though the broken pieces were still there, they were no longer slashing her heart; they were floating, as if they were almost ready to be joined back together.

"I shouldn't be so mean." Kate seemed to lean into her hand. "Sometimes I just need to feel the cloth. It helps me not forget." Fresh tears pooled in her eyes. "I'm afraid I'm going to forget. Daddy and Sammy are forgetting." Grace followed Kate to the window. "That's it." Kate pointed to a plot of ground between the pool and beach. "Down there, by the hammock. That's where Mommy and I planted the..." New gasps filled her voice. "Butterflies like red flowers." She moved away from the window. "Even when I try really hard, I can't remember what her hugs felt like."

"I know." She wrapped her arm around Kate, drawing her closer than they'd been in a long time. "My mommy lives in heaven too, and I really miss her."

She knew something else. She was holding more than this precious child in her arms. She was holding God's promise for a new family.

Grace put her pen down and ran her hand across the side of her face where hours earlier it had been wet with Kate's tears. There'd be more rough days, days when it would seem like the whole house would fall down around her.

But for now the girls were sleeping and the loudest sound in all the house was her pen looping and dotting its way across the page. *Help me, Lord Jesus,* she wrote. *And help Kate too. We both need to give you all our broken pieces.*

Grace didn't expect it to happen so soon. Just two days after she turned the corner with Kate, she was going through her nightly routine, checking on the girls before going to bed. When she peeked into Sammy's room, Sammy wasn't in bed. She was kneeling. "Jesus, I still don't know what to call her. I want to call her Mommy, but I'm afraid Kate will get really mad. How am I supposed to know what to do, Jesus?" Sammy raised her left palm. "Sometimes I think she wants me to call her Mommy." As if to weigh her dilemma, she held up her right hand. "And sometimes I think she wants to run very far away. Maybe one hundred or a thousand miles."

No, no, I've never wanted to run from you, Sammy. Grace wanted to scream her denial. Instead she stood in the door listening, not willing to miss a word of Sammy's soft prayer.

"Daddy told me you will let me know when it's okay. Just how are you going to do that, Jesus?" She refolded her hands. "In Jesus name amen."

Grace didn't know what to do, step into the room or back away before Sammy realized she was there. Before she could decide, Sammy whispered one word.

"Mommy."

She was still on her knees, holding the picture Adam had taken of them together in the pool. She watched her cover the picture with her little hand. The room, the whole house, was silent.

Say it again, Sammy.

"Mommy." Sammy nodded her head, bouncing her messed-up curls. "Yup, God, it's sounding better every day."

It didn't matter that she was holding her breath; a snicker too loud to ignore shot through her nostrils. Almost before Sammy could turn around, she made it half way across the room. "You're up?"

Sammy jumped onto her bed and with a shrug folded her hands in her lap. "I'm looking for Mister Derrick…I think"

"Don't see anyone, do you?"

Sammy shook her head. "Sometimes I think maybe he really isn't mean. Then sometimes…" Her voice turned to a whisper. "Sometimes at night he kicks our sandcastles. Uff-da, y'all not supposed to do that. They break really easy."

She sat on the bed and brought Sammy onto her lap. Almost immediately, her little girl head rested heavy against her chest. As Sammy's tiny fingers wrapped around the sleeve of her robe, Grace realized she'd never felt such softness. Soft pajamas, soft skin, soft voice.

She kissed the top of Sammy's head and rocked back and forth to the song that had moved from her heart to her lips.

Jesus loves me, this I know... It was more than a simple lullaby. It was a song of praise.

After she felt Sammy's body give in to sleep, she tucked the covers around her tiny shoulders. "Jesus, protect my…" She squeezed the word from her throat. "Daughters."

Chapter 11

"Oatmeal or waffles?" Grace placed the milk in the center of the table.

"Waffles please." Sammy scooted between her and the refrigerator and pulled out the syrup. "I like waffles, especially with lots of this stuff all over the top."

"She can't put the syrup on by herself." Kate took her place at the table. "You have to, Grace."

Neither had called her Mommy; but in her heart she knew it was coming, maybe when Adam came home for his birthday.

Life was full of promise. Her relationship with Kate had improved; the light stalker and Derrick were making themselves scarce. Best of all, just like this morning, Sammy followed her around most of the day, dancing and jabbering.

"Grandma always makes me get dressed first." Sammy raised onto tip-toes, absorbed in watching the toaster. "But I like this more better."

She swallowed the urge to correct Sammy's grammar, and was still buttering waffles when she caught a shadow out of the corner of her eye. In the next second, the door opened.

"Morning, ladies."

"Derrick." She set the plates in front of the girls and drew her robe around her tight, like a winter sweater. "You can't just—"

"How's Curly?" He tousled Sammy's hair. "Ready for a fun day?"

"No, we're going to church." Sammy grabbed the bottle of syrup and began pouring.

"Day's too beautiful to be sitting in a stuffy old church."

"Leave her alone." She took the syrup from Sammy and passed it to Kate. "She's uncomfortable with you doing that to her."

When he sat in Adam's chair, her skin prickled. "How about some coffee," he said. "You got any of that flavored cream?" He pulled a paper clip from his shirt pocket, bent it open, and dug it deep into his ear.

She held her can of ginger-ale next to her face. "Haven't been drinking coffee." With all that was in her, she wanted to push his tropical shirt and bare feet out the door.

"A day like today," he transferred the paper clip to his other ear and winked at Kate, "we should all go out on my boat. We can hit the upper island and grab a burger and beans and rice at Barnacle Bill's."

"Can we, Grace? Please." Kate brought the plates to the sink. "We can be ready really fast." She pulled on Sammy's arm.

"Kate, we're going to church." In an instant the *I-don't-believe-you're-doing-this* look covered Kate's face. "You need to shower and—"

Again, Derrick winked at Kate. "Be nice, Grace." Before she could move, he wrapped his arm around her shoulder. "Come on, when was last time you were on my boat?"

The last time she was on his boat? She wrenched away and started scrubbing the table. "Upstairs, girls. Showers. Kate, help Sammy."

As soon as the girls were upstairs, she turned to Derrick, looking him straight in his eyes. "Whatever game you're playing...you're pitiful." She wadded the dish cloth into a ball and threw it across the kitchen, all the way into the sink.

If only she could throw away the memory. Even though it had been years, she had no defense, no shield big enough to protect her from the memory of what happened on his boat. The shaking, the feeling of being the emptiest and lowest person on the face of the earth, things like that were too big to ever forget. She could still hear that one word: "Good." It was all he said when she told him she'd done what he wanted.

He didn't cry, not a tear.

She remembered how she lost it that day. Between violent sobs, she screamed every truth hiding inside her heart. "Good? You think it's good? There's something seriously wrong with you."

Just like this morning, there'd been a smirk on his face. "You got to get that thought out of your head."

That's when her anger had flared. She'd grabbed his half-full beer can and threw it across the bullet-shaped galley. "Baby, Derrick, our baby." She never liked the smell of beer, but that morning it disgusted her. By the time she stepped off the boat, every inch of her flesh burned, fueled by an endless well of rage. "You're okay with murdering your own baby." She didn't care if the whole island heard.

One week later she was home in Minnesota, as far away from him as she could get.

She didn't think she'd ever return to Tesoro. She still didn't know if it was God's providence, like their pastor claimed, that brought her back, but here she was, staring at the same fixed smirk.

And still longing to hold her baby.

She didn't know what gave her the courage to stand up to him. All she knew was she couldn't allow him to ruin everything. Not again. So she spent the next five minutes doing what she'd been putting off ever since the first day she was alone with Derrick. One-by-one, she listed the rules. From now on he would not step foot inside the house unless he was invited. It didn't matter if she and the girls were walking on the beach or sitting by the pool; he would stay away. And when Adam was home, he'd not go near him. That was it. Her last word, the way it was going to be.

She felt good about how she handled the situation. He hadn't interrupted, not even once. "If you have any questions, ask them now. We're going to church. Ought to give it a try sometime."

With a flick, Derrick shot his filthy paper clip across the table. "To church, pretty holy, aren't you?" A chuckle flared his nostrils. "Are those your rules or Adam's?" He walked backwards toward the door, looking her up and down. "We both know you're here to baby-sit. Babysitter with benefits, that's about it."

Her face burned. "Get out."

A fake mask of pity fell over his face and he took a step toward her. "Trust me; I feel sorry for you, Grace." He moved closer, until all he had to do was whisper. "Because Adam's using you."

Run or slap his face. Those were the urges beating against her mind. But she couldn't. The girls were upstairs getting ready for church. One word, that's all she could muster. "Leave."

He backed the rest of the way toward the door. Without looking, his hand found the knob. "Don't forget who knows your secrets, Grace." The room spun. "And, from where I stand, that means one thing." He slid his sunglasses over his eyes. "I'm the one who'll be making the rules."

Not even Derrick could steal the beauty and peace of the evening. After a day when the heat and humidity blistered temperatures into the upper nineties, the evening breeze felt as light and fresh as if it had drifted off a mountain, instead of a body of hot and salty water. Grace rested her head against the back of the chair and let the wind wash across her face. With every inch of her heart, she wished Adam was sitting next to her on the veranda, his bare feet skirmishing for equal space on the wicker ottoman. As silly as it seemed, that's what she missed most, his touch, even the unexpected touch of his toes.

As I hoped, she wrote in her journal, *Kate reneged on her no-swimming vow and together we coaxed Sammy into the deep end of the pool. First time. Hurray for Sammy! The only down side to the day was Derrick. Oh, Lord, how am I going to find a way out of this?*

She put her pen down and listened to the swash and roll of waves as they washed on shore. In many ways life had become equally predictable. She and the girls were growing closer and, even though conflicts popped up, there hadn't been any major incidents since the dispute over going out on Derrick's boat. Still, the stress of life without Adam was taking its toll. In the last week, she'd gone through enough ginger ale and soda crackers to last ten flu seasons. Two, at most three times each week the light-stalker shined his light, but she refused to call Derrick. Anyway, what good would it do? The stalker never came closer than the beach. And he always seemed to move on quickly.

Her cell rang and she scribbled the last line. *Another week till Adam comes home.*

As soon as she heard Adam's voice, she could tell he was exhausted. She could almost see him sitting at a hotel desk, one way too small, his papers spread in neat little piles across the bed behind him. "Only seven more days," she said. "Uff-da, the girls are so—"

"That's what we have to talk about."

"Not again." Every muscle in her body tightened and, like paint on one of those carnival paint wheels, one thought after another spun through her mind. *He wouldn't. Couldn't. His birthday…Adam knows how important birthdays are to his daughters.*

"Grace, I don't like it any more than you; but I have to stay. Another few days, that's all."

"You can't."

"I need you to understand."

She fixed her eyes on the moon floating like a giant balloon above the water. Right now, it was all that connected her to the man she loved. Then she closed her eyes, trying to come up with the right words, something that would help Adam see how important it was that he come home.

But when she opened her eyes, it wasn't the moon she saw. She darted into the bedroom and sat on the edge of the bed. "It's never been so close…the light...it's on this side of the pool. The stairs, he could—"

"Come on, Grace. I can't do this tonight." Irritation coated every word. "I need to know you and the girls are okay with—"

"Right now, I don't care what you need." The words were out before she could stop them. "All I care about—"

"Call Derrick. That's why he's there."

"I'm not going to call Derrick." She was pacing now, back and forth from the door to the bed. "I can't make you believe; but there is a stalker and what if he's not interested in me." The phone trembled against her ear. "Could be one of the girls. You hear about stuff like that all the time. Would you turn their safety over to someone like Derrick?"

"Grace, that isn't fair. I'll call Derrick."

It was obvious; all he cared about was getting off the phone. She pushed the corner of the drape back, sneaking a quick look outside. Darkness. Just as quickly as the light had appeared, it vanished.

But that didn't matter; her stomach still churned, worse than ever, and she knew she only had seconds to plead her case. "It is not okay for you to come home late…your birthday party…the girls and I have been—" Before she could say another word, a wave of nausea overpowered her. She had no choice; she dropped the phone and ran for the bathroom.

It seemed like she spent an eternity on the floor in front of the toilet, a damp rag draped across her neck. Maybe what Derrick said was true. The only reason Adam married her was because he wanted to use her. She sat back against the bathroom wall, pulled the wedding band from her hand and read the inscription. *Let us exalt His name together.*

Fresh tears ran down her throat. Together. That was it. Now that they were married, Adam no longer wanted to be together. And if that's how he felt now, she could only imagine how he would feel if Derrick tackled him with the truth. She wrapped her arms around her knees and rocked. If God had forgiven her, why did she feel so worthless?

Show me, God, she prayed. *Every part of my heart is open before you. There's nothing you don't see. You see me sitting here; you even hear the cries I hold inside. I'm a broken mess, Lord, a mess with Adam out of town all the time. What can I do? Just show me. Fix my broken pieces.*

Chapter 12

Adam yanked the price tag off his Minnesota Twins shirt. It didn't matter that his ticket was for tonight's game, there was no way he could tolerate the ear-piercing strain of cracking baseball bats and screaming fans with their smelly hotdogs and beers.

He couldn't because he was falling apart.

Why had he let things go so far? Grace was the part of him he needed most, more than legs or arms. It sounded corny, but that's how much he needed her.

All he had to do was tell her he was sorry, sorry she was sick, sorry he'd disappointed her. One way or another, he'd find a way home for his birthday.

But being sorry couldn't change the truth.

He was torn.

When he was home, in the bedroom he once shared with Beth, he couldn't help himself. There was a part of him that felt guilty.

Adam, I don't care what you need. He sat on the edge of the bed, Grace's voice still ricocheting between the walls of his mind. After all, it wasn't totally his fault. These feelings had to be normal.

Without warning, his heart lurched; his mind flew into a gallop, like a wild mustang. He had to escape.

Panic attack. That had been the doctor's explanation when the same thing happened years before. But he'd been certain he was having a heart attack and ended up in the hospital where Beth lay fighting for her life. He raked through his memory. What was the verse she had prayed over him, something about God quieting him? That's what he needed; someone to pray for him. But there was no one.

Not even Grace.

He'd taken care of that.

From the door to the window, into the bathroom, back to the door, he paced. Over and over again, and still he found no escape from the fire inside him. He snatched the ice bucket from the desk and cracked open the door. When he was certain no one was in the hall, he made his way toward the ice machine. Back in the room, he rubbed fistfuls of ice on his face and arms, allowing the freezing water to run down his neck and drip from his hands and elbows.

This was worse than before. Where was Beth's verse? He opened the Bible, leaving wet fingerprints on each page. But all he found were lifeless words.

And he knew why.

After treating Grace the way he had, God wouldn't talk to him.

With no destination in mind, he fled the hotel, using the back stairs so no one would see him. He made his way across the hotel parking lot, weaving between cars until he reached the paved walking path that ran along the highway frontage road. *Walk, Adam, walk,* block-by-block he urged himself on as impenetrable traffic whizzed past him. But the red lights were too red, green lights too green, darting like poison swords toward him. Horns honked, brakes screeched, voices pounded, louder and louder.

Still, nothing pounded louder than his heart.

He had to get back to his room or he would die, die out here alone on the street. *For heaven's sake, Adam, you didn't bring your planner. You must have your planner.* He saw himself, dead on the street, a circle of strangers surrounding him, smothering every breath. As fast as he could, he cut through restaurant and shopping center parking lots, back toward the hotel, incessantly punching Grace's number.

Answer, Grace, answer. I need to hear your voice.

After reaching the hotel, there wasn't much that stayed in his mind. He remembered waving down a taxi, remembered being trapped in the back seat, the bologna stench, the lights and noise. Even though the driver promised he could get him to the hospital in ten minutes, it took an eternity and the whole time he kept thinking maybe this was the real thing. Maybe this time he was going to die.

Grace had to know what was happening. She had to know he was sorry. He called the land line; he called her cell. But she didn't answer. He couldn't break down and send a text. He couldn't leave a message; it would only frighten her. There was only one thing to do.

Call Derrick.

CHAPTER 13

"Open the blasted door."

At first Grace thought it was a dream. Why would Derrick be on her veranda, screaming her name and pounding on her door? She took the pillow from Adam's side of the bed and positioned it like a roof over her head. But the racket continued. What was Derrick trying to do, wake the girls?

"Come on, Grace, at least come to the door so I can give you Adam's message."

"Go away." She couldn't believe that Adam had actually called Derrick. Hadn't she asked him not to?

"Not until I give you his message."

She had no choice. She grabbed her robe and opened the door just enough to stick her head out.

"You look like…" Derrick wrapped his hand around the door, nudging it open with his knee. "You're not doin' so good. Let me get you something."

She knotted her bathrobe belt. "Does Adam want me to call?"

"Didn't really say. Said he wasn't feeling too good, asked me to check on you."

"You sure he didn't want me to call?"

"Looks like some fresh air might do you some good." He stepped back and shoved his hands deep into his pockets. "Look, I'm sorry about before, shouldn't have said that stuff. No strings, just a walk."

She still felt queasy. Fresh air would help, but she couldn't take a walk, not with Derrick. It wouldn't be right. She looked over her shoulder. "The girls, I can't."

"Come on, they'll be fine. And if the light stalker returns, we can—"

"You saw him?"

"Didn't take my eyes off him until I got done chasing him away."

"He came a lot closer to the house this time."

"Won't get any closer," he vowed. "So are you taking that walk?"

Maybe God was answering her prayer. Maybe He was showing her that the way to get by was being kind to Derrick, treating him like a friend instead of her enemy. Besides, if he hadn't been there to chase the stalker away, who knows what might have happened. The possibilities were too gruesome to consider. A simple walk on the beach might help. On top of everything, why should she have to give up the things she loves just because Adam isn't around? Derrick was right; as long as she was with him and they stayed within eyesight of the house, they'd be safe. "Let me check on the girls. I'll meet you in five minutes."

She threw on a pair of jeans and a white blouse, rolling the sleeves up to her elbows. Her heart was divided; half of it telling her this was dangerous, even wrong, the other half telling her it was God's answer to her prayer.

She was almost to the beach when she realized she'd forgotten her phone. What if Adam called? She should go back. But she'd already come this far.

"I can't be long…the girls." She kicked off her flip flops.

And then she and Derrick walked like they had so many times before, close enough to the waves to catch the spray, making small-talk. "I painted the boat," he said. "Your favorite color, and made a bookcase. Put it in the corner, next to the head."

An uneasy feeling twisted her insides. Why would he remember her favorite color? She couldn't remember his. If she could, it wouldn't matter. "Bookcase?" She kicked her feet through the warm water. "You're reading? Really?"

"I'm planning to. Any suggestions?

She couldn't imagine Derrick curled up with a book. She thought about telling him the most important book he'd ever read was the Bible.

Trouble was, it was also the least likely book Derrick would open. Even so, she had to make the suggestion; it was her responsibility. What he did with the idea was up to him.

"Where are you?" The scream cut across the night air. Kate was on the beach, just yards away, hands on her hips, with Sammy behind her.

Grace ran toward them and wrapped Sammy tight in her arms. "Uff-da." She rubbed her little back. "I'm here."

"Sammy had a bad dream." Kate's hands flew to her hips. "Y'all left us. I checked Daddy's room."

Sammy wrapped her legs around Grace's waist and dropped her head on her shoulder. "I had a very bad dream and it scared me lots."

Once again Kate's hands found her hips. "I'm going to tell Daddy."

"Watch your mouth." Derrick stepped between them, his voice as demanding as Kate's. "Who do you think you're talking to?"

"Grandma says we're not supposed to be alone with the work people and Grace broke that rule."

She didn't have the energy to worry about Derrick's feelings. Without saying a word, Grace put her hand on Kate's back and led the girls into the house.

As soon as she locked the door, that's when she knew that walking on the beach was a mistake.

A mistake, she might not be able to make right.

Lord Jesus, how am I ever going to find my way through this? That one question had kept Grace awake all night. It wasn't until two in the morning that she'd been able to stretch out on the bedroom recliner where, according to Adam, Beth had spent so many nights.

The sun was up now, but she had no desire to move. She tucked the small blanket tight around her shoulders and looked across the room to where Sammy slept. After Sammy's nightmare, she'd invited both girls to spend the night with her, but Kate refused, stomping off to her room.

Sammy, though, had jumped into bed, resting her head on Adam's pillow. "The bad man chased me into the water." She pulled the covers tight, all the way up to her chin. "I tried really hard but my toes couldn't find the sand. Daddy was in a boat; but I don't think he saw me because he was laughing really, really hard." Sammy looked so tiny and terrified. "Even when I screamed like this." She sat up, cupped her hands around her mouth, and let out a screech. "He didn't even hear me." Fresh tears dripped off the tip of her chin. "Daddy should have heard me. It's way, way too scary to sleep."

Looking at her little face, her bottom lip tightly tucked under her upper one, her eyes large and filled with lingering fear, Grace knew exactly what she had to do. "I've been saving something just for you." She scooped Sammy into her arms and carried her to the closet where she pulled the treasure from its hiding place. Tenderly, she removed its pink tissue paper blanket.

"She needs a lot of love." That's what she said when she released the plush lamb into Sammy's arms. "And I know you're just the one who will love her."

For the first time since her dream, a smile lit Sammy's eyes. "Thank you, Grace. Can I give her a name?"

She'd told her yes. "And when you hold her close and feel her soft fur, she will help you remember that you are Jesus' lamb." She ran her fingers through the clean white fur. "And no matter what, Jesus will always take care of you because He loves you."

It was what her mom had told her when she was a little girl, and it was exactly how she planned to comfort her own children. That's why, even before she'd told Derrick they were going to have a baby, she bought the lamb.

She wondered if her heart would always grieve for the baby who would never cuddle the lamb or build sandcastles with the girls. But Sammy was here. It would be selfish to allow grief to stand in the way of love.

Sammy spent a good ten minutes studying the lamb before she announced, "I think I'll call her Snow." She'd kissed the top of the lamb's head. "Because you are white just like the snow." Minutes after Snow received her name Sammy fell asleep.

And the pillow her head rested on was not Adam's. It was hers.

It hurt, she wrote in her journal later that night. *But somehow I know it was a milestone. A miracle because for the first time ever, when I look at Sammy, all I see is Sammy.*

Sammy stirred, kicking the covers off. She'd be up soon, ready for another day, but it was still too early and she needed time to pull herself together before she had to face the girls with the news that Adam wasn't coming home for his birthday. She tucked the blanket around Sammy's shoulders, and was just about to head downstairs when her cell rang. She grabbed it from the nightstand, wrapping it in her hand as she quickly made her way to the veranda where she could talk without waking Sammy.

"Mrs. Will?"

"Yes."

"This is the discharge nurse from South Metro Hospital."

"Who? Adam, did something happen to—"

"Mrs. Will, your husband is fine. But when he was discharged, he neglected to take his copy of instructions. You're listed…and we just need to make sure Mr. Will schedules a follow-up with his personal physician. Should be within the next couple days. Will you pass on the message?"

She sat back and waited for something that would tell her the call was a joke. Why would he go to an emergency room in the middle of the night? Why hadn't he called? Wasn't she important enough? Maybe Derrick was right. Maybe she was nothing more than a babysitter.

As soon as the nurse hung up, Grace tiptoed downstairs to Adam's office, closing the door behind her. On the second ring, Adam answered.

"What's going on?" She hated the way her voice came across as cold and distant. What if something was wrong with him? Even if he pushed her away, she'd fight to be close. She took a deep breath and did her best to soften her voice. "I received a call from the emergency room. They want you to set up an appointment with your doctor." She plunked herself at his desk. "Adam, why didn't you call me?"

"What do y'all mean?" This time it was his voice that was icy. "Not even a phone call, Grace?"

"You told me not to."

"I specifically asked Derrick to have you call. He didn't tell you? Listen, the good part of this, I'm fixin to come home. Would you do a favor and call Dr. Wood?"

It wasn't that she wanted Adam sick. She wanted him home. She wanted him to need her the same way her Dad had always needed her Mom. This was her chance to actually prove to him that she could be the wife he needed. It was a small thing, just the first step.

CHAPTER 14

"Sit next to your Daddy." Adam patted the seat next to his.

Usually he didn't allow the girls to ride in the front seat, not even in the golf cart. But this time of year, with the island almost deserted, it would be safe. Besides, he needed Kate in the front seat where he could see her face. Ever since he came home, she'd gone back to being pouty. And he intended to find out why.

Kate set her red overnight bag on the floor. Without looking at him, she slid onto the seat.

With temperatures in the mid nineties, the day had been stifling. But summer days were as predictable as they were hot; in little time, the clouds would gather over the Gulf and slowly roll toward shore. Growls of thunder would follow, assuring islanders that cool relief was on the way.

"Tell me what y'all been up to." He turned right, toward Pastor Karl's where Kate had been invited to a sleepover.

"I don't know." Kate played with the cuff on her shorts, rolling it up, then smoothing it down. "I like it better when you're home."

He reached over and brushed her hair behind her ear. "I'm the one who should be sulking," he said. "First night poor old Daddy's home and you're off to a sleepover."

"It's a birthday, Daddy. I have to."

He was getting irritated. Kate knew how he felt about looking at people when she talked. "How are you and Sammy doing with Grace?"

"Sammy's doing fine, I guess. I don't know; sometimes it's just hard, Daddy."

"Kate, I need you to look at me when you talk."

He'd expected Kate to have a more difficult time adjusting than Sammy. She was the one who remembered Beth. But if anyone could win her over it was Grace. He reached over and covered his daughter's hand. "Have you decided to let Grace finish your quilt?"

Kate shrugged. "I don't know. I was going to and then…" She shrugged again. "I don't know."

"Something happen?"

"Daddy, she left us alone and Sammy had a bad dream." The words poured out like sour milk until at last she looked at him. "If she loves us so much, she should have been there."

"So that's it." He knew his daughter, could almost feel her confusion as she desperately tried to cling to a life that no longer was hers.

Another thing he knew, Grace would never leave his daughters alone. He couldn't ask for a more perfect woman to take Beth's place.

"Mommy would have never gone out walking on the beach when we were in bed. I just know it, Daddy."

"Mommy did. And I do. You're always safe, aren't you?"

"She was walking with Mr. Derrick. Grandma says we aren't supposed to be friends with people who work for us."

"Kate, sometimes Grandma is wrong."

He turned into Pastor Karl's driveway and before his keys were out of the ignition, Kate was out of the golf cart, running up the steps of her best friend's house, leaving him to carry her bag.

"Thanks," he said when Pastor Karl invited him in. "But Grace and Sammy are fixin to put in a movie and I promised..."

The truth was he needed time to put his thoughts in order.

As he drove toward home, he tried to erase the picture in his mind. *Grace walking on the beach with Derrick, what's that about?* He was hot, the kind of hot that made him dizzy. *There's something there, something between them, I can feel it.*

By the time he drove past the school, he could no longer hold back the panic. His hands gripped the wheel. Why hadn't he taken the car? Every minute lasted an hour, every foot the cart traveled, seemed like a mile. He urged himself forward. He needed Grace; and he needed to know the truth about Derrick.

But even more, he needed the bottle of tiny white pills the emergency room doctor had placed in his hand.

The time had come. Hiding the truth about Derrick had become too difficult. Grace had made her decision, and there was no turning back. Today was the day she would tell Adam the truth.

All of it.

She clipped a red hibiscus from the bush in front of their home. It wasn't that she enjoyed gardening or that she was like other islanders who kept hibiscus vases sitting on every ledge. Clipping the bell-shaped flower was the only excuse she could come up with for standing in the front yard, watching for Adam. Even if it started to rain, she'd stand there because she had to see his face the minute he returned from dropping Kate at Pastor Karl's.

It was the only way she'd know if Kate had told about her walking on the beach with Derrick, the only way she'd know where to begin.

It didn't matter how many times she told herself that taking a walk in front of their home was not a sin, a louder, more persistent voice insisted she was guilty.

And that's why, even before Adam flew home, she'd written the decision in her journal. Writing the promise to tell Adam everything about Derrick, their baby, and how ashamed and sorry she was, made it real, almost like an oath. If he really loved her, he'd believe there was no longer anything between them. His own heart would tell him that she was a new person.

When the gates swung open, an urge to turn away swept over her. It would be so much easier. She wouldn't have to look into his eyes; she wouldn't have to tell him the truth. But God wanted her to tell the truth, and he'd promised he'd give her everything she needed.

Even the words to speak.

She waved as the cart came to a stop in front of the house. But Adam marched right past her, into the house, up the stairs, two at a time.

"Adam?" It was all she could do to keep up.

"It's... I'm having another attack." Adam paced around the bed, his face watermelon-red as he pressed both hands into his chest. "What time is my appointment? Doc has to see me now. Call."

She didn't know what to do so she paced behind him. "Sit down. I'll rub your back. Your appointment is in three hours."

"Get the pills. I'm sorry, Grace, just get the pills from my briefcase."

What else could she do? Sammy was due to be dropped off any minute from her dance class. She expected to watch a movie with her Daddy. She couldn't see him like this. Grace laid the tiny pill in her hand and offered it to Adam.

Twenty minutes later, he sat quietly on the edge of the bed with a wet towel around his neck. He patted the spot next to him. "I'm sorry. It just came out of nowhere."

She took his hand, rubbing his ring between her fingers. "What happened? Kate?"

"She told me you and Derrick were—"

"Adam, there's absolutely nothing—" If she confessed now, just minutes after he'd suffered a panic attack and before he saw the doctor, it would hurt him, maybe even throw him into another attack. She almost felt relief when she took the first step away from her decision.

"She said you were on the beach together." He pulled his hand away. "What is it between you and Derrick? There's something. I can feel it."

"Adam, remember I never wanted Derrick here in the first place. Of course there's tension, nothing more."

As she assured him, she could see the tightness leave his body, and when he brought her hand to his lips, she knew she'd done the right thing.

This wasn't the first time; there'd been other times she'd heard God wrong. The truth was clear; God wanted her to hold her secret, at least until a better time.

Chapter 15

Adam gripped the steering wheel. Where had time gone? Two doctor appointments, a little time with his girls, even less with Grace, and just like that his two days home were gone. In less than ninety minutes he had to be at the airport. Not enough time to get stuck on the bridge waiting for construction workers to move little orange cones from one lane to the other. He pulled the seatbelt away from his chest and checked the rear view mirror. A line of cars, rare for this time of year, stretched behind him, well beyond the cluster of palms that marked the entrance to Tesoro Island Welcome Center.

He took his planner from the seat next to his and paged to the first week in August. July, where had it gone? Every month seemed to move faster than the one before. Grace was right about his birthday. He should have acknowledged it from the start. But when he came home for his doctor appointment, he promised Grace and the girls he'd return in time for his birthday celebration. The promise that gave him only two days to accomplish over a week's worth of work.

He could still see his doctor looking over the top of smudged glasses. "Adam," he'd said, "you're sacrificing your health, maybe even your life to the demands of that planner." He ripped the paper from his pad and handed it to him. "I won't give you refills unless you talk to someone, even your pastor, about these attacks."

Eighty minutes to get to the airport. Even though the last couple days had been hectic, he enjoyed being home with his family. He'd gone to the Bible study group with Grace and it felt natural sitting next to her on a sofa, holding her hand and taking part in a discussion about the power of prayer. Old Fisher Johnson, with yellow teeth and breath that smelled like stale chewing tobacco, made the evening delightful. He cut through all their jargon and sanctimonious equations. "All yaw gotta say is, 'Lord Jesus, help.'" A shabby black Bible trembled in his crooked hands. "Why waste time telling God how to do His job or tellin' things He already knows?"

One thing he didn't have to explain to God or anyone else was that he'd missed a lot this summer. He missed the first time Sammy jumped into the deep end of the pool. He missed listening to Kate recite her poems. He missed going to sleep to the steady whoosh-whoosh of the ceiling fan and the soft scent of Grace's lotion.

The blast of a horn shattered the stillness and he inched forward. In seventy-five minutes he'd be officially late. He took a deep breath. What was the song Kate and Sammy spent the morning singing? He rested his head against the back of the seat as traffic inched toward the mainland. It was from the movie they'd watched the night before. Maybe it was childish, but like the movie suggested, he ticked a list of his favorite things off the top of his mind. *Kate and Sammy's tickles, Grace's soft hand in his.* His grip on the wheel relaxed. *Sitting next to Grace on the bedroom veranda, watching dolphins play, the sunset, making breakfast…*

As the list grew, he could feel the muscles in his jaw relax. He didn't know where the voice came from. It was like an inner nudging. *Adam, why do you spend so much time running from your favorite things?*

Sixty minutes. He was off the island now and traffic moved at a steady pace. Still, his mind lingered at home. Last night when they watched the movie, he spent most of his time watching Sammy snuggled next to Grace, pulling on her hair, trying to braid it the way she braids her dolls'. It was as natural as the unplanned moments Beth had spent with Kate.

He'd have to admit sometimes it seemed Kate was the most immovable child. After the movie, right in front of Grace, she told him she was afraid Beth would get angry if someone else finished her quilt. Grace didn't say a word. She simply got up, gathered their empty popcorn bowls and soda cans and brought them into the kitchen. That's the way she was.

Mommy might get angry. When Kate's words weren't playing over in his mind, his own questions bobbed to the surface. *Is Beth angry because Grace is completing the plans we had?*

Twenty minutes. He was pulling onto airport property when his cell rang.

"How's traffic?"

"It's been cruel, but I'm fixin to park."

"I made the appointment," Grace said. "She fit me in, tomorrow at three."

It had been like selling sugar to a dentist to get Grace to agree to a doctor appointment for herself.

Last night when he crawled into bed and wrapped his arms around her, her bones poked painfully into his flesh. Without meaning to, he pulled away. "Grace, you're getting too thin. I want you to make an appointment," he'd said.

Of course she argued, telling him it was stress. But he insisted until she agreed.

He pulled his suitcase from the back seat. Fifteen minutes. He had fifteen minutes to get to the gate.

And little more than forty-eight hours to get back home.

Grace couldn't sleep. The house was too quiet, her thoughts too loud.

She tucked the sheets around her shoulders and tried not to think; but she could still see Dr. Rich's round face and her curly black hair. "We'll give it another month, and then we'll have to do something about your weight loss." Grace turned onto her back and searched for assurance that the doctor's next words were true.

If she could tell Adam, then maybe she'd believe. But it wasn't fair to tell him over the phone; that's why she hadn't said a word when he called. If only she knew how he was going to handle the news. She pulled herself out of bed and made her way to the veranda.

Heavenly Father. She rested her hands on her stomach. *You know the truth about yesterday, today, and tomorrow; but still I'm afraid. What if it's true…what is Adam going to do?* She looked out beyond the pool to the beach where the full moon floated moon-diamonds on the Gulf's black waves.

At least for now, the light stalker was gone and Derrick was too busy working on his boat to irritate her. He'd met someone, at least that's the way he made it sound the night they walked on the beach.

"Boat's ready for us as soon as hurricane season is over." He sounded so proud.

"Us?" She couldn't hide her shock. "Do you have someone going with you?"

"Surprised?" That's all he would say.

Once again, her attention was drawn to the moon's reflection on the waves. Ever since she put the girls to bed, she'd longed to go out there. She slipped into her sandals and robe. All she needed was a few minutes, enough time to dip her toes in the water.

Enough time to hear God's voice.

Her toes were barely wet when he stepped out of the darkness. "Derrick." It felt like her heart flipped into her throat. "You scared the life right out of me."

"Need some company?"

"That's okay." Without brushing the sand from her feet, she stepped back into her sandals. "I'm heading in."

Derrick's steps matched hers. "I'll walk you back."

"It's not necessary, Trick." She retied the belt on her robe. "I'm fine alone. And I don't want Kate…it just doesn't look right."

But Derrick didn't seem to care how it looked, because as they walked across the sand, he moved closer. "I was wondering." He took her elbow and helped her step around a small sand dune. "Could you tell me where I can buy some of those books you write in? I want to get a supply before I leave."

"Don't tell me you're journaling, or is it the mystery woman who's going with you?"

She didn't know how long they stood at the foot of the stairs. Long enough to hire him to paint the girls' playroom, and long enough to find out he was thinking of leaving early, maybe late September, before hurricane season was officially over.

"Figured you'd be happy if I left early—kind of the sooner-the-better." He sat on the steps and looked up at her with his familiar grin. "You jealous I got someone going with me?"

"Dream on." She'd forgotten how much she enjoyed ending the day bantering back and forth like this. "On that boat, I'd be your worst nightmare." She stepped around him and started up the stairs.

Derrick didn't move. "Thanks for tonight."

"It's okay." She turned to face him. "We need the room painted."

"Well, that too. I can use the money" He looked up at her, and for a minute she thought he might try to follow her up the stairs.

But she didn't have to worry. When Derrick stood, he came no closer. "Thanks," he said, "for calling me Trick."

Chapter 16

Grace couldn't explain the way she felt, so on edge, as if her world was about to turn up-side-down. She ran Sammy's comb under the kitchen faucet before gently pulling it through her tangled curls. "So what color should we paint your playroom?"

"Red for Kate and blue for me."

"Not white or brown?"

Sammy's nose was still wrinkled in disapproval when Kate clumped into the kitchen wearing a red sundress accented by bright yellow flip-flops, ones that were years away from fitting her little-girl feet. "Derrick's going to paint up there?" Kate grabbed a banana and plopped herself at the table. "Does Daddy know?"

"Of course." Grace snapped Sammy's barrette into place and helped her down from the stool. "We're picking out the paint today."

She couldn't remember ever talking to adults the way Kate did. One day she was as sweet as apple juice, the next as bitter as apple vinegar. There was a time when she thought it would be easy to pull Kate out of these mood swings. "You know, a smile isn't going to crack your face." As soon as the words left her tongue she wanted to take them back. "What happened? I never know when…" She stood at the end of the table, as close to Kate as she cared to get. "Uff-da, I love you. I'm doing my best. Kate, will you just give me a break for one day?"

Kate rolled her eyes before turning away.

And that's when she snapped.

"Those shoes are too big for you, young lady." Certainly, Kate could hear the anger that had set her stomach on fire. "Take them off. Find some that fit." She took her keys off the kitchen hook. "Sammy and I will be waiting in the car."

It wasn't until she turned back toward Kate that she noticed the tears spilling from her eyes. "All I'm asking for is a chance." She laid the keys on the counter.

"I don't care." Kate took a bite of her banana.

She could barely hear Kate's voice. But Kate did care. If she didn't, she wouldn't be sitting at the table crying, unable to swallow the small bite of banana that puffed her cheek. "Help us pick out the paint." She pulled out the chair next to Kate's. "If you don't, who knows what color we'll end up with? Maybe princess pink or—"

"Fine." Without looking up, Kate picked up her half eaten banana and walked it to the trash. "But the flip-flops." By the time she sat back at the table, tears were rolling off the tip of her chin. "They were Mommy's."

Her Mommy's shoes.

She wrapped a strand of Kate's hair around her finger. "Oh, Kate, I promise you're going to be okay." She pulled two napkins from the holder in the center of the table, handed one to Kate, and kept the other for her own tears. "Uff-da, wear the flip-flops. It won't be long and they'll fit perfect."

Perfect. Even with Kate tripping over the flip-flops, perfect was the word that described the rest of the day. After picking out paint, they headed across the bridge to shop for curtains and a rug. They were almost done shopping when she felt a tug on her pony tail.

Before she could turn around she heard the familiar voice. "Grace, Grace Andrews, when did they let you out of the pool?"

If she had known when she woke up that in hours she'd be reunited with her friend, she wouldn't have cared if Kate wore purple mittens on her feet. "Abby? Where have you been? I tried to find your address so I could send you—"

Abby grabbed her left hand. "Look at that," she said as Sammy pushed between them. "And who are these pretty ladies?"

She wanted to tell Abby they were her daughters; but she didn't want to lose the ground she'd gained with Kate that morning. It felt like an hour passed before Sammy spoke up. "She's our new mommy. Who are you?"

Mommy. Since the day she and Adam spoke their vows, she'd waited for that one word. *Mommy*. Now, she wanted Sammy to say it again and again.

But Sammy could barely fit in a word. As was common, Abby drove the conversation, explaining to the girls how they'd been friends when they taught swimming together. "That was before we both moved away. One day maybe I'll have my own daughters, just like you."

"And you can bring them over to play with us." It was as if Sammy was making plans for next week. "They can come to my birthday party. I'm having a real circus with clowns, right Mommy?"

"God knows what's ahead." Abby took both Sammy's hands in hers "Who would have guessed He had two such beautiful daughters planned for your new mommy?"

Abby lowered her voice to little more than a whisper. "Have you heard from Derrick?"

She should have known the question was coming. Her stomach twisted. Even though she hadn't been open to her friend's nagging any more than she'd been open to her invitations to attend church, Abby had never stopped warning her about Derrick. In the end, it had been cause to avoid her friend.

But not anymore. She left the mall with Abby's phone number tucked inside her purse and plans for Abby to come over the next day for lunch.

On the way home Sammy said, "God answered my prayer."

"What prayer, honey?" She pulled down her visor so she could see Sammy's reflection in the mirror.

"Kate isn't angry anymore. I think she likes you now."

How much better did it get than this? "I love her too. I love both..." The words were a gift, and she delighted in each one. "I love both my daughters." As soon as the words were out, that's when she realized she'd been right that morning.

Today was the day her world turned up-side-down.

CHAPTER 17

Grace still didn't eat much more than crackers and soup, but Abby hadn't changed, so she placed the bowl of chicken salad within easy reach.

"Is it the curry or cashews?" Abby licked her fingers before scooping a heaping second portion onto her plate. "It's the best. I mean, if Adam's business goes belly-up, you could sell this to the island deli and save the day."

"Don't go saying that around him," she warned. "The economy and all, he's worried enough."

It still amazed her how Abby could eat like a football player and never gain one pound. But that wasn't the only unchangeable thing. Abby still asked the snoopiest questions, the kind that always seemed to get under her skin, like those little no-see-um bugs that swarm the beach at sunset.

"Why does Derrick have a key to your house?" They'd finished eating and were sitting on the edge of the pool when Abby brought it up. "I'm warning you, Grace, you have to be careful."

Grace tossed the diving rings into the middle of the pool and waited until Kate and Sammy splashed out of ear-shot. "Ab, he wouldn't do anything. Anyway, he has someone new and they're—"

"I saw the way he looks at you."

"You never liked him." Grace slid into the warm water. "Uff-da, he's taking her to Jamaica, maybe South America." She splashed two armfuls of water at Abby. "The important thing, did I mention Adam comes home tomorrow?"

"Not in the last thirty seconds." Abby grabbed a foam noodle. "Too bad you're not missing him."

Later that afternoon Grace put in one of the girls' movies, hoping it would give her at least an hour of uninterrupted conversation.

"Sit here, Ab." She moved the small stack of Adam's mail to the far end of the table. Derrick pushed something that sounded like a ladder or can of paint across the playroom floor. She wished she'd told him to hold off on painting until after Adam's party. "I've got pictures." She set a plate of brownies on the table. "Would you like to see them?" She only turned her back for a moment, just long enough to retrieve the album from the family room bookshelves. But that's all the time Abby needed.

"What's this?"

When she turned around, there was Abby holding up an envelope.

"His first wife still gets mail?"

"Abby, don't." She plucked the envelope away and moved the entire stack of mail to the counter. "You shouldn't. It's private."

"Grace, how long has it been; it's not private."

She handed the album to Abby, opening it to the page where Adam stood tall and tan in his white dinner jacket, the Gulf of Mexico behind him. "He's gorgeous and good, so much more than I deserve, Ab. Really."

"What are you talking about? No one's too good for you. But did you say he has a brother?"

One-by-one, she showed Abby the pictures, explaining each detail—how the sunset had created the perfect backdrop for the simple beachfront ceremony and how she and the girls had secretly decided to go shoeless. "Adam still calls me his barefoot bride," she said.

"No shoes with a dress like that?" Abby reached for another brownie. "So, how's his relationship with the Lord?"

The question shouldn't have taken her by surprise. "Ab, why do you always make me feel like I'm under some kind of spiritual microscope? On our honeymoon we prayed every morning." Her heart flew back to the days she and Adam spent alone in the mountains. At the beginning and end of each day he would blanket her hand with his and they would pray. She had never felt so safe and cherished, as if their actual home was inside the cup of God's hand. "I don't know, Ab…we're both so busy now."

"Something's going on here."

"What do you mean?"

"Your eyes." Abby slid her chair closer. "It's not just peaches and a creamy cottage by the sea."

"Nothing is going on. Just this morning when he called he told me he'd been reading his Bible again. I was busy with the girls and didn't have time to..." Grace could feel herself squished even tighter under Abby's microscope. *Didn't have time.* She watched the impact of her words make their way across her friend's face.

Despite Abby's look, this was what she'd been missing, a friend to open up to, someone who would understand. And so she told her everything—how they'd cut their honeymoon short and how Adam took off for Minnesota the morning after they returned. "I don't think he even believed me when I saw some guy out there shining a light into the bedroom. And then he ended up making matters worse by hiring Derrick. I'm fine with it now; except for being terrified that Derrick will tell Adam everything."

"You haven't?"

"I can't." She couldn't force herself to look at Abby. "I love Adam and I love the girls, Ab." Her eyes traveled to the family room where Kate's head was at one end of the couch, Sammy's at the other, their bare feet mingled together in the middle. "Derrick thinks Adam married me just so he can have someone take care of the girls."

Abby scooted closer and drew her into a hug. "You can't believe that."

"I'm starting to." Her eyes burned as if someone had sprinkled salt onto them. "And I think I'm willing to settle for it. That's how much I love Adam and the girls."

"This I know." Abby took hold of her left hand and held it inches from her face. "Look at it. Not the diamond. Almost anyone can buy a diamond. The words engraved into your ring. He deserves the truth. A man like Adam doesn't have anyone else."

"I'm not talking about that, Ab. It's his first wife. You're right; she still gets mail, almost every day. And I don't throw it away; I save it for him." She dropped her hand into her lap. "When he's away from me, he's alone with Beth. It doesn't matter that it's only memories."

"Wow." Abby blew out the word. She had more to say; Grace knew it. But at that moment Derrick bounded down the stairs.

"What do you have to drink?"

Even before she handed Derrick his water, Abby's eyes shot darts. And for the first time since Derrick came back into her life, she felt sorry for him, even guilty as she watched him finish off his water in one long guzzle. What was wrong with her? She'd made all this food, and hadn't even offered Derrick a glass of water. It was the same way Adam's mother treated *her people.*

"Room's almost painted." Derrick swiped his hand across his mouth and handed her the empty water bottle. "You should see."

"We want to see." The girls' movie had just ended, and before she could respond, they were on their feet, leading Derrick upstairs.

"You want them up there alone with him?" Abby lowered her voice. "Didn't you feel absolutely sick when he walked in?"

"I guess I'm getting used to him being here."

With the girls upstairs, they sat knee-to-knee on the sofa, trying to stretch their time together. "I almost forgot," Abby said, "how are your nightmares?"

"Better." She forced her lips into a smile as she reached for her ginger ale.

"You sure?"

"I thought once we were married they'd stop altogether."

At any minute the girls or Derrick might walk into the room. Now wasn't the time to admit she could still hear the baby's cry, still see her tiny mouth…open…close, and little hands reaching for her. "I just wish I didn't see her floating in darkness." She searched Abby's eyes for understanding. "The worse thing, there's nothing I can do."

Abby's hands wrapped around hers. "Hold on. Listen to me."

She didn't want to hold on. She wanted to escape, escape Abby's counsel and the tears that were beginning to gather behind her eyes.

But she didn't.

"Grace, your baby's not in darkness. That dream, it's of the enemy. You know that." Tears glistened in the corners of Abby's eyes. "And our loving God, the Light of this world, is taking care of your little one."

She looked toward the empty stairway; and she knew it wouldn't stay empty long. She had to pull herself together. "It's two-thirty. What time do you start work? I don't want you late because of—"

"Pray first?" Abby didn't wait for an answer. "Heavenly Father, help Grace see that her baby is safe. And when Adam comes home, give her the strength to tell him the truth...all of it."

Before she put her beach bag over her shoulder, Abby took the last brownie. "Your past doesn't matter. God gave you the desires of your heart. And they're wonderful." She held up her half-eaten brownie. "Better than chocolate, those two girls."

She had to tell someone, who else but Abby? "There's one more thing."

Abby pretended a tortured response, "No, don't do this to me."

She took a deep breath, one that reached all the way to her heart. "There may be more than two daughters. The doctor says I'm—"

"Pregnant?" Abby stuffed the last bite of brownie into her mouth.

"Ab, shhh." Grace put a finger to her lips. "No one knows, not even Adam. A baby, Abby, can you believe?"

"Absolutely."

At that moment, for the first time since she walked out of the doctor's office, she felt joy soar across her soul.

The kind of joy that only comes with a miracle.

CHAPTER 18

Grace scolded herself. After searching from one end of the house to the other, she had no idea where she left her journal. She stepped out on the veranda where the heat and humidity hung heavy and pushed her sleeves above her elbows before inscribing the date on the inside cover of a new book, one that felt like a chilly stranger instead of a warm friend, one that could never replace the most important journal of her life.

The journal she started after Adam asked her to marry him.

At first she thought maybe Adam had taken it. How many times had he wanted to know what she was writing? But he would never.

She couldn't wait for him to come home, couldn't wait for the little things, like the way his eyes smiled, especially when he looked at the girls, and the way it felt every time he took her hand in his.

Most of all, she couldn't wait to give him the news. She'd already decided on the perfect time and place—after his birthday party, as they walked together along the beach. It would be his best gift of all.

At least, she prayed that's the way he'd receive the news.

All day, ever since he told her how he started reading his Bible again, she'd felt a pull to do the same. If she did, maybe life would go back to the way it had been on their honeymoon when they prayed together every morning and talked about Bible verses that seemed to be written just for them. That was the type of home she wanted to raise her children in. Not only that, maybe her nightmares would stop.

Lord, I want to do the right thing. Those were the first words she wrote in her new journal. *But how can I know…*

When the wind picked up, she pulled a beach towel from the back of her chair and wrapped it around her shoulders. Far out in the Gulf a streak of lightening flashed across the sky. As she sat there, watching the wall of weather move closer, her mind passed over the day—lunch with Abby, and getting ready for Adam's party. Sammy's bath time. The picture would forever be in her mind—Sammy stepping out of the tub, her curls all squishy tight. She could still feel the warm water drip from Sammy's body onto her toes as she wrapped a towel around her tan shoulders. "Mommy." Sammy pulled back, wrinkling her wet forehead. "You don't have to worry when you take a bath; and you don't have to stay all the way under the bubbles because Jesus closes His eyes. He does not look, not even one teeny peek."

How long had Sammy worried about Jesus seeing her naked?

A bowling ball of thunder rolled across the waves, striking the beach in front of their home with so much force that the windows shook and pictures rattled against the walls. She grabbed her journal and headed inside. Just as she closed the veranda door, Sammy ran into the room carrying Snow by her front leg.

"We're scared. Lambs don't like storms." She jumped into bed and laid Snow's head on Adam's pillow. "We want to sleep with you."

Less than an hour later, after the storm passed and Sammy's eyes were almost closed, the phone rang. "It's Daddy." Sammy sprang up. "I want to talk." For five nonstop minutes, that's just what she did, telling Adam about the storm and how she and Snow had a bad dream. "But we're safe now." With a yawn, she laid her head back on Adam's pillow. "Love you too, Daddy. Here she is."

One more time, she tucked the covers around Sammy and Snow, and then she took the phone into the hall where she could be close to Sammy without disturbing her sleep.

When she switched on the brass floor lamp, a gentle splash of light stretched across the floor. It was incredible how much peace the light shined into the hallway. "It's late," she said. "You must be tired."

"I am. Had a lot of paper work, so I'm afraid I can't talk long."

She curled herself onto the small chair at the end of the hall. "Sorry I didn't have time to talk this morning."

She didn't mind when Adam cut their conversation short. Maybe it was the weather. Even now, her mind seemed to be darting. She stayed in the hallway long after she and Adam said goodnight. It was one of those nights when her pen pushed to admit things her tongue wasn't brave enough to express. She was still worried about the light stalker, afraid to believe he was really gone. *I'm even more afraid,* she wrote, *to allow myself to believe Adam will really be home tomorrow...even though he promised.*

But the truth that frightened her most was the one she'd struggled to hide, even from herself. The words came almost without thought, so fast her pen could barely keep up. *What if Adam never loves our baby the way he loves Kate and Sammy? Lord, you know I couldn't take that.*

She placed her pen in the fold of the journal. "God, it's the past. Why can't I let it go?" Her words came in a desperate whisper.

All the pieces, Grace, I want all your broken pieces. The impression stirred across her mind.

"God, I've given every piece."

All your broken pieces, Grace. She turned the words over in her mind.

Was God actually talking to her? Maybe not. Maybe it was just her own thoughts.

After all, both she and Adam held their pasts tight.

Tonight, Grace, release what was. Commit to what's ahead.

Could it be that God was telling her he didn't expect her to tell Adam about her past? Was it actually better to pretend the past never was? Ignoring what was in the past could be the safest way to commit to what was ahead.

She dropped to her knees in front of the chair and rested her head in the cusp of her folded hands. "Lord, by the time Adam comes home tomorrow," she prayed, "I will decide whether to tell him everything... or tell him nothing at all."

She laid her hands across her stomach where God was forming a new life, a life she already loved.

"Oh, God." She pulled her hands away from her stomach and held them out, forming an empty cradle. "Whatever happens please let me hold my one broken piece. Just a little longer."

CHAPTER 19

Grace stood at the foot of the stairs, savoring the aroma of barbeque sauce and fresh bread as it whiffed its way through the house. "Make sure Daddy stays in his office," she said as she swiped her hands across her white shorts. "Mommy's going to shower."

She took one final look, allowing her heart to fill with pride over the way the girls had chipped in, giggling their way through projects, especially when she gave them free reign with the red and blue confetti. With balloons and banners filling the family room and the house smelling like a celebration, everything was perfect.

Kate opened the office door a peek. "Don't y'all come out now, Daddy," she said.

With that, Sammy pushed her head in alongside Kate's. "Because don't you know, we will catch you, Daddy."

Since Adam came home, the girls had been stationed outside his office door, paper and crayons strewn across the floor as they made last-minute birthday cards. A good hour remained before Adam's parents would arrive, just enough time to shower and fix her hair the way Adam liked. She popped open her can of ginger ale and turned toward the stairs.

But before she made it beyond the second step, the doorbell rang and the door pushed open. "Hi, all. You don't mind we're a little early, do you, dear?"

A little early? Her skin tingled. Her hair was going in every direction and her clothes were an absolute finger painting of food. Did she mind? "Uff-da." She pulled on the hem of her blouse. "I'm...we're not quite ready; but certainly, come in."

Adam's mother stood just inside the door, her eyes camouflaged behind sunglasses that were so perfectly round and red that they looked like they were made to cover lady bug eyes. Without turning even a neck muscle, she handed the glasses to her husband. "Gordon, put them in my case, will you?"

The girls scooted across the floor, picking up crayons and paper. With a shrug, Adam stepped from his office hiding place into the front hall and gave his mother a quick hug.

As usual, Gordon stood quietly in the background, waiting as his wife made her entrance. He held the gift bags and Marjory's red leather purse which was as large as a piece of carry-on luggage. "Where would y'all like Adam's gifts?" he said.

Before Grace could answer, Adam's mother cleared a spot on the living room coffee table. "Here's fine."

Ten minutes later Grace stood in the shower fighting off a guilt attack. *But it's not all my fault,* she told herself. *They come when they want, put gifts where they want.* She rubbed conditioner between her hands and massaged it into her hair. *Rude.* When she stepped out of the shower, her thoughts still raced. *Thanks to them, I don't even have time to fix my hair.* She pulled it into her usual pony tail. *Uff-da, if it wasn't Adam's birthday, you bet I'd say something.*

She slipped a coral print sundress over her head and zippered the back. Adam was right. She had lost weight. And tonight he'd find out why.

But first, she had to make it through the party. She stood at the top of the stairs listening to their laughter, urging herself downstairs where she would do her best to make this Adam's best birthday ever.

Almost before she entered the room the struggle began. "Kate, darling, anyone can see those shoes are too big. Never mind. Grandma will take you shopping before she goes back to Georgia."

Grace placed her arm around Kate. "We've talked about it, Marjory, and sometimes she just likes wearing them." She could feel Kate's shoulders loosen. "Girls, did you show Daddy how we decorated the family room and patio for his party? Maybe we should move in there."

"Fabulous." Adam's mother pulled a DVD from her purse. "We'll need the big screen for this."

It didn't matter that it was a small accomplishment, Grace felt proud that without being rude or bossy she'd managed to move the party out of the formal living room to where it was meant to be. After everyone was seated, she squeezed onto the sofa next to Adam, so close that every time he moved the sleeve of his sweater brushed against her bare arm. When he took her hand, every twisted rope of tension seemed to relax.

"You didn't cater in?" Adam's dad dipped a chunk of fresh pineapple into the cream cheese dip. "Made it all yourself? How about that, Marjory?"

Adam draped his arm around her and, out of the corner of her eye she was sure she saw his chest inflate with pride.

She'd just replenished the fruit tray when Kate pulled a red balloon from one of the bouquets and swatted it to Sammy. After a few back-and-forth's, Sammy missed and it was about to bounce off Gordon's Q-tip head, when he raised his eyes over the top of his glasses and gave the balloon a mighty whack. Before long, they were all laughing and contorting like double-jointed pretzels, just to keep the balloon from landing in the fruit or on the floor.

By the time the balloon popped everyone was breathless. Gordon reached for his inhaler. Even with it protruding from his mouth, the smile never left his face. As soon as he could, he spoke. "I haven't had that much fun since…I don't know when."

Then, just before dinner, Kate and Sammy presented Adam with his gifts. Sammy went first. "Here, Daddy." Grace had never seen her eyes as bright as they were when she handed him the package she'd wrapped almost by herself. "I made it for you."

Adam pulled her onto his lap and rested his chin on top of her head. Seconds later, he held a matted and framed Sammy original. *My Famly.* The words were printed in purple crayon across the bottom of the drawing.

"Daddy, the lady sitting on top of the cloud is mommy, you know, my mommy that lives in heaven." She moved off his lap and stood next to him, pointing to each figure. "And this is you and Kate and me and Mommy…this mommy. Do you like it, Daddy?" She didn't wait for her daddy's answer. "And we went to the store and picked out all this stuff." She pointed to the matting and frame. "So it looks even prettier."

When it was Kate's turn she stood in the middle of the room holding a frame that matched the one Sammy had given him. "I wrote a poem. And Sammy forgot to tell you, you can hang these in your office, by your desk, so you can see them when you're working and all stressed."

"Oh no, you don't." Adam patted his knee. "You're not standing way over there."

Kate rolled her eyes. "But it's hard to read if I'm so close."

"I'm fixing to come get you."

Reluctantly, Kate dropped into Adam's lap and took a deep breath. "You're my Daddy, Strong and kind" On cue, Adam flexed his muscles. "Yes, you are the best Daddy, Better than any girl can find. And that's why Daddy, I'm glad you are mine."

Adam's nose turned red and his chin quivered as he brought both girls into his arms. "I couldn't ask for more, not in my entire lifetime, than I have right now."

"Don't cry." Sammy patted Adam's cheeks.

"It's only because you're happy, right Daddy?" Kate looked into Adam's eyes.

"Happy and hungry." he took the girls by their hands and led the way to the table.

Grace felt like a child on a merry-go-round. If she could have stopped time and made the meal last forever, she would have, right up until the moment Marjory refolded her napkin and laid it on her plate. "Adam, if you haven't found someone to finish the quilts, I have a girl." It was like someone slammed the brakes on the celebration.

Grace put down her fork and reached under the table for Adam's hand. If she didn't hang on, she would either fall off the ride or push his mother off. She wasn't sure which.

"Not necessary, Mother." Her hand relaxed in Adam's. "Grace has been working with Sammy to finish hers. And Kate hasn't decided if she wants her quilt finished or if she just wants to keep the pieces."

It wasn't until Gordon took the last rib from the platter, that she found her way back to enjoying the party. "Birthday cake now or later?"

"A little later." Marjory looked at her watch. "I'm afraid we barely have time for the DVD."

CHAPTER 20

"Look, girls, that's Daddy when he was a baby." Adam held the girls close, resting one on each knee. Never in a hundred years, would he have guessed his mother saved all his old photos and movies. Now, here they were on a DVD with his favorite songs looping their way across the background, connecting photos and video clips. "Mom, this is wonderful," he said.

The DVD took him back to the Christmas when he received his first tool set. He remembered how, before the day was over, he'd used his hammer to pound a dent in the coffee table, and the measuring tape to determine the size of everything, even the opening in the fireplace where Santa came down. He relived other Christmases too, like the year his grandfather gave him his first Bible with his name engraved in gold, and there were Easter egg hunts around the pool with his cousins and birthday cakes with magic candles that he couldn't blow out.

Then, without warning, there was the picture of him standing alone next to his father's blue convertible, trying his best to smile when all he wanted to do was cry. His mother would never understand why the picture didn't belong, why he wanted to forget that day, forget riding in silence in the front seat next to his dad, the man he'd trusted to rescue him, to never leave him standing alone on the steps of Hawthorne-Louis Academy.

"Daddy, why are you so sad?" Sammy grabbed his chin.

But before he could put the words together, his mother answered. "Boarding school. Sometimes good things make children unhappy. It's like vegetables."

It was the same logic she'd used on him. To this day, he didn't understand why parents sent their children to boarding schools. All he knew was that he'd do anything to make sure his girls always came home at the end of the school day. They'd learn to enjoy vegetables at their own table and experience the satisfying security of sleeping in their own beds.

After he entered boarding school there were fewer pictures until… no, his mother wouldn't do this to Grace. He thought of reaching for the remote, but the girls were already off his lap.

"Look, that's Mommy." Kate pulled Sammy by the arm. Soon they were both touching the screen, patting Beth's cheeks, tracing her hair from the top of her head to her shoulders.

Just like he wanted to do.

Sammy stood next to Kate. "She looks like a real queen, doesn't she, Daddy?"

"She was perfectly gorgeous, Sammy," his mother answered, "and those eyes."

He didn't mean to go there, not in front of Grace, but before he could stop himself, he was in Atlanta on their wedding day.

Beth. His heart whispered her name.

It wasn't until his dad mentioned it, that he noticed Grace had left the room. He glanced out the window. There she was, outside, blowing out the lanterns she'd arranged around the pool. He should be out there with her. But he had to stay. There he was with Beth, standing in front of their home and waving. In one swoop, he picked her up and carried her over the threshold.

I never carried Grace. The thought slipped through his mind. A few photos later, Beth was pregnant and still enjoying the pool even though he teased her mercilessly about the way her stomach floated above the water like a basketball.

They were still laughing over Beth's stomach when he caught Grace out of the corner of his eye, making her way into the kitchen, struggling to open the door with her arms full of decorations. "Let me help you." He started to get up. Somehow he had to put a stop to what was going on. It wasn't fair to Grace; but she had to understand; he couldn't turn the DVD off, not in front of the girls.

"It's your birthday." He could barely hear her voice as she made her way inside.

"Daddy, look. It's the flip flops Kate always wears." Sammy pointed to Beth's feet. The DVD had moved from photos to video. One minute Beth was swinging in the hammock with Kate cuddled by her side. The next, she was walking along the beach, the two of them leaving mommy-daughter footprints, and there she was drinking from one of Kate's tiny tea cups.

"If only you could remember, Sammy." Kate's voice was soft and sad. "She was the best Mommy in the whole wide world."

He could see Grace standing in the kitchen, just feet away. There was no way she hadn't heard. He wanted to cover Kate's mouth, anything to put a stop to this so he could take Grace in his arms and tell her she was perfect, perfect for him and perfect for the girls.

He'd do anything to get rid of the guilt burning inside him.

And even more to see Beth, just once more see her alive and filled with joy.

There she was, pregnant again. For the first time, he noticed that she looked more tired than she had with Kate. Her steps weren't quite as bouncy and there were puffy purple circles under her eyes. Why hadn't he noticed back then? Why hadn't he stayed home when she asked? If he had, maybe things would have turned out different. The doctors told them they'd caught it too late.

Stop, he told himself. *You have to stop this.* He got up from the sofa. *Go to Grace.*

He was close, with only the breakfast bar between them, when Sammy started jumping up and down. "That's me. Look, Daddy." She grabbed his knee and drew him back toward the television screen. "Mommy and me."

As he lifted Sammy into his arms, he turned toward Grace. Everything in him told him to go to her, to wipe away the clouds of hurt that had darkened her eyes. The words were there, ready to leave his heart. *That's the past, Grace. I want you to know; I love you. Only you.*

But he didn't move and the words never left the gate of his heart because the truth had grown to full-size. No matter where he was, in a Minnesota hotel room, or in his own home, Beth was never far away.

Grace was certain Adam didn't even turn his head when she went outside a second time. Her lungs needed more air than they could find in the house; and her mind needed the sound of waves. She sat at the patio table, closed her eyes, and listened to the safe, steady roll. It wasn't until she opened her eyes that she saw Derrick walking along the beach. Like a shock of electricity, a sickening shiver passed through her, a knowing that was charged with truth. She was more comfortable out here with Derrick than she was inside with them.

And she knew why.

She belonged with a man like Derrick. If she didn't know it before tonight, she knew it now. Never in this lifetime could she measure up to Beth. It was easy for God to love Beth, easy for Adam and his parents and the girls because she was so good and she had the perfect smile and perfect love for them. As unthinkable as it was, Derrick was the man she deserved.

The house grew quiet and she took it as a sign that the DVD had come to an end. She tensed her shoulders, making them as strong as they needed to be. She'd go in, make coffee, and light the candles on Adam's cake. She would sing with them, just like she planned. Then his parents would go home and the girls would go to bed. And she and Adam would be alone.

Alone, but not alone.

When she walked into the kitchen the DVD was still playing. Purposefully, she spread a smile across her face, and pushed herself into the family room where she came face-to-face with Beth. And there was no escape. Adam patted the empty place next to him, inviting her to sit and watch.

"That's okay," she said. "I'm fine." She backed toward the kitchen. It wouldn't be right to sit next to Adam, not with the girls still snuggled on his lap staring at all they'd lost.

Sammy stroked Adam's arm. "Where's Mommy's hair?"

"Cancer." Marjory's voice cracked.

She stood between the kitchen and family room as frozen as the rest of them, watching as Beth sat on the family room floor rocking Sammy in her arms while Kate cuddled at her side. Her legs were crossed and on her feet she wore the flip flops that had become such an important part of Kate's life. Beth smiled at the camera.

From that moment on, even more than before, the air was filled with Beth. "I've written letters to each of you." She brought Kate's little hand up to her lips and kissed it. "Because there are so many things I want you to know, so many important things I may not have time to teach my little loves." Sammy squirmed in her arms and she kissed the top of her fuzzy head. "God is good, even in this. I pray my babies never doubt His absolute goodness and power."

When Grace could take no more, she scooped coffee into the coffee maker. How was it possible? Beth was days away from death; yet peace sparkled in her eyes like the richest jewel.

When the DVD came to an end all that was left on the screen was Beth's picture. The same picture Adam kept on his desk.

After the girls' bedtime routine, when she and Adam should have been marking his birthday with a celebration of their own, Grace struggled to ignore him, swiping barbeque sauce from the top of the stove while he stood behind her. She could feel him, could smell the familiar aroma of his gum.

"How much longer?" His hands moved to her shoulders, massaging them; but she refused to take even a peek into his eyes. She didn't have to because she knew exactly who was there. Beth, more alive than she could ever pray to be.

"Listen, you have to know." He turned her to face him. "I'm sorry about tonight."

"I have to get this spill." She focused on a splat of coffee on the floor. Her very existence depended on staying away from Adam's eyes.

"Look at me, Grace." He squeezed her hand. "I had no idea mom would do that."

"I can't..." She pulled away and ran a wet paper towel across the floor, her knees shaking until she didn't know how much longer they'd hold her. "Your mother put a lot of thought into your gift."

"I'm fixing to take a walk. Come with me?"

She didn't pull away when he led her toward the door. How many nights had she sat alone on their veranda, longing for exactly this? She saw it in her mind a hundred ways. The moon was always full and she was alone in his arms and in his eyes.

But that was her dream.

With his arm around her, he led her toward the waves. Close, they were so close that with every step his leg brushed hers. "I have a gift for you," he said. "It's back at the house."

Again she felt herself drawn into the dream, to places she didn't deserve to be. The only way to protect herself was to pull away. But she couldn't. Not all the way. "I have something for you too; but not tonight. I don't think I can."

"Grace, about tonight, I want you to understand. If I could drown my memories out there in the Gulf, I'd do it right now."

She wanted to kick the sand and water, kick it and kick it until she could make him see. "That's not it. I don't expect you to bury your memories. Adam, I'm not stupid." She took the folded tissue Adam offered. "Face it. If Beth were here right now," she squeezed the words out of her heart, "I wouldn't be."

He let go of her hand and threw his arms in the air. "You know that's not fair." She could hear tears gurgling in his throat. "I came home with a plan; I really did. A plan so you would know how much I love you. So you would stop making yourself so small. And I get this."

"And I get this." She followed him back toward the house, stomping through the damp sand. "You'd choose her, wouldn't you Adam? I know because every time you call and tell me you're not coming home, every time you put off calling until it's so late that you're too tired to talk, you're choosing her over me." They were feet from the patio now and every inch of her body, inside and out, was trembling.

Adam took her by the arm. "Come on, Grace, can't we just bury this entire night and start fresh?"

"If it were just memories, I wouldn't care." She had no choice; if she didn't say it now, she never would. "But there's a difference, Adam." She took a deep breath and stood silent before her husband, waiting for the courage to go on. "There's a difference between remembering the past and living in it."

"You think I'm living in the past?"

"I do."

"Then maybe we both are." Adam pulled two chairs away from the patio table.

She no longer had strength to argue or pull away. In at least one way, he was right. "Adam, do you ever think of heaven…you know, what it will be like?"

"Sometimes." He reached for her hand. "I think everyone does."

When he started fidgeting with her ring, moving it back and forth, she didn't pull away. The touch of his hand made her feel safe. "When you think about heaven what do you see?"

"I don't know. Clouds. Angels. Children laughing and skipping down streets of gold. How about you?"

Maybe now wasn't the time to ask. But she had to, because she had to know the truth. "Do you see homes?"

Adam's tone grew thoughtful. He no longer looked at her; he looked into the night sky, as if he was trying to seize a glimpse of the place they would one day call home. "Jesus said there are many mansions." So, yes, we'll live in homes."

"Who do you see yourself living with? Beth and the girls? Me? All of us together? What do you see?"

"Grace, why are you doing this?" Frustration dripped from every word. "Heaven's going to be different. Better. That's all I know."

Frustrated or not, Adam was right. Heaven was a place beyond their imaginations, a perfect place. There'd be no tears, no regrets or broken dreams like the ones that took over tonight.

It was like neither of them knew how to end. And so they sat next to each other without touching, without talking. At last, Adam stroked his hand across her cheek.

"My Grace," he said, "if only everything…the answers…our marriage…just everything could be easy. Better yet, if only everything could be perfect, as perfect as you are for me."

Chapter 21

Grace sat across the tiny table from Adam, her eyes fixed on his hands as he broke two pieces from a loaf of pecan bread and handed one to her. The night she had waited for was finally here.

Over the last few days his words had proved themselves right. Married life was anything but easy. But for every difficult moment, there seemed to be two magnificent ones. And now here they were at Duke's, sitting at the same table they'd sat at the night he'd asked her to marry him.

She'd never forget how they held hands that night, and how her name seemed to quiver on his tongue. After the sun went down, Claude lit the candle on their table. She still remembered the flicker of its shadow across their hands.

Out on the patio the same bare-foot musician strummed his guitar and sang those beach songs the tourists love to hear. "Grace." He had pulled a small black box from his pocket. "I want to spend forever... together with you." She had no idea it was coming, no idea how her life was about to change.

But tonight it was her turn to change his life.

Forever.

"I'll never get used to this." She was afraid if she looked into his eyes, the dream might end. She placed both elbows on the table and rested her chin in her hands. "It's all so perfect." Stroke by stroke, the setting sun's brush colored the sky and water, even the sand, a soft and rosy tone.

Adam unfolded his napkin and laid it across his lap. Unlike the slow sunset, the last few days had flown by. During the day they'd devoted themselves to the girls, playing in the pool, building sandcastles and watching movies. One day while Adam spent time with his parents, she and Abby took the girls shopping for school clothes.

But the nights were theirs. They spent hours walking on the beach. They laughed. And they prayed. And not once did the light stalker shine his evil light.

They were both trying. But there was no denying it; moving out of the past was difficult for both of them. Tonight would either push them ahead or make it more complicated. She wasn't sure which it would be.

"Mr. and Mrs. Will." The waiter opened their menus before placing them in their hands. "How are you this evening?"

After ordering a ginger ale for her and coffee for himself, Adam excused himself. "Do you mind? I want to talk to Claude for a minute… make sure he's doing okay."

She watched him make his way through the restaurant, stopping twice to chat with couples she'd never met.

Claude, Duke's owner, stood close to the entrance, his back toward her as he and Adam made conversation. Like Adam, sometimes she worried about him. Built as if he made it his responsibility to sample every dish on the menu at least once, maybe twice daily, he'd put on even more weight.

Even before Adam proposed, the tiny beach front pub had been their favorite. It went beyond the fact that they served the freshest seafood on the islands, beyond their pastry chef who baked the best breads and desserts. There wasn't another restaurant that felt so welcoming or offered a more breathtaking view. And, even though Duke's didn't accept reservations, all it took was one quick call from Adam and they were guaranteed a window table at sunset.

She hadn't known what to think when Adam made arrangements with his folks to take the girls for a couple days; but she was glad he had. "Hon, it's what they've done with Kate every year before the new school year, and now with Sammy starting kindergarten…let Mom do her shopping with them." He'd stood behind her and kissed her neck.

"We need time alone, maybe go out for dinner, and I still have your gift in my office."

That evening before they left for dinner, he gave her the gift, an absolutely beautiful painting. "Oh, Adam, it's magnificent." It was all she could say.

"Like you." He'd draped his arms around her waist and drew her close. "God takes great delight in you." Adam read the words engraved on a plaque attached to the frame. He told her how he'd found the little gallery, almost invisible between Ole's Pizza and Ted's Pharmacy, on the main street of a tiny riverfront town in Minnesota. "The artist is amazing. He has something wrong with his legs and spends most of his time in a wheel chair."

Already, she cherished the painting of the long-haired man with a rugged face, his arms wrapped around a young woman with a pony tail about the same color as hers. Her face was turned up and it was easy to see she was captured by his love.

If only she could believe the painting's message.

Adam had every word of the verse the painting portrayed memorized. "The LORD your God is with you, he is mighty to save." When he spoke the words, it was as if they had come to him directly from the breath of God. "He will take great delight in you, he will quiet you with his love, he will rejoice over you with singing." The words felt like a blessing. "Zephaniah 3:17, it's my verse." Tears pooled in the corners of his eyes. "I've been looking for this verse to help me through the attacks, never expected a painting to lead me there."

As Adam talked about the painting and artist, it was as if she had two eyes, one in the front and one in the back of her heart, and she didn't know which eye to close, which to open. With one she saw God's love and Adam the way he was last night, and this morning, and the way he said their life would be from now on. But what she saw with the other eye spotlighted another truth, the truth captured on his mother's DVD, and the words he spoke that birthday night, words that still rang like a gloomy gong in her heart.

In my entire lifetime, I want no more than I have right now.

Even here at Dukes, she didn't know if she was good enough for the promise of Zephaniah. Her history with Derrick was still a secret, only buried deeper, since she'd convinced herself it was the best way to move forward.

Adam pulled out his chair. "Sorry it took so long, hon. Claude and I got talking. Have you decided? He says they have some beautiful lobsters tonight."

"Grouper." She attached a tease to her smile. "Lobster can surprise. Are you able to handle two surprises in one night?"

They both ordered grouper and there were no surprises. The flaky white fish melted in her mouth. They were waiting for a slice of key lime pie when Adam leaned across the table. "So, how long are you going to make me wait for this surprise of yours?"

She rubbed her hands together. "Adam." She couldn't look into his eyes. What if she saw disappointment, the same disappointment she'd seen all those years ago in Derrick? She and Adam hadn't talked about babies. With Sammy starting school, Adam might look at having a baby as a step back. What if Kate and Sammy really were enough? What if the only person he wanted to have children with was Beth?

In my entire lifetime, I want no more than I have right now. One last time, she replayed his words.

"Adam." She reached across the table for his hand. "Uff-da, Adam. I'm...we...we are going to have a baby."

"What?" A mixture of bewilderment and joy danced together in his voice. "When? I gave all the nursery furniture...we'll buy new." He leaned across the table until his lips touched hers. "You're happy, Grace, aren't you?"

This had to be what it was like to know God was rejoicing. She rested her hand against her flat stomach. God rejoicing over them, that's what gave her the courage to look into his eyes, to look and see pure joy. The most impossible dream of her life was coming true.

Adam wanted their baby.

"A slice of key lime and two forks." The waiter set the plate between them. "Anything else for you this evening?"

"Nothing, thank you." Adam held up his hand. "Wait. Ask Claude to come to our table, would you please. And tell him to bring his toasting glass."

She had just covered the tip of her fork with a swirl of whip cream when Claude pulled up a chair and set his glass on the table. According to Adam, the strongest thing Claude mixed with his soda was a squirt of key lime. He'd seen too many businesses go under, too many families and lives destroyed by alcohol. Sure, Duke's had a well-stocked bar; but it was not the place to come to get wasted. Islanders knew it. And it didn't take long for tourists to find out.

"Mrs. Will, good to see you. At last you are able to pull him from the house. I am so pleased." Claude put one hand on her shoulder and the other on Adam's. "And what happy occasion do we toast this evening?"

"Claude, the night I proposed, where did I bring my beautiful wife? Here, right?" Claude nodded and, as if he were getting ready for the latest bit of island gossip, scooted his chair closer to the table. "Tonight we're celebrating something just as wonderful. I just learned we are going to have a baby."

"No." Claude shook his head. "She is a-way too thin. We must fatten her up. Make-a-that baby nice and strong." Without taking his eyes off her, he waved the waiter back to the table. "A dish of the fresh raspberries and put-a-very much cream on top. Yes, a-very much."

The rest of the evening Adam did not take his eyes off her. She ran the spoon around the inside of the bowl of raspberries and cream. "Adam, what are you gawking at?" Her voice held a slight giggle.

He touched her lips with the tips of his fingers. "I haven't seen you smile like this since coming back from our honeymoon and I'm trying to picture you with a tummy. Ever had one?" Adam's eyes were glittering more than she'd ever seen.

Even on their wedding day.

CHAPTER 22

Adam stuck his head into the playroom where Derrick was hanging pictures on the girls' freshly painted wall. He pointed to his phone just long enough to stop Derrick's hammer. "Want to give me some quiet here."

Before continuing his conversation, Adam backed into the hall. He closed his eyes, reminding himself that Derrick really didn't matter. Before the start of tourist season he would be long gone.

"Okay." his voice still held edginess as he picked up his conversation with the florist. "Two dozen—no three—a dozen of each, red, pink, yellow. Is there a way they can be delivered in an hour?"

True, his mother's DVD had hurt Grace in ways she didn't deserve; but at least it had forced them to face the unspoken truths that stood between them.

"Thing's hung." Without as much as a knock, Derrick stood in the center of their bedroom. With the claw end of his hammer he pointed toward the playroom. "Might need to do a little touch-up on the paint. Those girls got to learn to keep their stuff away from the walls."

For a minute he considered telling Derrick it wasn't up to him to decide what his daughters learned or didn't learn, but he'd only be wasting his breath. There were more important issues.

"Listen, Derrick, I want ya'll to understand there's just no reason for you to wander around the house." He motioned for Derrick to follow him downstairs. "And our bedrooms are off-limits." He'd already made these restrictions clear, but as he tried to reestablish boundaries, his insides rolled with uneasiness. "You're not just walking into our house without knocking, right? Grace and the girls tell me you just walk in. That's not acceptable." They stood face-to-face at the bottom of the stairs. "We're on the same page here?"

He hated that he couldn't see Derrick's eyes. The man wore sunglasses when he shouldn't. On top of that, his clothes were wrinkled. He had to wonder if this guy even knew what a hanger was. He wanted to pull the sunglasses off his face and hand him an iron and some starch. Normally he didn't consider himself a judgmental man, but the more he was around Derrick, the more his skin crawled. His eyes fell to Derrick's feet. "And shoes, man. I want you to wear shoes. You need money; I'll give you—"

"Didn't know...." Derrick backed away. "I have shoes." A ridiculous grin flashed across his face. "Spend the money on another dozen roses, like white, since they're her favorite."

He had to admit he didn't know Grace felt that way about white roses. Maybe she didn't. Maybe Derrick was playing another one of his games like the one he'd played the night of his panic attack.

Even though she rarely complained anymore, Grace had been right about Derrick. If he could find someone to replace him, he would. He'd tried; but seasonal workers went north this time of year and those who stayed were already employed. The important thing was that Grace and the girls were safe.

"If you don't have questions, go ahead and hang Grace's picture." He turned her painting over to Derrick before heading into his office.

It felt good to check picture hanging off his to-do list. As much as he hated it, in a few days he'd be back in Minnesota, far away from his girls.

Far away from Grace.

As soon as he pulled his chair up to the desk, his eyes fell on the framed photo Grace had placed on the far back corner. The day they shot the picture seemed a lifetime ago, but he'd never forget how thrilled Grace had been on their honeymoon as she followed the muddy trail that ran along the shallow mountain creek. To be on the safe side, he called the florist and added white roses to his order. After the call, he took the picture of Beth from his desk and ran his hand across her beautiful face. "This is the right thing to do," he said as he set Beth's photo on the bookshelf behind his desk. After all, he'd been fixing to this do for a long time.

Place Grace's picture where Beth's had been.

When the doorbell rang, he reached for his billfold. Hopefully fifty would be an adequate tip for such speedy delivery. The bell rang a second time before he could make his way toward the door.

But when he stepped into the hall his legs froze. Derrick stood at the door holding Grace's roses, talking to the delivery man. "Little lady's going to love these."

Adam did his best to nip his rage. The dim-wit was passing himself off as the one who'd ordered the flowers.

"I'd invite you in; but he's here. Out of town most of the time, but this week…" Derrick leaned against the door frame as if he owned the house. "Guy's not at all plugged into meeting her needs, if you know what I mean."

His blood had to be on fire. That didn't matter. He stood frozen for what seemed like an eternity. When at last he was able to move, he pushed past Derrick and stuffed the tip into the delivery person's hand.

"Derrick, put the roses on the kitchen table. We need to talk."

Their talk lasted no more than five confusing minutes. With less than a foot between them, he felt his anger grow. "Take the sunglasses off. I don't want y'all hiding behind them." His fists hung stiff at his sides. With everything in him, he wanted to smack the grin off Derrick's face.

"Just doing a little leg pulling. You don't have to worry." Derrick's grin had never looked more malicious. "Nothing's happening between me and Grace. It's all cool."

"What I want to know is this." He couldn't believe he was actually going to give his fear the power of words. "How cool is it when I'm not here? What needs of hers do you feel you have to meet?"

"No, Man." A chilly snigger escaped his nose. "It's not like that anymore. Listen, if you're looking to get rid of me, just say so." He pulled a paper clip from his pocket and bent it open. "But there's someone out there. Grace isn't the only one who sees the guy. I have." He poked the paper clip deep into his ear. "Twice. So has your kid. If it was my wife and kids, I wouldn't leave them alone in a big old house like this. Who knows what could happen." He stepped back, and for the first time their eyes met. "Anything, alone out here at the end of a stupid island." He held up his hand like he was preparing to testify in court. "I swear, I don't want that anymore than you."

Not like that between us anymore. The words were too gargantuan for Adam's mind. When the time was right, he'd check with Grace, have her tell him again just how well she knew Derrick.

And just how long ago their friendship was.

He watched Derrick's eyes for a sign that would tell him something more. But they were cold silent.

"Understand." He sliced his hand through the air between him and Derrick. "My job is to make sure we have the right person providing security. Are we on the same page with that?"

"Most definitely, Sir. You can trust me on that."

As soon as she walked into the kitchen, she saw the roses. "What did I do to deserve roses?" Grace set the grocery bags on the counter, expecting Adam to emerge from his office wearing a proud grin.

But Adam must have been in the middle of something important because the first she saw him was well after the groceries were put away and all but the white roses had been arranged in vases she'd placed in the family room and kitchen. "I love them all," she said when he stepped from his office. "But these..." She cradled the bouquet, breathing in their sweet fragrance. "These are going in our room."

As Adam walked up the stairs behind her, it felt as if his heart didn't follow. Once the flowers were arranged, she sat next to him, resting her head on his shoulder. "You okay?" She moved the vase so it was half on his lap, half on hers. But Adam nudged it back and walked across the room. She hated it when he stood with his back toward her, closing her out. Why hadn't he looked at her, not even once since she came home? "Adam, what's—"

"Why did you save the white roses for our room?" He stood in front of the veranda door, looking toward the water.

"Adam, I don't understand." She moved next to him and placed her hand on his arm. "Please, Adam, look at me."

"What's the deal with white roses?"

"They're my favorite." At that moment she saw a look of betrayal cross his eyes. "Did I say something wrong?"

"That's what Derrick said."

"It's not a secret."

"I ordered the ones you left downstairs." Adam pointed in the direction of the garage apartment. "Didn't know about white roses until your Derrick told me."

"He's not my Derrick."

"How would I know you like white—"

"What about when we got back from our honeymoon and you sent me white roses. You even had them wrapped in the newspaper story on our wedding. You remember, don't you, Adam?"

"What are you talking about?" Adam sat on the edge of the bed. "I sent flowers, but not white." Confusion clouded his eyes. "And I don't know anything about a wedding story."

"You have to." She sat next to him and took hold of his knee. "The article had our picture."

Listen to what I'm saying." He turned to face her. "Until today, I had no idea. If you told me white roses are your favorite, I don't remember."

"Derrick." She searched Adam's eyes, trying to find just a hint of understanding. "You've got to know he's up to no good. I told you it would be like this."

"There has to be something else going on." Adam stared at the ceiling and held his breath, as if he expected an answer to float by. "Something you haven't told me. Even creeps like him, don't start trouble without a reason, Grace."

Just the thought of Derrick having any part in sending her flowers, gave her sick shivers. It wasn't Adam who picked out that first bouquet, it was Derrick. And it had been his idea to wrap them the way they'd been wrapped. It was all too much. She felt like a bucket of cement had been dropped on her chest. And it left her no choice.

She had to tell Adam at least some of the truth.

Very cautiously, that's what she did.

She told him that once she and Derrick were more than friends. Much more. "It was a long time ago, just after my parents and Grady were killed." Without looking at her, Adam stuffed his hands into his pockets. How was she going to make him understand she'd been intimate with someone like Derrick? "I'm sorry, Adam. I wasn't walking with God."

More than ever, she longed for him to take her in his arms, to tell her he still loved her; but he didn't. He stood there as still and frozen as a January lake. "I was young and I made a lot of mistakes. I promise it's all in the past."

But it wasn't. There was no way she could let him see the part of her heart that would never heal, the corner where she still cradled an innocent baby. A baby she'd never see grow, but who was with her every single day. What if he thought her baby was a creep, just like he'd called Derrick? For the sake of the baby growing inside her, she would hold on to the final piece of truth. She would not tell Adam that his baby was not her first child.

When Adam turned to face her, there were tears in his eyes. "If only I could find someone to take Derrick's place. But businesses are already gearing up for tourist season."

"You have to know I'd like nothing better," she promised.

Before she could say one more word, Adam cupped her tear-soaked chin in his solid hand. He brought her face close to his. "I don't like it," he said with a kiss that stood up to her fear. "But I love you. Nothing will ever change that."

"I'm putting your love to the test." At last they had the strength to look each other in the eyes.

He kissed her again. "No more secrets, right?" He reached for the vase and, in one clump, pulled the roses from the water, holding them at arm's length. "Do you mind if I get rid of these?"

That afternoon they went to a movie and when night came, Adam insisted he owed her a walk on the beach. They walked under a perfect night sky for over an hour as warm waves broke against their legs. Every now and then, she thought about Abby's latest warning. *The only way to love him is to trust him with the truth.* But every time she thought she might, there was always a reason not to. Adam would laugh or kiss her hand, or start talking about their future and how he couldn't wait to see her face the first time she held their baby.

When the girls returned, she and Adam told them about the baby. As expected, they were ecstatic. Sammy bounced with joy. "I always wanted to be a big sister like Kate," she said.

And Kate, proud of her biggest sister status, took her own money and bought the baby a soft yellow blanket.

There were so many memories to cling to. Despite the one secret that stood between them, despite the fact that between now and September's end, Derrick would be close, reminding her of that one broken piece, Adam still loved her.

And she loved him more than ever, all the way to eternity.

Chapter 23

Adam set his Bible on the corner of Pastor Karl's desk. He couldn't explain feelings like this, an inside certainty that God was ready to do something. Maybe it was because he was back after months of being away from the routine of praying with Pastor Karl before service. From now on he was ready to take on his responsibilities, the ones at home and the ones here at church.

"The visitors are on my heart this morning." Pastor Karl's hand landed in a firm grip on his shoulder. "Will you pray for them?"

Adam cleared his throat and picked a few donut crumbs off the top of Pastor's desk. "Heavenly Father, guide Pastor Karl as he preaches this morning." He stroked his chin, searching for the right words, but they had never been more difficult to find. "And, Lord, the visitors…I ask, especially for the visitors, that those who have never heard about your love and forgiveness will hear and receive Jesus Christ as their Lord and Savior. Bring each person here safely and may they feel welcome as they worship with us this morning." Once he got started, it was as if God gave him the words. Not only that, the words took on power, enough power to make him care about visitors like he never had before.

"Amen. Amen." Pastor Karl placed the bulletin on top of his Bible and walked toward the door. "Thanks, Adam. Good to have you back."

Adam checked his watch, hoping there might be enough time to fill Pastor in on what was going on since he'd been in for counselling, how he and Grace were beginning to open up and move out of their pasts. "Do you have time this week just to catch up? Maybe lunch at the Lighthouse"

Pastor Karl held the door open. "Everything okay? I have a minute if you—"

"Haven't told anyone." He tucked his Bible under his arm and stepped into the narrow hall, where it was still safe to talk without being overheard. "Grace and I are expecting."

"Congratulations. Grace must be beside herself." Pastor slapped his back. "Be sure to let her know how happy we are for both of you. Our God certainly is a God of amazing mercy."

Adam made his way down the side isle to where Grace was seated and took his place alongside her. *Mercy.* Crazy how one word could get hooked inside his mind. Everyone was singing now. *What can wash away my sin?* Every so often his ear caught Grace's voice, or his arm brushed hers, drawing him to the edge of worship. But it didn't take long before his mind snapped back to Pastor Karl's comment. *Mercy. Amazing mercy.*

Why had he linked Grace's pregnancy to mercy?

It was a good ten minutes after worship began when he heard the door open and close, not a quiet close, one that was almost a slam. Shoes scuffed their way toward the front. With everything that was in him, he wanted to turn and give the culprit a look that said pick up your feet.

But before he could do anything, Grace grabbed his leg and squeezed. Except for a red chin, her face was as white as a cotton ball. "Adam, he's here. Look." She gave his leg one more squeeze. "Derrick."

He turned just in time to see Derrick take a seat directly across the aisle, right alongside old Fisher Johnson.

From that point on, his face burned and all through the service he battled an inside voice that was louder than Pastor's preaching. *What is he doing here? The facts are clear, he doesn't belong in our church.* He laid his hand over the top of Grace's and tried to calm their trembling.

He couldn't help himself; every few minutes, he looked. He was there all right, next to Fisher, paging through one of the paperback Bibles the church provided those who didn't have means to purchase one. He felt Grace's leg shake against his. And there was nothing he could do except scribble a message across the bottom of his bulletin. *Want to leave?*

Without looking at him, Grace shook her head. And as she did, his heart hooked another word. *Visitor.* The prayer came back as fresh as the moment God put it in his heart. *I pray for the visitors…that they'll hear and receive Jesus as their Lord and Savior… bring them here safely… may they feel welcome as they worship with us this morning.*

God knew he meant the prayer. But Derrick? There was no question about it; he had a right to feel this way. He didn't care one iota about Derrick's safety.

And he cared even less about his salvation.

CHAPTER 24

Today was Sammy's first day of school.

Adam gripped the steering wheel as he watched his daughters walk under the school's green and blue welcome banner. Even though it was Grace sitting next to him, her hand gently resting on his knee, she was little more than a shadow. He assured himself it was just for today, just for this moment, that he wished the woman sitting beside him was Beth.

This day had come too fast. Wasn't it just days ago that he grumbled endlessly about sour Sippy cups and soggy Cheerios left scattered in the backseat?

For the first time since his birthday, memories gripped him by the neck, twisting until he had no choice. The only way he could look was back, back to when Beth was alive and Kate was about to begin her first day at Tesoro Elementary.

Beth had gotten up early that day. While he made breakfast, she sat at the kitchen table with Kate on her lap, brushing her hair. Once it was perfect, she took a rainbow ribbon from her bathrobe pocket and tied it into a bow around Kate's ponytail.

"Mommy, that's your favorite," Kate said.

And it was.

No. It had been—before the chemo.

The picture of Beth straightening the collar on Kate's white blouse was as fresh as this morning's coffee. "Yes, it's my favorite, all right." She wrapped Kate's hands in hers and looked straight into her eyes. "But I want you to wear it and remember that even though you're a big school girl, Mommy and Daddy are close. And we'll be praying for you all day." She touched her nose to Kate's. "Eskimo kisses," she said. And for the first time that morning, Kate laughed.

They'd parked in the same spot he and Grace parked today, and held hands just the way they were doing right now. But everything else was different. He could still see Beth's straw hat, the one with a wide brim that made her look like she was going to pick strawberries. He could still taste his tears as she explained how with every stroke of the brush she'd prayed over Kate's mind, asking God to shield it from falsehoods, asking him to use her education to lead her to knowledge of the truth.

That's why he knew one thing for certain, nothing could keep Beth away from celebrating Sammy's first school day. It didn't matter how thick the barrier between heaven and earth was, nothing would keep her away from today. It was one of those days when God would take Beth by the hand, lead her to heaven's window and invite her to look. Beth was watching as Kate wrapped her arm around her little sister. When he counted Sammy's steps…past the American flag…under the welcome banner, Beth counted with him. He couldn't believe anything different.

Does she know who fixed Sammy's hair? The question had barely bounced across his heart when Kate and Sammy turned and waved. A dash of fear seasoned Sammy's voice. "Bye, Daddy. Bye, Mommy."

At that moment Grace scooted closer. Squishing herself between the steering wheel and him, she waved out the window, tears pooling in her eyes like they'd been doing all morning. "Love you," she said. "Pick you up at three."

And then they were gone.

Lord Jesus, keep the window open just a little longer. Once again he reached for the hand that was there. *I know this is silly, God. But let Beth stay by the window so she can watch Sammy all the way through her first school day.*

Back and forth, he ran his thumb across Grace's hand. He had no idea why he wasn't driving away—no idea until Grace rested her head on his shoulder. "Lord, protect them." Her voice was soft. "Protect their little minds. Be with their teachers and classmates all through today."

It had taken Sammy's shaky little voice to bring Grace back to where she should be—sitting next to Adam, watching the girls make their way across the school yard.

The spinning in her head hadn't stopped all morning, even when she was celebrating with Kate, listening to her little girl chatter as they filled her new backpack. And when she was comforting Sammy's Kindergarten fears, holding her on her lap, gently moving a brush through her tangled curls, it was all she could do not to close her eyes and run away from everything this morning reminded her of.

But she didn't. She stayed strong, listening to a myriad of Sammy's questions. *If I don't like school will you come get me really, really fast...what if they have yucky food...what if there's a mean boy who pulls my hair?*

In the middle of it all, right there in the front of her mind, was the knowing that this was the day her baby should be starting school. She should be in Sammy's class. They should be best friends, defending each other against boys who pull ponytails.

Now, as she sat next to Adam, watching the school door close, she could feel herself tripping over a tombstone of regret. Her baby would never have a first day of school with Sammy. She'd never watch her carry a book or report card through the front door, wouldn't hear her stories about struggles with trays of cafeteria food, or hear her sing a silly new song.

Adam took her hand, rescuing her from her thoughts. Back and forth, he rubbed his thumb over her knuckles. And when he did, the spinning that had plagued her all morning slowed, making room for a new spinning, the good kind she always felt when her hand was in Adam's. For as long as she lived, she'd never get used to the power of her husband's touch.

But this morning his touch stirred more than romantic love. It stirred security, the security of love that never walks away. Adam loved her that way. She was beginning to feel it. And that's what gave her the courage to tighten her promise. She would stop finagling the truth, stop finding reasons to delay telling Adam everything.

He was leaving for Minnesota today, but as soon as he came home, whether he wanted her to or not, she would tell him about the child who should have started school today.

Chapter 25

Grace scraped the last spoon of chocolate chip cookie dough from the mixing bowl and set the oven timer for ten minutes, just enough time to run upstairs and gather the girls' towels.

The last few days she'd felt much better, well enough to enjoy the buttery aroma of freshly baked cookies, and well enough to complete the forms she needed in order to return to college in time for the next semester. She felt freer than she'd felt in a long time. Of course, classes would have to be online to fit her schedule. Adam was all for it, encouraging her to take this step toward her dream of becoming a teacher.

With Adam in Minnesota and the girls in school, she played her favorite music loud enough to sound through the entire house. "Tears of joy and tears of shame…" As she picked Sammy's towel off the bedroom floor, she sang along. "Washed forever in Jesus name."

This is what she loved. It seemed every day brought new blessings and new reasons to sing.

Already Sammy's biggest school complaint wasn't homework or mean boys. "Mommy." Grace chuckled at yesterday's conversation and the way Sammy had crossed her arms around her tummy. "Schoolwork makes me lots hungrier than swimming." She'd pulled a crinkled pink slip from her backpack. "I ate a cookie when it wasn't snack time. How was I supposed to know?"

She took the paper from Sammy, unfolding it slowly. "Did you tell Mrs. Webber you were sorry?"

Sammy nodded. "And I made her a picture with flowers."

"Will you bring home a note like this again?"

"No, promise, even if I'm starving to death."

"Good enough for me." She tore the pink paper in two pieces and placed them back in Sammy's hands. "Toss it in the trash. That's the end of it."

"Yep. The end of it," Sammy echoed.

She wrapped her arms around the bundle of dirty clothes, pressing it under her chin and against her abdomen as she carried the laundry downstairs.

At least her stomach wasn't as flat as it had been back when she existed on ginger-ale and soda crackers. In no time, there'd be one more child's laundry to fold, a child who might have problems settling into the restrictions of school, a child to love—a child who every day of his or her life would remind her of God's inexhaustible mercy.

It didn't matter that her music had finished playing; her heart continued to dance as one-by-one she dropped the towels into the tub of soapy water. Every line of the song captured her life, rich words speaking of Christ's mercy and healing rain reaching the lost.

Reaching her.

Soaking her once dry heart.

She stood in front of the washing machine, her arms wet almost to her elbows. Without God's love and mercy, she wouldn't be here washing clothes for daughters she loved.

That's why, even in an empty house, she was content. The only things she dreaded were the nights, nights alone in bed, never knowing when the light stalker would show up, or if one of her dreams would wake her.

She moved into the kitchen and took the last batch of cookies from the oven, placing them on a platter. Just as she was about to check the dryer, she heard the patio door click open.

"What you trying to do?" Even before she turned, his voice took over the room. "Play little Miss Suzy Homemaker?"

Her heart scrambled into her throat. "Derrick. That door was locked."

He dangled two keys inches from her face. "Locked doesn't matter when I have these."

As much as she tried, she couldn't figure Derrick out. Ever since Adam returned to Minnesota, he'd been waffling between extreme thoughtfulness and increasingly brazen behavior.

It wasn't that she was afraid of Derrick. She was uncomfortable with him and his antics. Besides, the two of them alone in the house didn't look good. She kept her voice cool. "Do you want something?"

"Since I can't have what I want..." Even though sunglasses hid Derrick's eyes, the force of his stare pushed her back. "Cookies would be nice." He pulled the last gallon of milk from the refrigerator. "And a glass."

With an intentional clunk, she set a glass on the table. Why today? He'd been spending almost every day at the marina, getting his boat ready to sail. Now here he was in her kitchen, eating the girls' cookies.

"You can make these for me anytime." He grabbed another handful and wrapped them in a napkin.

"Does Adam know you still have the keys?"

"Try to get them?" He pushed the keys deep into his front pocket.

"That's enough." She turned her back to him, doing her best to sound unruffled. "Before you leave, drop the keys on the table."

She wanted to throw him out; but with his new interest in church, God would want her to be kind. Anyway, she understood him well enough to know he would never hurt her. In his own strange way, he cared. At least he seemed to. Besides, if she really believed the things she claimed to believe about heaven and hell and God being willing to wash His mercy over anyone who asked, her history with Derrick really didn't matter.

"Hey, I've been reading that Bible your Pastor gave me." He followed her into the laundry room. "He said to read John first. Who starts reading a book that close to the end?"

She brought an armful of towels into the kitchen and set them on the table. "I'm sure Pastor Karl wants you to know God loves you. That's why he told you to read John." She reached for a towel and folded it just the way Adam liked.

"Here, let me help." Derrick pulled a towel from the pile. "Don't know if I buy into the whole God thing, you know about some old book being God's word."

In that split second, before she could tell him that's exactly what the Bible is, the worst thing that could possibly happen, did.

Adam's mother walked through the door.

Standing out on the veranda, Grace did her best to come to terms with the clammy night air, which smelled like a blend of rotten eggs and discarded fish. Other than the light coming from Derrick's window, it was totally dark. She stared at her phone and pushed Adam's number, hoping it would go to voice mail; but Adam picked up on the third ring.

"You've talked to your mom?" Even before the words left her mouth she knew the answer.

"Just got off the phone."

"It's not what it sounds like, Adam. I swear." She dropped onto the wicker chair. "I was just baking cookies and doing the laundry. I'm sorry."

"Why wasn't the door locked?"

"It was."

"I told you, we're done hiring him for jobs around the house."

"He just walked in behind my back. Want me to call your mother?" She could still see the woman's tight face.

"It's simple. Lock—"

"He has keys, the ones you gave him."

"I don't care who gave him the keys." Adam released a lungful of air. "Just get them back."

There was no point telling him she'd already tried. It would only make matters worse. And if she couldn't tell him that, she certainly couldn't tell him that despite all Derrick had put them through, she was actually beginning to feel sorry for him.

Icy teardrops fell on Grace's shoulders, rolling down her arms, forming red pools that flowed into a rancid river. In bare feet, she stood in the middle of the river holding a tiny body. *Help. Can't you see; something is wrong.* She waded to the far shore of the river to where she stood frozen perfectly still in center of a circle of people wearing long coats. But it was no use; the baby floated out of her arms. And it didn't matter how much she loved the child; her love wasn't strong enough to pull her back. Why weren't the coat people helping? Couldn't they see the tiny hands? Couldn't they hear her weak whimper? This was a baby. Why was she the only one who cared? If only she could touch the little face. *Over here. Look into my eyes. Come; and let me wipe your tears.* For an instant, the baby turned toward her. That's when she saw the teeth, full-size and black with decay, teeth that didn't belong in a baby's sweet mouth. "Help." The scream pulled Grace from sleep.

Minutes later, she sat in her usual spot on the veranda, her Bible open to Psalm 103, the same words Pastor Karl had written on the inside cover of her Bible.

When she wasn't scanning the darkness for the stalker or Derrick, she read. *Who redeems your life from the pit and crowns you with love and compassion…* She ran her fingers across the page. *He does not treat us as our sins deserve or repay us according to our iniquities…as far as the east is from the west…*

Tears ran down her neck, soaking the front of her robe. If only Adam were here. "Lord God, help." She searched the sky, wondering if God really had time to listen. "Help me make it till Adam comes home. Keep me strong, strong enough to tell him everything."

She read the verse again. *As far as the east is from the west, so far has he removed our sins from us.* "And, Lord Jesus, I know how Adam feels about these things, how Beth volunteered at the pregnancy center, how generous Adam is because he cares about children. Make him strong enough to hear the truth. Strong enough to continue loving me."

Tiredness filled her body. She sat taller, uncurling her legs and placing her feet flat on the floor, willing herself to stay awake long enough to finish her prayer.

But drowsiness urged her to relax.

She reached for a pillow and curled herself on the outdoor lounge, slowly floating...floating…unable to make herself get up and move into the safety of the bedroom.

It wasn't until it started to rain that she woke, but she didn't go in. She sat there, allowing the healing drops to wash over her, to soak her. And as they did, she was no longer afraid of the light stalker, or Derrick.

Or telling Adam the truth.

CHAPTER 26

Grace fastened the top of her swimsuit and slipped into the knee-length cover-up Adam had brought back from one of his trips to Minnesota. This was the time of year islanders routinely tracked the weather on their hurricane maps. But the season had been calm. Rain only came late in the day, sometimes not until after sunset. In the grocery stores and at the girls' school Grace listened to lifelong residents' predictions. "Made it through another season," they'd say. It was almost as if they believed hurricanes no longer hit Tesoro.

She tapped the bathroom door where Abby was changing clothes. "Lunch will be waiting out by the pool."

A few minutes later Abby sat across the table. "You've told Adam, right?" She opened the deli container, scooping two generous scoops of shrimp salad on to her plate. "Everything's okay?"

"I told you; he's been gone over two weeks." She handed Abby the plate of melon slices. "I'm going to tell him everything, just not over the phone."

"You're sure this time." Abby pointed her fork across the table. "Right?"

"As soon as he comes home." She rested her head against the back of the chair and closed her eyes. When she opened them Abby was looking straight at her. "And what happens is in God's hands."

Abby shook a fresh layer of pepper on her salad. "But haven't you promised this a zillion times?"

Abby was right. Every promise to herself, and every promise to God had ended up broken. "All I can tell you is this time nothing can stand in my way."

"Wow." Abby scraped the last of the salad from the container's lid and licked the spoon. "The two of you totally need to be alone when you tell him. If it will help, let me take the girls to a movie or something."

At that moment Abby's eyes got the look. She'd seen it before. Every time Abby crafted some crazy idea her eyes grew into perfect circles.

"I've got it. This is way beyond good."

Grace slid a piece of key lime pie onto a plate and passed it to Abby. "So when your eyes are back in their sockets, do you want to fill me in?"

"You're going to love this…really. And so is—" Before Abby could say another word, the phone rang.

"Adam." Grace reached for her cell, anticipating the sweet sound of Adam's voice."

"I'm fixin to go into a meeting." Adam talked fast and businesslike, poking holes in her anticipation. "Just checking to see if you've gotten the keys from Derrick?"

"Not yet. Abby is here."

"Perfect. Ask her to go with you. Mom's going nuts over this. Once you have the keys, give me a call."

Next to handing out advice, Abby loved nothing more than being in the middle of adventure. That's why, before she could stop her, Abby was on her feet, heading toward Derrick's apartment. Without hesitation, or fear, or any of the feelings Grace felt churning inside her, Abby led the way up the stairs and knocked on Derrick's door.

"Uff-da, Ab." She double-knotted the sash that held her cover-up closed. "I don't feel good about this." She backed down a step. "Let's go. I'll tell Adam he wasn't here."

But it was too late. Abby had already opened the door.

"Don't, Ab, please" Grace couldn't stop her heart or knees from shuttering as she followed Abby deeper into Derrick's space, scanning the oversized room for any sign that he was there. In one corner there was a small kitchen, in the other a sofa and coffee table, and in the center, taking up most of the space, an unmade king-sized bed. It was the first time she'd been up here. "We have to leave." She pulled on Abby's sleeve.

But Abby was already on the move, picking through the heaps of clothes that were scattered across the floor, shaking shirts and turning pockets inside-out. "You really need rubber gloves for this," she said.

With the shutters closed, the apartment was dark. Somewhere, in the kitchen or bath, she wasn't sure which, a faucet dripped. She stood in the middle of the room, breathing as little as possible. Stale grease, fish, and filth, the combination was more than her stomach could tolerate. "I don't know where to start."

Abby moved into the kitchen. "Check the table," she said. "I'm telling you, the keys have to be here."

She did as Abby ordered, moving crusty paper plates and empty beer cans across the plastic tablecloth, scooping them into a trash can that was already full. *Keep Derrick away, Lord, until we're done,* she prayed.

When she found no key on the table, she went to the sofa and ran her hand between the cushions. Abby was right; she could use rubber gloves. One hand landed in goo. The other pulled out a few small coins and an oily paper plate. She used the back of the plate to scrape what looked like a wad of chewed gum from between her fingers.

"This is too gross, Ab. And they're not here." She opened a shutter just wide enough to peek out and scan the beach for Derrick. Even though she couldn't see him, she was sure he was there, maybe only seconds away. "Let's go. He's going to walk in any minute. What then?"

"I swear this guy has never washed a cup or fork." Abby continued to rattle her way through the cupboards. Another drawer slammed open, this time with more force. "Oh, Yow." Abby motioned her toward her find. "Look here. You're not going to believe this. There's an entire box of these. I'm not kidding you." She released a large black flash light into her hand. "It's Streamlight, the kind my Dad used when he was a cop." Abby's eyes were large and Nancy Drewish, as if she'd just come across what she'd spent a hundred pages in search of. "Do you know what this means?" Abby leaned toward her, looking her straight in the eyes.

Grace stared back, maybe even harder. They'd been friends long enough that she knew Abby wasn't interested in anyone's answer but her own.

"Cops use these because they're the most powerful flashlights out there. Derrick is the light stalker," Abby said.

"I'd believe almost anything about Derrick. But not that." She tossed the flashlight on the bed. "No way. Let's just get out of here."

"The keys, Grace." Abby dropped to her knees at the foot of Derrick's bed. "Check that side; I'll check here."

It was too late; something more important had already caught her eye. Her cookies sat in plain view on top of the nightstand, and alongside them, a paperback Bible. "If Derrick's the light stalker, how do you explain this?" She slid the book across the bed. "This should prove something. Do you think someone with a Bible next to his bed could be a stalker?"

"Doesn't mean anything." Abby fanned the pages. "I don't see any underlining or highlighting. He probably hasn't cracked it open." Abby was standing now, tall and with the same confidence that once drove Grace away from her best friend.

She didn't know how she could make Abby see that she wasn't always right. Sometimes she was wrong about people, and just as judgmental as Adam's mother.

"It worries me that you trust this guy, Grace. It really does. Anything under that side of the bed?"

Other than a red tackle box, a few stray socks, and a scattering of candy wrappers and food-coated plates, she found nothing. She pulled the tackle box toward her, thinking if she checked inside for the keys Abby would be satisfied enough to leave. But just as she was about to lift the lid, she heard steps.

"Derrick." She pushed the box and garbage back under the bed. "Abby, it's him."

"Stay cool. You have a right to be here, you know."

The faucet dripped louder. "There's no way out." She stood next to his bed, waiting for the door to open. When it did, an alleyway of sunlight divided the room.

Derrick on one side. Abby and her on the other.

"Find what you're looking for, ladies?" He looked directly at Abby.

"You know what we're looking for." Abby put her hands on her hips. "Empty your pockets."

Grace stepped back, away from her friend, away from Derrick. This had to be worse than a hundred hurricanes. She wanted to run. What was Abby doing, confronting Derrick like that? "Come on, Ab, let's go." She tapped her friend's shoulder, but Abby wouldn't budge.

"Grace, you should be more careful who you hang out with." The skin around Derrick's eyes tightened, drawing them into slits. "Hate to see you getting into trouble for breaking and entering."

"She won't; it's her property."

"We're leaving. Come on, Abby." She moved toward the door.

"Tell me this, Abby." Derrick took a step closer. "If you're so fearless, then why do you look as frightened as a raccoon caught with garbage between its teeth?"

Grace could see him scanning the room, checking to see what they had touched. All she wanted to do was get out of there before he found something out of place. "Come on, Ab." She looked into Abby's eyes, pleading. "We have to—"

"First, he needs to tell us what he's doing with an entire box of flashlights."

Derrick closed in on Abby until there was little more than a thumb's width between their noses. But Abby didn't back down, even when he waved his finger in front of her face. "You just say what you want, don't ya? You step on toes, and the whole time that self-righteous look is plastered across your face." He opened the door and stepped back, giving them barely enough room to escape.

Abby huffed down the steps ahead of her. But before their feet touched the sand, he called after them. "Grace, they're the best flashlights." When she stopped and turned to face him, Abby kept walking. "She had no right to make such a big deal out of my flashlights." No matter how loud he yelled, Abby refused to turn back. At first she thought he might go after Abby; but, after going down only two steps, he stopped. For the first time she noticed he was wearing the earring she'd bought him in Key West. His hair was clean and brushed, his shirt unwrinkled.

"Grace, the flashlights..."

She reached for the railing. There was no shade and the sun was beating down on her. She needed water. Or a ginger ale. Why did she want to defend him? She had to stop feeling this way. If she didn't, it would be just like before. She'd go from having pity to trusting him.

"What about the flashlights, Derrick?"

"All I want you to know is that they're the best."

She squeezed the railing, hanging on as if her life depended on that one piece of rough wood. "And all I want are the keys to my house."

"You don't have to worry." Grace sat next to Abby on the edge of the pool, dangling her feet in the water. "He'll give me the keys." Not far from shore, a boat raced, its hull thumping the waves. She lowered herself into the pool. "Come on, get in." She lay back and allowed the swizzle from the pool jets to float her across the warm water. "Anyway, are you ready to tell me about your hot idea?"

Abby kicked her way toward Grace. "It's the best plan I've had since I can't remember when." She bobbed face-to-face with Grace. "How would you feel about making reservations to fly to Minnesota?"

"I can't. The girls—"

"That's just it. I have vacation. I'll stay here; take care of the girls and your other problem." She nodded toward Derrick's apartment.

She'd never thought about surprising Adam. "Abby, it's too much to ask. I don't want you to spend your vacation babysitting."

"You don't want me to spend my vacation here? Have you gotten so used to all this that you forget people actually save for a lifetime just to spend a week in a place like this. The girls are great. Derrick's the only one I'll have to keep in line."

"That's what scares me."

As she swam to the other side of the pool, Abby's offer floated across her imagination. She could almost picture Adam and her alone in Minnesota. He'd never seen the house she grew up in. They'd buy lefse at the Scandinavian bakery, and she'd show him how to roll it into a tube after covering it with butter and a thin layer of lignonberries. There'd be lots of time to talk. That's the only reason she'd take Abby up on her offer, to tell Adam the things she should have told him long ago.

And if, when everything was said, Adam no longer loved her, at least she'd be close to home.

Abby's idea made perfect sense.

"Are you sure? I mean, it's a huge commitment. It's not only the girls; it's Derrick. You have to promise me that no matter how you feel about Derrick, you'll call him if the light stalker shows up. He's really not such bad a guy anymore."

"If you think that, then you really need to get away from here."

"I can't wait." She pulled herself out of the pool and wrapped herself in a towel. "Hopefully I'll have time to check for flights before I pick up the girls."

"I can take a hint," Abby said as she grabbed her beach bag. "I'll be out of here in ten minutes."

But by the time Abby left, there wasn't time to check flights. On the drive to pick up the girls, all she could think about was her trip. They'd never really finished their honeymoon. She'd take him to the waterfalls where her family enjoyed summer picnics. They'd climb the rocks and follow the path along the creek. On Sunday they'd go to her old church. And they'd absolutely have to take a day for the state fair with the tunnel of love and the best foot longs anywhere. She'd wait in the hotel lobby, her face hidden behind a magazine. She'd give him just enough time to get up to his room before she walked down the hall and knocked on his door.

She could almost feel the excitement of standing there, waiting to be taken into Adam's arms.

CHAPTER 27

Adam clicked send. One tap and his plans were sealed. Grace didn't know yet; but she was coming to Minnesota.

They needed time together, especially with the big deal he'd been making over Derrick, and the position he'd put her in, asking her to present the Elizabeth Award at the Pregnancy Center. Clearly it seemed to be something she wasn't comfortable doing.

For the first year since Beth's death, he wasn't going to make it home for the fund raiser. Without asking, he'd assumed Grace wouldn't have a problem presenting the award. After all, she was just as passionate about babies as Beth had been. As he looked back on his decision, he realized he needed to find a way to show her how grateful he was. One thing he was learning, no matter how many miles separated them, he couldn't make it through even a single day without Grace, even if it was just the sound of her voice or the vision of her on face-time. That's one reason this vacation was important.

But not just for the two of them. The girls needed a vacation too.

"Are you close to the computer?" he said when she picked up the phone. "I want you to check your mail."

"The computer, how did you guess?" Her voice held the kind of tease he hadn't heard in a long time, a reminder that only a few weeks ago she would have been too sick to make a trip like the one he'd just booked.

He opened his planner and drew a long red arrow across the first week of September. "This time of night, I pictured you writing in your journal. You know, about how miserable you are without your husband. Frankly, I'm disappointed."

"You won't be," she promised.

He pulled the picture of Grace and the girls from his wallet and laid it next to his planner. So much had happened since that day on the beach when she became his wife.

More and more, Kate and Sammy looked at her as their mommy. He was even beginning to believe that Beth would be pleased.

"By the way, Derrick gave me the keys," she said. "He dropped them off after I picked the girls up at school."

He could hear the click of her fingernails. If only he could be there to see her face. More clicks and then a swallowed gasp. "Adam, I don't believe this; tickets for the girls and me? Is that what this is?"

"Ten days. I'll have to work some; but I'll keep my days short." He closed his planner. "So what do you think?"

At first he was disappointed in her response. He'd expected her to be ecstatic. Instead it was almost as if she were making excuses not to come. "Adam, the girls have school. I'm not sure I can get them excused."

"Don't worry," he said. "With Labor Day, it's not a full week anyway."

But it wasn't just her words. There was something in her tone. If he didn't know how much she missed him, he'd say she was reluctant to make the trip.

He leaned back, balancing his chair on two legs the way he told the girls they shouldn't do. "It's your turn; what's your surprise?"

"Nothing," she said, "compared to yours. I can't wait to tell the girls."

After they said goodnight, he felt more alone than he had in a long time. Maybe it was because now that the plans were set for Grace to come to Minnesota he missed her all the more, or maybe at night he had too much time to think about all he was missing. He clicked on the bedside lamp. Strange how it wasn't the big things he missed. It was little ones, those moments with Grace, watching her study a quilting book or write in her journal, or the way she nonchalantly brushed the hair out of her eyes.

He loved her hair.

On the day they met, that was the first thing he'd noticed. He had been eager to leave church that morning. All of a sudden, there she was, her hair almost the color of a winter sunset, blowing across her eyes as she bent to catch Kate's hug. It had been against everything in his sensible mind to invite her to breakfast. After all, he was still grieving. And what would people say? The words that came out of his mouth had shocked him. "Would y'all like to grab breakfast with us?"

It didn't take long, a few lunches with the girls. They loved her; and he loved watching them with her in the pool and in the kitchen making peanut butter sandwiches, using Beth's heart-shaped cookie cutter to cut the crusts away. When Grace was in the house, it was almost like Beth was back.

A month later he invited her to dinner without the girls. That's when he learned about her family, how they died and how she dropped out of Bible College and after that dropped out of life. He understood. After Beth's death, he'd dropped out too, letting his mother take over with the girls. And he stopped trusting God, stopped finding any joy in living.

That's the way it was until Grace stepped into his life. She was like Beth in many ways, yet different. Gradually, he started moving out of his grief; and he grew to love Grace.

But, no matter what he did, his love was mixed with guilt. It was like he was cheating on Beth. And he was not that kind of man.

Then on one of his trips to Minnesota he realized he missed her, missed her voice, her laugh, her imitation of nosey Mrs. Cramer who served coffee and donuts at church. He missed the way she could pull a couple words out of a Bible verse and turn them into a prayer. He loved the patience she had with Kate and Sammy.

He loved her. And because of that love, he bought a diamond and asked her to marry him.

Sure he'd sensed her hesitation. She wouldn't give an answer right away.

As he looked back, he couldn't help but wonder; did that hesitation have anything to do with Derrick? And the hesitation he sensed tonight, was that Derrick too? It couldn't be; she'd told him a dozen times she didn't even want him there.

He remembered how, when they started planning the wedding, she insisted on simple. A wedding on the beach at sunset, that's what they agreed to. Grace was beyond beautiful in her long white gown. There were no ruffles and no shoes as she walked toward him across the white sand, hand-in-hand with his girls.

He still couldn't understand why things changed; but in the nights that followed, even while they were on their honeymoon, he began to see Beth's face.

Now, with God's help, he was changing. He was moving out of the past. He pulled his Bible from the bedside table and opened it to Psalm 27. *I am still confident of this: I will see the goodness of the LORD in the land of the living.*

The land of the living. Every time he read the promise, the words seemed to dance in his heart. These were the words that had given him the idea to have Grace and the girls come to Minnesota.

Now, in just days, the goodness of the LORD would be coming to him, all the way from home.

Grace stood in front of the mirror struggling with the zipper at the back of her knee-length dress when Kate's giggle carried up the stairs. "Abby is here. She brought pizza."

She wished her dress was longer. Mid-calf would be ideal. She had longer dresses; but they were too colorful. And something as important as presenting the Elizabeth Award at the Life Pregnancy Center called for appropriate, simple black.

"Now, don't you look gorgeous? And heels? Let me help you with that," Abby said as she walked into the room and took hold of her zipper.

"You're spending the night, aren't you?" Grace pulled her hair over her shoulder. It was almost time to leave; and all she wanted to do was crawl into bed. "Close the door, will you, Ab?" She slipped a lipstick into her purse and sat on the bed. "You're not going to believe this. Adam called last night with a surprise."

Abby sat next to her. "Sounds great."

"Same dates as my surprise, Ab. Just different plans. He made reservations for all three of us to fly to Minnesota."

"Not great." Abby reached for her hand. "Had you made your reservation yet?"

"Almost. He was so excited, so proud of what he'd done; I didn't know what to say. What could I do? On top of everything, I'm only going tonight because it's important to Adam. If they only knew who was presenting Elizabeth's award, they'd push me off the stage."

"Grace, stop." Abby's voice was softer than normal. "Every minute of tonight is part of God's plan. I can feel it."

"But the award is in memory of Beth. Imagine me in front of all those people." Abby stood over her, looking down, like a teacher over a difficult student. "The more God wants you to do something," Abby grabbed both her hands and pulled her to her feet, "the more the enemy will work to keep you from doing it. And he's going to use every trick in the book to stop you from going tonight."

"Don't worry." She slipped the strap of her purse over her shoulder. "I promised Adam." She knew Abby meant well. Her eyes, her entire face, flushed with understanding as she took on the role of wise counselor.

"And he'll use every trick in the book to stop you from telling Adam."

The more God wants you to do something, the more the enemy wants to stop you from doing it. Thirty minutes later, Abby's words gave her strength to walk into the award ceremony and take the place reserved for her at the front of the banquet room.

Flowers and music, information tables covered with adoption literature and sculptures of unborn babies, testimonials from several women who had chosen life—it was almost too much for Grace to take in. The elite were there, the ones with deep pockets, as well as the passionate faithful.

But it was Carrie, a woman about her age with gelled brown hair and a butterfly tattoo just below her shoulder, whose message caught Grace's heart. Carrie stood at the front of the room with both hands wrapped around a microphone, her voice confident, yet bearing a delicate southern drawl. "I thought it was going to be simple. Quick and simple and my problem would be removed." Grace heard tears gathering in Carrie's throat, choking her, forcing her to pause until every fork in the room lay silent. "But what no one told me was that no doctor or machine, no boyfriend, could ever remove my baby from my heart." The microphone thumped against her chest.

Even the servers were still.

For the next half hour Carrie abandoned her stack of note cards and talked about the nightmares and flashbacks, her preoccupation with her unborn child. She talked about God's healing and later how He led her to start a group for women suffering as she had suffered. "All I can tell you is that in a gathering of this size, there's more than one woman who knows firsthand what I am talking about." She held up a pink and blue brochure. "This is for you. You're not alone."

More than one woman. Grace scanned the room, looking into each woman's face for a clue. Who else? Not in a group of Christians, it couldn't be. Who besides her understood the pain of being pregnant and unable to find a way out that didn't end up making the pain worse?

The ache and guilt of empty arms and burdened heart was pain that would last forever. She was sure of it.

Before the evening was over, Grace stood on the stage, side-by-side with Carrie and presented The Elizabeth Award, a small trophy and a check to be used in her work.

As she drove home, a light rain began to fall. She set the wipers to their lowest speed and allowed her thoughts to wander backward. Her child wasn't with her, wasn't sharing school clothes, toys, and a bedroom with Sammy.

Derrick still had no idea; but she ran from the clinic that day. Their child was alive. She was in a home with parents who loved her. God had been good to her. He'd stopped her from making the same mistake that so many were struggling to move beyond. *I will tell Adam about my first baby,* she promised herself, *there's nothing stopping me now.*

She opened the window just a crack, and with the windshield wipers providing the only rhythm, sang the song she could not chase from her heart. "Healing rain, it's coming down."

CHAPTER 28

By the time Grace parked in the garage, the drizzle had turned into a steady rain. Before she opened the door, she slipped out of her jacket and held it over her head like a limp umbrella.

As she readied herself to run, an uneasiness grew inside her, pushing down the joy and confidence of just minutes before. At first she comforted herself with the assurance of patio and veranda lights to guide her between the garage and house. But as soon as she stepped beyond the garage she noticed the lights were out, leaving the patio as black as the sky, her veranda even darker. For the first time in days, she thought about the stalker. Was this his doing? She'd only seen him once since Adam left.

She stepped back inside the garage and pulled the cell phone out of her purse. Who could she call? It was too late to bother Abby. And there were no sounds coming from Derrick's apartment.

She leaned against the car and whispered the words to Adam's prayer. "Lord, quiet me with your love." How many nights had she walked alone on the beach barely giving her safety a second thought? She took off her heels. There was no reason to believe the light stalker had anything to do with this. Lights burned out all the time. No big deal. *Lord, quiet me with your love.* In less than ten minutes, her head would be on her pillow. *Quiet me, Lord.* She opened the garage door and covered her head with her jacket.

And then she ran.

By the time Grace was ready for bed, she had only enough oomph to check on the girls.

As usual, Kate had fallen asleep under the glow of her reading light. When she removed the book from her hands, she didn't budge.

Sammy was different. The minute she walked into her room, she sat up and rubbed her eyes. "Mommy, I forgot Snow outside and he's very, very lonesome."

"Oh, honey, he'll be fine. Lambs like to sleep outside." She kissed her forehead and wrapped the covers extra snug around her shoulders. "We'll get him first thing in the morning."

There was no way she could go back out there tonight. It was more than the rain, it was the question that had been plaguing her ever since she had to run through the dark. The outside lights should have been on. Adam had recently changed them. What if Derrick had done something to the timer? What if he really wasn't her rescuer? What if he was the light stalker, just like Abby said?

Her phone rang, rescuing her from her thoughts. While she talked to Adam, she slid between the sheets, tucking the phone between her shoulder and ear as she rested her head on Adam's pillow.

"I knew you'd be a hit at the banquet," he said. "Wish I could have been there to hear you."

It wasn't until she answered all his questions that their conversation turned to the upcoming trip. "You're right," he said. "I picked up a brochure. We have to go to the state fair." She could hear the rustle of paper and she wondered if they still used the same pictures—baby animals, carnival rides, and the Minnesota Gopher playing with children.

"They have this milk booth, any flavor, drink as much as you want. The girls will have a ball. Be sure to pack the camera." His enthusiasm was so commanding that before long she was no longer tired. "Kate will have to go to the horse show," he said, "and Sammy's never seen a real lamb."

"Don't let her hear you say that. Did you forget about Snow?"

She was just about to say goodnight when Sammy stumbled into the room. "Mommy, Snow." She climbed into bed and snuggled into her side, looking up at her with eyes that could melt the North Pole. "Can you get her, please?"

"Maybe you left her in the family room, Sammy."

"No, she's by the pool, under Daddy's chair. That's where I put her so she would be really safe. And then I forgot." Sammy's eyes told the story. She wasn't going to sleep until Snow was safely inside.

"Adam, this is when I miss you most. If you were here, you'd be the one going after Snow."

At least the rain had stopped, so she didn't need to bother with her robe. "Talk to Daddy." She handed the phone to Sammy. "Mommy and Snow will be back in a minute. If you need me, the door's open."

As her eyes adjusted to the dark, her steps quickened and soon Sammy's sweet voice danced across the night air. She guessed that Sammy had followed and was peeking through the veranda railing. "Y'all are kidding me, Daddy. Uff-da…Strawberry milk…Really…really…as much as I want?"

Even out here in the dark she had to laugh. Right in the middle of her sweet southern talk, Sammy dropped a Minnesota *Uff-da*.

"Honey." She turned to tell her to go back inside, but before the words left her lips she lost her balance.

In less than a heartbeat, it was as if the step fell away. There was no time to grab for the railing. Her body rolled and bounced, painfully slamming against rigid steps. She heard herself scream, "Der…rick," and felt ragged slivers puncture her legs and arms.

"Mommy." Sammy's cry pulled her from dark silence. She didn't remember landing in the sand, didn't know how long she'd been there, but when she opened her eyes the first things she saw were Sammy's tiny feet. She tried to reach for them to calm their dance of fear, but her fingers were too numb to catch her daughter's toes. Excruciating pain shot down her right arm.

Keep your eyes open, she warned herself. *Don't sleep.* She tried to talk, tried to tell Sammy everything was okay; but her tongue was caked with shell grit and salty sand.

"Grace." All of a sudden Abby was there, kneeling beside her, the cell phone tight against her ear, and Kate tight against her side.

"Sammy's Snow…please, Ab."

"Already taken care of." With her delicate fingers, Abby brushed the sand from her lips. "Listen, don't try to get up." She laid the phone against the side of her face. "Adam's still on the phone."

Even before Abby touched the phone to her ear, she heard Adam's voice. "I need to talk to her. This can't be."

"Adam." As she struggled to say his name, the tears came; and like rivers of fear, they flowed, pooling in her ears. "I don't know what…I turned…lost my balance, that's all I can remember."

Before Adam could respond, Derrick was there, bending over her, his damp pony tail brushing her neck.

"I'm here, Grace." He covered her shoulders with his jacket. "Anyone think to call 911 or y'all just standing around as useless as…" He pulled the phone from her grip.

With all that was in her, she longed to take her phone back, but pain walked up and down her body. She had to hear Adam's voice, had to hear him promise everything would be okay.

But it wasn't. Soon every voice, every move, every light melted together. Abby handing out orders…the girls' soft hands and the drip of their tears on her face…her own voice telling them she was fine… Derrick's and Abby's flashlights moving together, up and down her body…the sweet smell of the girls' strawberry shampoo…flashing lights… sirens...questions.

"How'd you fall?"

"It was dark. I don't know."

The ambulance was moving now. She couldn't remember being put inside. "My girls?" A man in a blue shirt sat close to her head. "Are they okay?" She wanted to look into the man's face long enough to ask more questions, wanted to see the inside of this emergency room on wheels, but her neck wouldn't move.

"We've got you in a brace. Don't try to move. This is just oxygen." He poked a rubbery tube into her nose. "It will help. Can you tell me your name?"

Her name? Of course she knew her name. "Grace." The beach still coated her tongue. "Some water, please." She pointed to her mouth.

"A little later. We need to get you to the hospital."

"Please." She touched her dry lips.

"Have you been drinking? Any drugs?"

Fresh tears ran down her face all the way to her bare shoulders. Why couldn't he see the kind of person she was? She would never do anything like that. With both hands, she covered her stomach. "My baby?"

"She's pregnant." His voice was louder than before. Then he patted her hand. "How many months?" For the first time he sounded like he cared. "You know, they're pretty tuff little guys; don't you worry."

But she did. The rest of the way to the hospital, while she was in x-ray, and as they settled her into a room, one dark terror filled her mind.

What did I do to harm this baby?

CHAPTER 29

W*hat are you doing the rest of your life?* Adam couldn't push the song he and Grace danced to the day they returned from their honeymoon out of his head.

And he missed her all the more.

He poured the last drop of coffee from the carafe room service had delivered the night before. What was wrong with him? He should be on his way to the airport. More important, he should have been the one to go after Sammy's toy. He should have been the one who fell down the stairs.

He tried to convince himself to focus on the good instead of the guilt. Grace and the baby were safe. Abby and Derrick had been there to help. Still, all through the night his mind had been tormented not only by his culpability, but by one word—the first and only name Grace called when she plunged helplessly through the night air.

Derrick.

She'd screamed his name only once; but it had echoed a million times in his heart. *Derrick. Derrick. Derrick.*

Why had Grace called his name? Did she see him as her rescuer? What if she was actually pointing to him as the one responsible for her fall? He fought back the thoughts. Of course she called Derrick's name. It had nothing to do with who she wanted, any more than who was responsible. But he had to admit the truth. Only one word defined the look in Derrick's eyes when they were on Grace.

Worship.

In his own pathetic way, Derrick worshipped Grace. And that sent shivers down his spine.

He goaded his heart back to the miracle. Other than a few cuts and bruises, something called cervical spine strain, and a mild concussion, Grace would be fine. He replayed the conversation he'd had with the doctor the night before. "Commonly, it's referred to as whiplash."

"How serious? Let's be clear; I want a specialist to look at her." When he heard the rustle of pages, he wondered how thick Grace's chart was. Beth's had been volumes.

"Dr. Stare from the Ocean Walk Group will follow-up with your wife in the morning, Mr. Will." He'd gone on to explain that her neck had whipped back and forth causing her muscles and the connecting tissue to stretch in ways they were never meant to stretch. "We don't believe there was any trauma to the baby. Of course, we'll know more in the morning. In the mean time, she's been fit with a neck brace. Just so you know, she reports all the lights were out."

He'd wanted to defend himself, tell the doctor he'd just spent a fortune to have those long-life bulbs installed on the house, inside and out. He was a contractor; his house did not have dangerous steps. But, more than defending himself, he wanted to hear Grace's voice. "May I speak with Mrs. Will?" he said.

"Our baby is safe." Those were her first words, spoken scratchy and weak.

"I'm fixing to fly home in the morning, the flight at six."

"Stay where you are. I don't want our vacation ruined." He had to admit, she was right. Abby had promised to stay with Grace and the girls until they left for Minnesota. If he came home now, the Minnesota trip would be pointless. Her voice grew even more tired; but still she forced a quiet giggle. "I haven't looked in a mirror; but I've a feeling you shouldn't expect to see beautiful when I step off the plane."

"You'll never be anything but gorgeous to me." That's what he promised. And it was true. Grace's beauty went deep, all the way to a place bruises couldn't reach. "How's your pain? Are they able to give you anything?"

"I won't. The baby, Adam. Uff-da, it's not like I have broken bones."

Two quick taps on his door pulled him from his thoughts. The door opened a crack. "Cleaning lady. Would you like your room cleaned today, Mr. Will?"

He told her no, just fresh towels. When she handed him a stack of bleach-stiff towels, he missed home all the more…soft towels…daytime chatter…and nighttime quiet.

He stared out the window at a city that was already busy. Cars zoomed this way and that. And inside the cars, people…busy people. If only he had someone to talk to, someone who could assure him that Grace—and every uncertain thing—would be okay.

He leaned against the window sill, his eyes scanning the empty room until they landed on his Bible.

"Lord, thank you." He pulled the drapes all the way open. But this time, instead of looking down at the city, he looked up. "I praise you for protecting Grace and our baby." He pulled a tissue from the box. "But I might as well be honest; I don't feel peace about this. Show me. Show me how to be a godly husband for Grace." He bit down on his lip, trying to decide if he should end his prayer there, where it was safe. But he'd already promised honesty. Anyway, didn't God already know his thoughts? "Lord." For the first time since he started praying, he closed his eyes. "Give me strength enough to go after the rest of the truth. I know Grace has more, Lord. Somehow I don't think any of this will come to an end until..."

As if in answer to his prayer, his phone rang. "I'm getting out today." Grace's voice was stronger than it had been before. "As soon as the doctor checks my brace, I'm out of here. Abby, the girls, and Snow are on their way."

"You mean Snow isn't grounded?" He tossed the tissue in the trash and sat at his desk. Her picture was still there, on top of his planner, and he ran his fingers across her beautiful face. "Are you sure you don't want me home?"

"Stay there," she said. "It's just a few days."

He didn't argue. Now that she was well enough to leave the hospital, it was most beneficial to stay. Over the next four days, he'd dive into work and fill his mind with all the wonderful things God was doing, like the miracle of His protection over Grace and their baby and His promise to create a new family.

A family that would no longer look back in sorrow.

CHAPTER 30

Grace stared out the kitchen window at Derrick who was busy digging through one of Adam's tool boxes. The plans had been for him to fix the wobbly step after she and the girls left for Minnesota. But Derrick wasn't a man who stuck to plans. In fact, she doubted if he even owned a calendar.

"Mommy, when can we leave?"

Grace turned toward the clip-clap of Sammy's suitcase. "Excited to see Daddy?"

"Very, very excited."

The red ribbon she'd tied in a bow around Sammy's pony tail was ready to fall out. "Wheel your suitcase back to where it belongs," she said as she retied the bow. "Make sure Kate has hers ready to go. Where's Abby?"

"She's jumping in the shower." Sammy shrugged and raised her hands, palms up. "That's what she said. Really. I don't think that's very safe because she could slip and get hurt just like you. Right, Mommy?"

"Right." She kissed the top of her daughter's head. "I'll be sure to talk to Abby about shower jumping."

As soon as Sammy was gone she turned back to the window, still unable to decide if she believed the things Adam and Abby said about Derrick. Could it be, just like Sammy didn't understand what jumping in the shower meant, they didn't understand Derrick and his unconventional ways?

Or was she the one who didn't understand?

She stepped outside. No matter what they thought, Derrick at least deserved a thank you. Since coming home from the hospital, she'd kept her distance, but from everything she remembered, he was the one who'd taken charge the night she fell.

"You look like you could use this," she said as she offered him a bottle of water. Sweat dripped from his forehead and chin. His shirt and swim trunks, the ones he wore when he worked on his boat, clung to him like soggy skin.

"You're not leaving already." He pulled a wrinkled hankie from his back pocket and poured water over it before draping it across the back of his neck. "Are you sure you should tackle a trip like this?"

"I'll be fine."

He pointed to her stomach. "The doctors think the kid's okay?"

"My baby is fine."

He finished off the water and threw the bottle next to the tool box. "I better help you with the suitcases."

"Derrick, I want to thank you for being here for me when I fell." She felt like her hands needed someplace to hide, but her dress didn't have pockets.

"Someone had to do something." Derrick leaned a board against the patio table. "Abby was useless, letting the girls slobber all over you. And Adam was no better." Derrick's upper lip curled the way it always did when he felt taken advantage of. "You might still be laying there in the dirt, if it was up to them."

"I just wanted to let you know I appreciated your help." She wished she could see inside him, not into his mind, but into his heart so she could uncover his intentions.

"Mommy, the taxi is here. And guess what color it is." Sammy ran across the patio and hugged her arm. "Orange. I always wanted to ride in an orange car."

She took Sammy's hand. "Let's go see Daddy," she said as Derrick followed them inside where Abby stood in the entryway, her hair still wet from the shower.

Like a worried grandmother, Abby dispensed instructions. "Remember, Mommy doesn't carry any of your stuff." She waved a finger at the girls and turned to Derrick. "Got the suitcases?"

Sammy was right about the taxi's color. *Why ride in a lemon when you can ride in an orange,* was scrawled across the bumper. The driver, who looked like a sixty-year-old Elvis, wore a Hawaiian print shirt, his neck accented by several thick gold chains. He opened the trunk, and stood back with his arms crossed and resting on his belly as Derrick lifted their suitcases inside.

She looked at Abby, hoping to see a hint of warmth; but there wasn't even a spark. "When I come home…" She elbowed her friend and spoke close to her ear. "I don't want you telling me you've fed Derrick to the sharks."

"Don't worry." With an ominous smile, Abby pointed toward the sky. "I'll leave that to the man up there."

Grace rested her feet on top of the bag that held the girls' snacks and coloring books. Her neck couldn't breathe and her ankles were getting puffier by the minute. For almost two hours she'd been scrunched between the girls, Kate in the window seat and Sammy on her other side.

She patted Kate's knee. According to the girls' agreement, it was Sammy's turn for the window seat. "I know." Kate didn't look up from the palm-size screen in her hand. "Is it okay if I finish this game first?"

A few minutes later Sammy settled into the window seat with Snow's nose pressed flat against the window.

It didn't seem to matter how many times they'd told Sammy there'd be flowers and swimming pools, with all her heart Sammy believed she'd look out that little window and see snow. She'd even asked Adam to buy her boots with fur and a fast sled. Sledding, building a snowman, sleeping in an igloo fort, those were Sammy's impossible dreams.

Were her dreams for this trip just as impossible?

She could almost see the four of them posing for a family picture in front of the waterfalls at Minnehaha Park. They'd explore the hillside trails and finish the day with hot buttered popcorn and strawberry ice-cream cones from the concession stand. On Sunday, they'd go to her old church, and later she'd take them by the house where she'd lived most of her life. Pastor had e-mailed that the Jorgenson's left to go back on the mission field; so it was empty, at least for a while.

But the dream she most longed for seemed as impossible as snow in August. In her dream she stood before Adam, the secret fresh off her tongue. At first she can't see his eyes, but then their eyes meet and he tells her he still loves her. He still wants her to be the mother of his children.

Telling Adam would be more difficult than she first thought. He'd moved out of his business hotel; but with the state fair in full swing, his plans to get a two-bedroom suite with a living room and kitchen hadn't materialized. Instead, he'd reserved two adjoining rooms at a family resort. It wasn't ideal; but with the door between the two rooms closed, they'd have enough privacy for conversation.

"Ladies and Gentlemen…" While flight attendants gathered the last cups and napkins, the Captain made his announcement. "We're beginning our descent into the Twin Cities, Minneapolis and St. Paul." Sammy took a deep breath and held Snow close, her nose next to hers against the window. "And the temperature in the Twin Cities is a sultry eighty-seven degrees."

Sammy's shoulders fell. "It's all blue and green down there." She kissed the top of Snow's head. "Maybe we just can't see the snow yet because we're too high up in the sky."

Kate turned off her game. "Sammy, you've already been told a hundred times…anyway, trust me; you'll have more fun without snow." She leaned in front of Grace, stretching to see out the window. "Just think, Daddy's down there waiting for us."

Grace looked too. Before long, lakes and fields gave way to skyscrapers she could still identify by name. For the first time since they started planning the trip, the truth hit her.

Even if it was for just a few days, she was going home.

CHAPTER 31

The closer Kate and Sammy came, the brighter their faces beamed, watering the lump that had been growing in his throat ever since he made the temporary move into the water park resort on the outskirts of the city.

He stepped even closer to the security barricade, watching Grace weave between travelers, doing her best to keep up with the girls. With all that was in him, he wanted to push past security, past the machines and boarding pass checkers, and run toward his family.

"We made it, Daddy." Kate threw her arms around him. The girls' giggly voices and sticky hugs, the smell of their shampoo, it all melted together like honey butter on a warm biscuit. He struggled to lift his daughters into his arms, stunned at how much heavier they were today than the last time he held the two of them together like this.

It wasn't until he set the girls down that Grace took a slow step toward him. "Hi," that was all she said.

As the girls jabbered on about the plane ride and their plans for the week, he couldn't take his eyes off Grace standing there with the neck brace, and her beautiful feet, so puffed they bulged over the straps of her sandals. "I should have been there." He traced the top rim of her brace. "I don't want to hurt you."

"You won't."

"Stop me if…" With travelers rushing past them and the girls dancing in circles around them, he took Grace into his arms.

"No sitting on the beds in your swim suits." Grace stood back against the door as the girls giggled their way into the room.

"What about your towels?" Adam's voice sounded stern, but the smile never left his face as he pointed to the trail of damp beach towels and swim goggles the girls had scattered around the room.

She could barely believe almost a full day was behind them. While Adam tucked the girls into bed, she put her feet up on the chaise in the room she and Adam would share for ten glorious days. At least she prayed it would be glorious. Tonight she would tell Adam the truth.

And when she was done, the last broken piece of her past would be out in the open.

She listened as Kate read from her book and Adam told the girls about the state fair and how much fun they'd have. Maybe she was a little crazy; but as far as she was concerned, a good father was even more attractive than a golden tan or handsome features.

And when he was around, Adam was a good father, a man who would accept nothing but the best for his daughters.

Like a well-timed affirmation, Kate's voice carried from the adjoining room.

"Everything's so totally awesome, Daddy. This is the best hotel I ever saw."

"Me too." Sammy's sweet laugh landed in the center of Grace's heart. "Take a picture of me, Daddy. I can fly all the way from my bed to Kate's."

She expected it would take half the night before the girls were calm enough to sleep; but in less than twenty minutes, the only sounds making their way through the door were whispers. *They must be praying,* she told herself as she pulled her journal from the front pocket of her suitcase. It wasn't until she'd filled half a page that she noticed the crumpled paper lying in the middle of the floor. She put her journal aside and pushed her feet as far as they'd go into slippers that no longer fit. If the paper was one of Sammy's little drawings or a poem from Kate, she'd have to thank them before they went to sleep.

But as soon as the paper was in her hands, she knew the truth. It wasn't from Kate; and it wasn't from Sammy.

It was from Derrick.

Dear Grace. Penciled letters smudged a path across the wrinkled paper. *I don't understand why you had to leave so soon after that fall. I will be thinking of you every day, and I wait for you to come back to me so I can keep you safe. Derrick.*

She wadded the paper into a ball. What kind of game was Derrick playing? He had someone else, someone he was taking with him when he left. Why would he even spend a minute thinking of her? Her neck had to breathe. She loosened the Velcro straps that held the brace firm. Why would he think something so ridiculous? He couldn't believe that when she returned to the home she shared with Adam that she was coming home to him. He'd gone crazy; that's what had happened.

And if Adam ever found the note, he'd go crazy too.

Abby was right; the way Derrick behaved was creepy. Maybe Abby was also right about Derrick having something to do with her fall down the stairs. Thankfully, she didn't have to worry about that for ten wonderful days. There wasn't time to rip the note into tiny enough pieces, so she stuffed it back into her suitcase and settled back with her journal, as if nothing had happened.

Even with the note hidden, she couldn't think clear enough to write. She rested her head against the chair's high back and closed her eyes. Kate's words were true; this had to be the best hotel, a child's paradise, complete with an indoor water park boasting slides that reached stories high and a lazy river that meandered its way through an imaginary Northwood's wilderness. She wasn't going to let Derrick and his stupid note destroy everything because this wasn't just the girls' paradise.

For ten days, it would be her paradise as well.

All she had to do was look back over the day to have the sensations grow fresh in her heart...Adam walking toward her, the boyish bounce in his step, his hair sticking up, swimming-pool-wet, and his eyes filled with more joy than they'd held in a long time.

"We have an hour," he said as he opened his beach towel and spread it over the chair next to hers. "When I made reservations, I checked out the children's program and signed the girls up. I just sent them off on a scavenger hunt."

She'd loosened the Velcro strap and removed her brace.

"Grace, what are you doing?"

"Come on." She grabbed a two-person tube from a stack at water's edge and waded into the river. "Float with me."

Of course he argued, insisting that what she was doing was nothing short of insane. "Uff-da, I don't need a brace when I have you to lean on," she said, coaxing him into the water. "Besides, the doctor said when I'm ready; I can leave it off for short periods of time."

When Adam stretched his strong legs alongside her, she rested her head against his chest, allowing the current to take them where it willed. He pulled her hair off her neck and kissed her across both shoulders. "You know, pregnant women aren't supposed to look so gorgeous in swim suits," that's what he said. And when he wrapped his arms around her, resting his hands on her stomach, the thrill of the highest and steepest water slide belonged to her.

She was still looking back over the day when the door to the girls' room slammed open and with a typical Sammy smile, one that said the party was about to begin, Sammy ran across the room and flew onto her lap. Kate followed, her smile just as large as Sammy's.

Inside and out, she loved moments like this. But she'd worked hard to establish bedtime routines. "What about bed?" Her eyes moved across the room to Adam who was standing back, leaning innocently against the door, the camera in his hand and goliath grin across his face.

"Careful, Sammy, of Mommy's neck." Kate scrunched herself into the chair. "Daddy, take a picture of us, okay?"

Something was up; she could feel the girls' excitement and Adam's peace when he snapped their picture. "The girls have something they want to say."

"You may have Daddy wrapped around your little fingers but it's past bedtime. Tell me; then its straight to—"

"We want you to be our for real mommy." Sammy jumped off her lap. "Daddy said it's okay because he wants you to be our for real mommy too."

"Me too." Kate folded and unfolded her hands. "And I'm very sorry for when I was so mean because…" Her nose turned pink, and in the corners of her eyes Grace saw tears. "If Mommy could come back from heaven for just a little while, I think she would choose you to be my Mommy."

"What are you saying?"

"Daddy said if it's okay with you…if you want to…" Kate looked up at Adam. "Come on, tell her, Daddy."

"They want you to adopt them."

"If you adopt Sammy and me, then nobody can ever take us away from you," Kate said, "even if—"

"Yup, it makes good sense." Sammy spun around like she did when she was pretending to be a ballerina. Then, she climbed back into her lap and placed her sweet hands flat on Grace's cheeks. "Mommy, it's okay; you don't have to cry."

It didn't matter how much pain she was in; she didn't know if she'd ever be willing to pull away from their hugs.

Adam wanted her to adopt Kate and Sammy.

Not in a thousand years, could she dream a gift like this would be offered to someone like her.

Seconds later, Adam stood behind the chair, his chin resting on top of her head and his arms gently stretched around her and the girls. His tears or hers—she wasn't sure which—ran down her neck.

"Yes," she said, "I want to adopt you. I'd give anything to be your for real Mommy."

Once again Sammy moved off her lap. "Daddy said adoptions don't hurt. Even if the judge looks scary, he won't give you a shot or anything."

Could this actually be happening? Adam only gave his daughters the best, the best clothes, the best hotels, the best food.

Just who do you think you are? The thought appeared like an under-the-bed monster. *If you tell him the truth now, that will be the end of it. Remember, only the best is good enough for Adam's girls.*

Sammy was dancing, Kate laughing, Adam ordering ice cream from room service. It was all so close.

Yet, all so far away.

"It's been way too long." Adam tossed the extra pillows on the floor and slid between the sheets, moving closer until his body lined up perfectly with hers.

Tell him now. The impulse shot across Grace's mind as Adam wrapped his arm around her. *God, I can't.* For the first time in weeks, the pillow next to hers wasn't empty. Adam was there; his face turned toward her…close enough to kiss.

"The girls are excited." He curled a piece of her hair around his finger. "Are you too tired to pray?"

"You mean together, without a phone stuck to my ear?"

"That's right." Adam reached for her hand. "Heavenly Father, thank you for today, for bringing my family safely here. Thank you for my wife and that she loves Kate and Sammy and wants to become their for real Mommy." A chuckle caught in his throat, and for an instant he released her hand. She raised her eyes and saw him swipe his fingers across his face. "Fill our home with love and peace. Even when we're surrounded by storms, quiet us, just quiet us, Father, with your love. In Jesus' name Amen."

Once again Adam squeezed her hand. It was her turn to pray. But what she most wanted to say, she couldn't, not in front of Adam. "Thank you, just thank you, Lord." It didn't matter that she was praying; she opened her eyes and stared into the face of the man God had put her together with. His eyes were closed and a look of deep peace was etched into his face. "Sometimes I feel so unworthy, Lord Jesus. You know I want to be the best wife and mommy…" For a moment, she was silent, not sure how to wrap words around the feelings that filled her heart, but then her thumb brushed Adam's ring. "And, Lord Jesus, Adam and I want to glorify you together. Don't let anything come between us or stand in the way."

Then, in a silent corner of her heart, she added a secret plea. *Lord, please forgive me. I promised; but I can't. Not on a night like this.*

The night Adam asked me to adopt his daughters.

CHAPTER 32

Grace had been standing alongside the lazy river, looking for Adam and the girls, only a few minutes when Adam spotted her. "You didn't happen to put my phone in your bag?" he said as he waded toward her.

She dug through her bag, even though she knew it wasn't there. "Sorry."

"I guess it doesn't matter."

But she could tell that it did matter, even when he spread his towel over the chair alongside hers. For the next few minutes they sat together, holding hands and talking. "You know, there's not a slide I haven't been down at least ten times," he said as he checked his watch.

They'd barely had ten minutes alone when Kate and Sammy showed up, dripping wet and begging for more adventure. "Take us on the big slide again. Please, Daddy."

"I'm fixin to relax a bit with Mommy."

"Come on, Daddy. Just one more time." Kate pulled on one arm and Sammy on the other. "Please," they giggled.

That's all it took. "Be back soon." he said with a shrug as his daughters led him away. "If it's not in ten minutes, send a rescue party."

When she was a little girl, it had been the same way. No one's time, no one's attention, was as important as her dad's. She could still see him sitting at the kitchen table, creases running like white rivers down his shirt sleeves, his open Bible alongside his blue coffee mug and a yellow box between them. "Cheerios?" He'd pour two bowls, sprinkling bonus crystals of sugar over hers. "I'm so happy this morning," he'd say, "that my heart is dancing."

Most people in their church didn't care much for dancing. But her parents were different. "Put your feet on mine," her dad would say. He'd hold her hands, bend his knees and they'd polka back and forth, from one end of the kitchen to the other, bumping into chairs and laughing.

"Mommy, up here." Kate's voice pulled Grace from her memories, drawing her eyes to the platform at the highest point of the water park where Adam stood between his daughters, the three of them waving down at her. Even in a crowded place, Grace could single out their voices. She waved back, swallowing the urge to tell them it wasn't safe to stand so close to the railing.

Amazing how simply knowing they needed her made her feel almost whole. They needed her love. They needed her to take care of details, just like she'd done that morning when she gathered all their forgotten necessities—Adam's camera left on the dresser—the baggie of first-aid supplies lost under Sammy's bed—Kate's forgotten towel. Carefully, she'd tucked their left-behind belongings into her beach bag.

Every forgotten item, except Adam's phone.

Actually, she'd wrestled with the knowing that she should toss it into her bag. How many times had it already rung? *Enough is enough,* that's what she told herself. After all, in the most wonderful moments of their vacation, Adam's phone had managed to get in the way.

Their day at the zoo was a perfect example. In the middle of the seal show, Adam excused himself. They found him a half hour later, sitting on a bench, snow cone in one hand and phone in the other. She still had to chuckle over the way the girls ran to him, exploding with joy over the seal that played with a beach ball and clapped his "hands."

She pulled her cover-up off the back of her chair. The only right thing to do was bring Adam's phone down to the pool. But before she could slip the cover-up over her swim suit, he was there. "The girls are fixin' to float in the river." He pulled the room key from her bag. "I'm going up to the room. Do you need me to grab anything?"

She watched him walk away, his towel wrapped around his broad shoulders the way it had been earlier that morning when Sammy finagled Adam and Kate down to the water park as soon as it opened.

Being left behind hadn't bothered her. She needed time alone to grapple with the doubts she'd been having ever since she'd gone back on one more promise to tell Adam about her first baby. Was she really breaking her promise to God, or was she actually doing what He wanted? As she looked back, she saw one constant truth. God was the one who kept putting roadblocks in her way. Even Abby would have to agree. Adam's panic attacks, the change in vacation plans, the adoption. Those were just a few examples.

God knew exactly what impact telling Adam about her first baby would have. What if it would mean the end to their marriage? God hated the pain of divorce; He wouldn't want that. Besides, for the first time since her parent's death, she felt truly at home in Minnesota.

She draped her cover-up over the foot of Adam's chair and removed her neck brace. Already her fall seemed far in the past. Their days together had gone fast. Here it was Saturday. This afternoon they'd enjoy a picnic; tomorrow they'd go to church and after that make one last visit to her parent's home where they'd already created some of the best memories of their vacation.

As far as Kate was concerned, her old backyard was as exciting as the water park. Not even Adam's camera could capture the look of pride on Kate's face as she climbed the same apple trees she once tackled. Sturdy branches and an abundance of fruit made the trees perfect for climbing. She'd never forget the sight of Kate biting into a crisp red apple without checking for worm holes.

They'd saved the best for last, the State Fair. Adam had bugged her all week. "I need to know what I'm in for. Ye Old Mill, is that what y'all call it?"

Every time he brought it up she gave the same answer. "Uff-da, Adam, not everything has to go into that old planner." She loved teasing him. "What do you think it is?"

"Better not be one of those up-side-down coasters. I don't do those."

If she had the time, she'd spend all day looking both ways—back over the week and ahead to the days before them.

The best thing, there wasn't anything to dread, not even the day they'd leave, because Adam was coming home for Sammy's birthday.

And that's when she would take her first step to becoming Kate and Sammy's "for real Mommy." The details were set. In two weeks, just two days before Sammy's birthday, they'd meet in the attorney's office to initiate the paper work.

On top of everything, Adam's baby was growing inside her. One day soon she'd feel the first poke of an elbow or knee, the first gurgle-glop of a silent hic-up.

Before wading into the water, she took a sip of lemonade. Then she looped her arm around an empty raft and waited for Kate and Sammy to float into view. She heard them first, above all the other children. "Hooray." Sammy squealed when she waved them over to the river's edge. "You fixin' to float with us?"

And in that moment she was certain. It was all the proof she needed to know her decision not to tell Adam was the right choice.

In fact, she'd go as far as saying it was God's perfect will.

CHAPTER 33

Three, that's how many calls Adam had missed. It didn't matter that they were on a little vacation; this was totally unacceptable. If only he or Grace had remembered to bring his cell down to the water park, none of this this would have happened.

He sat on the edge of the bed with his planner spread across his lap, listening to the latest message. "Good news, Adam. Phase-two on the Stillwater project…other bid fell through…Adam, I like your work…but I need to hear something today…decision is less than two weeks out."

He'd almost worked himself into the grave on the Stillwater proposal, and then when they were on their honeymoon, a huge piece of it had been pulled from his grasp. Now, if he played his cards right, that piece could be his again.

Today…less than two weeks. He played the deadlines over in his mind, trying to blend them with Sammy's birthday party and their appointment with the adoption attorney.

There was no way.

Here he was standing on the brink of what he'd always envisioned for his company. Would it be prudent to let a child's party stand in the way? He could feel his heart beat faster as his mind hunted for a solution. Sammy's party, even the appointment with the attorney, all of it could be rescheduled. This could not.

But, what about breaking his Sammy's heart?

He paced between the two rooms, searching for the words he could use. He could tell Sammy this birthday was so special that they'd celebrate early at the fair. After all, there'd be balloons and an entire midway. He'd let her go on as many rides and play as many games as she wanted. She'd love it. It would be better than some little circus party. Grace could order a cake from that bakery she was always bragging about.

"Daddy, we're hungry for our picnic." Sammy's wet hug pulled him away from his predicament. How could he do this to his sweet Sammy?

Within seconds, a trail of flip-flops and towels littered the room. "Girls, please," he said motioning to the soggy trail. "How many times do I have to tell you?"

"Adam, are you okay? You didn't come back and…" Even with the brace around her neck, Grace's movements were elegant. She sat next to him on the edge of the bed, reaching for his hand. "You should have seen Sammy."

"Ya, Daddy." Sammy poked her head around the corner. "You should'a see'd me."

"Seen, Sammy." He pulled his hand away from Grace's. "I'll see you later; now get ready."

He held up his phone. "Grace, I should have had this."

"I'm sorry." She moved her hands across his shoulders. "Maybe we should cancel the picnic. If you need to spend the rest of the afternoon working, I can take the girls—"

"No." He paced to the window. "Forget it."

He didn't have to look at Grace to know she was still sitting on the bed, her hands folded in her lap, her eyes and lips turned down as she waited for him to do the impossible.

Tell her the truth about the change in plans.

Grace couldn't sleep. This wasn't the way it was supposed to be. She scooted to the edge of the bed, as far away from Adam as she could get.

Almost every detail of the picnic turned out just as she dreamed it would. But that didn't matter, not anymore.

They'd had sunshine with a gentle breeze, the kind that wasn't strong enough to scatter their paper plates from one end of the park to the other. Fried chicken and potato salad from the Parkway Grill, topped off by strawberry ice-cream, created the perfect feast. And the girls loved climbing the rocky hills and following the same sumac lined trails she had followed as a young girl. Just as she hoped, the waterfall took their breath away. So did the creek water which turned out to be colder than their little Florida toes had ever been dunked in. She'd never forget their giggles and the feeling in her heart when she took their hands and led them, rock by slippery rock, across the creek, all the way to the statue of Hiawatha carrying Minnehaha.

But it was obvious Adam only pretended enjoyment.

He made one creek-crossing, mumbling the entire time about the frigid water and slimy rocks. It wasn't until the end of the day, while the girls played on the swings while they watched from a nearby picnic table, that he admitted the obvious.

Something was wrong.

"I don't like this any more than you." His words came slow and not even his daughters' daddy-calls were strong enough to pull his eyes off his knees. "I should have kept my phone closer and now...I'm not blaming you, Grace…but this absolutely demands my attention."

"Uff-da, the fair? That's what's been bugging you?" She took his hand in hers. "Life will go on without the fair."

He shook his head. "The fair's still a go."

A nickel-size splotch of strawberry ice-cream smeared the front of his white shirt; and she dug through her bag for her stain removal pen.

"Something's come up; and it's going to be difficult to make it home for Sammy's birthday."

"No. Adam." She rubbed the pen across his shirt, but he wouldn't look at her. As far as she could tell, he wasn't looking at anyone but himself.

"Look, I knew you'd do this," he said. "It's just this new deadline."

"It's your company; you set the deadlines." She did her best to keep her voice reasonable. "It's not just Sammy's party, what about the attorney?"

"Can you reschedule the attorney?" He took the stain pen from her hand and capped it. "But you're right; I simply have to find a way to make it home for the party. I just don't know how yet."

"How can you do this? Why can't you figure out a way to come home for both Sammy's party and the attorney?" She dropped the stain pen into her bag. It was as if all the joy of the last few days, all the promise of becoming the girls' forever mommy, had been blown away. "How long would it take, half a day? Making us a real family is not worth half a day?"

Adam didn't give in. After that, he acted like everything should be okay. But it wasn't. Not for her, and she wouldn't pretend it was. How could he even consider missing Sammy's birthday? And the adoption, couldn't he see how important it was to her and the girls?

And now here they were at the end of the day, and about the only thing they shared was a bed. As far as she could tell, she cared more about Sammy's birthday than Adam did.

And that was wrong.

As quietly as she could, she slipped from bed and made her way to the bathroom where she locked the door and slumped to the floor, clutching her journal and pen.

Even Adam's breathing fed her anger. How could he sleep? It was an insult. She probably wouldn't sleep all night.

It wasn't just the adoption. It was how easy it was for Adam to break his promises.

It's not fair, God. Those were the first words she wrote in her journal. *How can he even consider missing his own daughter's birthday party, and then sleep as if everything's okay?*

She thought about what happened before he went to bed, how he stood with his hands flat on the marble vanity. She could still see his red eyes. "You have to believe me; I'm doing this for us."

For some crazy reason, she did believe him, at least almost. But for another, even crazier reason, she was not about to let him off the hook. Without a word, she turned away and crawled into bed as close to her edge as possible.

When she felt him slip under the covers, she didn't turn, and when he kissed her goodnight, she just stayed there, as stiff and silent as a slab of Minnesota granite.

She was making him pay.

And, in the process, she was paying too, tearing down her own home instead of building it up.

And in the middle of it all, she remembered Derrick's crumpled note. He missed her. He probably even missed the girls.

For the first time in a long time, she doubted her place in Adam's heart. Maybe Adam was doing this because deep down, he didn't think she was good enough to adopt his girls.

Or maybe, even though she hadn't told him about her first baby, he'd found out.

Her face burned, and she felt as if there wasn't enough air to keep her alive. It wasn't out of the question. Adam had been in the room alone for a long time. He had more than enough opportunity to answer her phone or check her messages. And the truth was, there were only two people who would have called.

The same two people who believed they knew every detail of the truth she was keeping from Adam.

Chapter 34

Adam opened his laptop, and like he'd done almost every morning since his family left, forced himself to sit in front of the screen. *Concentrate. You have to concentrate.* He massaged his temples, counting off the hours till the deadline for the final proposal. *Help me here, God.* With everything inside him, he tried to pull his thoughts away from Grace and gather them together on the task before him.

But instead of coming together, all his thoughts were breaking apart.

Into a million unwieldy pieces.

He covered his eyes, holding the lids closed with his fingertips. *Beth would have understood; why can't*—he did his best to capture the thought. But it was too late.

The thought had already captured him.

Why couldn't Grace be more like Beth? He closed his computer. *The adoption...maybe all this is a sign that it's too early to be thinking of such things. If only I could talk to Beth.*

From the inside-out, his body burned as he dredged up last night's conversation. He'd done his best to make Grace understand why he couldn't make it home before the morning of Sammy's party. At least he'd be there on her birthday. But the conversation ended just like before, with him insisting she didn't understand.

Grace knew that he was a man who thrived on everything going according to schedule. Making snap decisions rarely ended well. That's what his decision to give in on the birthday had been. He'd felt pushed into a corner.

And now he stood in front of the window, looking down, but seeing nothing. It didn't matter how much time had passed; the wounds were just as raw as they'd been on Labor Day when they made their way through the fairgrounds, pretending, doing their best to ignore the hurt they were dragging each other through.

Even the smells of that day wouldn't escape his memory—farm fresh hay, hot cinnamon doughnuts, and sausages smothered in onions. He could still see Sammy's eyes; how they lit up each time she was given a thumbs-up for one of the scary rides. Inside the Children's Barn, when it was her turn to pet a tiny lamb, she snuggled her curly head into the animal's fur. "Look, Daddy," she said. "He really loves me." The sight of her little cotton candy chin was a vision he'd carry with him until she was a grown woman.

At the end of the day, when it was time for Grace's Ye Old Mill ride, Kate wanted to sit next to him. Grace knew. She knew the boat ride was actually a tunnel of love; and she didn't even try to convince Kate to sit with Sammy. By the time their boats came to a stop he was actually fuming. "You knew what this was." She was struggling to help Sammy out of the boat, but he was so hurt that he hadn't even thought to help. "Maybe next time we can sit together."

And that was the first time the craziest fear swooped into his heart, a fear that kept coming back.

Maybe there won't be a next time.

He turned from the window, and using the back of his hand, brushed tears to the side of his face. *Maybe there won't be a next time at the fair.* The list of next times waved like a parade of banners in front of him. *A next birthday party…a next tunnel of love…a next walk on the beach with my daughters…with Grace.*

"Lord, I should have never considered missing Sammy's party, never cancelled the adoption appointment." He closed his eyes until all he could see were the faces of his family. "It just seemed the easiest way. I am a good father. Jesus, you know I am. Show me how to get through this." Even though he felt like his words echoed against the walls, the words kept coming. "I need to know. Please, Lord."

The prayer had barely left his lips when his eyes landed on the camera, forgotten on top of his empty suitcase. He sat on the edge of the bed and pressed the button that would allow him to review the pictures.

The first photo brought him back to his birthday. Sammy sat on Grace's lap and Kate on his, a balloon hiding half of her pretty little face. It was their first family photo since the wedding.

He clicked forward, through pictures of Grace and the girls on the beach and in the pool, to a picture of him sitting in the passenger seat of the golf cart. Kate sat behind the wheel as proud as she could be, paying close attention to his instructions. "You don't try this without Daddy," he'd told her. "And only in the driveway." All too soon she'd be driving alone, beyond their gates, on the side roads, over to a friend's house or to the marina for sailing lessons.

"Oh, Grace," he said when the next picture appeared. There she was standing with the girls in front of the resort, her Minnesota Twins shirt stretched over the brace.

He moved slowly through the pictures, taking time to remember details, the smells, the sounds, and feelings that each photo brought to life. And as he did, Grace's words came back to him, pushing their way into a place they hadn't reached before. *Adam, please, don't you want me to adopt the girls? Is that what this is about?*

Was his business worth breaking Grace's heart?

He closed his eyes and took a full breath, releasing it slowly. If only he could go back. But he couldn't; so he focused on the next picture, the one Grace had taken of him and the girls at the zoo. Kate walked on one side, Sammy on the other, her little hand reaching up to hold his. But she couldn't because his hand wasn't available. It was wrapped around his phone.

He couldn't help it; the photo reminded him of a story his friend Joel had shared about his daughter's wedding, how through the entire ceremony he couldn't take his eyes off his daughter's hand, resting safely in the hand of the man she was marrying. "I know it sounds crazy," he'd said, "but with all the beauty before me, my eyes were glued to her hand. Life was never going to be the same. My daughter no longer needed my hand to help her through life. She had his, and I longed for the days when she was just learning to walk and needed my hands to steady her…for the days when she was your daughters' age and letting go seemed so far away."

He returned the camera to his suitcase and pulled a white towel from the bathroom shelf, saturating it with icy water. Without wringing it totally dry, he covered his face. Slowly, the cool water drew the heat from his body and, within minutes his heartbeat slowed.

Maybe there was a way to stay a few days beyond Sammy's birthday. He opened the drawer on his bedside table and reached inside for his planner. But as he did, his hand brushed his Bible. For the first time since Grace and the girls left, he wrapped his hands around its cool, soft leather.

He moved the Bible onto his lap. *Quiet me,* he prayed. *Quiet me with your love.*

And God did.

A silk ribbon marked the page in Isaiah where he and Grace had stopped reading. Pulling the ribbon tight, he opened his Bible.

And there, before his eyes, was the picture of the three most important people in his life, snuggled close, smiles taking over every inch of their precious faces. He held the photo close, remembering how he'd taken it the night Kate and Sammy asked Grace to be their for real Mommy. He had no idea how the picture ended up in his Bible. Maybe it was Grace. Maybe one of the girls.

He knew only one thing. Whose idea it was to put the picture there.

God's.

There was no other explanation.

With the picture still in his grip, he read from Isaiah forty-three. *Fear not, for I have redeemed you; I have summoned you by name; you are mine. When you pass through the waters, I will be with you…*

I will be with you. The words of Isaiah washed over his mind; and when he read them again, it was as if God was speaking to him. *Adam, don't be afraid of the future…I am with you.* He reached for his planner and laid it open on top of his Bible. Then, all the way to the back, past the calendar boxes, to the blank white pages, that's where he turned. He never wanted to forget. So he did what he'd seen Grace do a thousand times. He wrote the Bible's words as a promise made specifically to him.

The LORD God knows my name. I am His. When I pass through the waters of panic and doubt, He is with me. When life sweeps over me, He is there. He takes my hand and pulls me through. Life's storms will not destroy me because my Heavenly Father promised, "I am the LORD, your God. I will save you…I will quiet you with my love."

At last his thoughts began to settle back into their proper boxes. He'd stay up all night if he had to, anything to finish the Stillwater proposal. And if they wanted more changes and meetings, they'd have to wait, or go on without him.

He was going to do the right thing. He was going home.

Home for the party, home to meet with the adoption attorney.

Home to hold the hands of the three most important people in his life.

CHAPTER 35

Adam opened the door and stood back as T. Ralph, the man who'd brought him meals more times than he could count, and probably knew more about him than all of his country club friends put together, placed a tray with a bowl of wild rice soup on Adam's desk. "Anything else, Mr. Will?"

"All I need now are your prayers." Adam placed a more generous tip than usual in T. Ralph's hand. "I'm planning to go home a day early, finishing up here and catching a flight first thing tomorrow morning. It's my daughter's..." He pulled his wallet from his pocket and took out Sammy's picture. "It's her birthday."

"Beautiful." T. Ralph gave the picture a knowing nod. "I see much joy in those eyes."

He wondered what kind of father T. Ralph was. According to his story, his family immigrated to America when he was a just a boy. It wasn't long before a man who drove an old bus—one that never warmed up in the winter or cooled down in the summer—started coming every Sunday to pick him up for church. By the time he was ten T. Ralph had memorized more verses than anyone in his Bible class; and just before he turned twelve he became the first in his family to give his life to Jesus Christ.

"May I pray for you now, Mr. Will?" Before he could answer, T. Ralph reached up and wrapped his hand around his shoulder.

As soon as he closed his eyes, uneasiness shot through him. For a moment he wondered what he was getting himself into. His shoulders tightened. Was this going to be some kind of crazy experience where

T. Ralph would proclaim all the secrets of his soul? If that happened, he'd stop him in his tracks.

"Heavenly Father" T. Ralph's grip tightened around his shoulder. "Give my brother peace, peace that passes all understanding…"

T. Ralph knows everything. He knows about my panic attacks. He knows I've not been the husband and father I should be. Adam felt like a child wanting to squirm out of the grip of a giant.

But he couldn't. T. Ralph was still praying. "Yes, Lord. Protect Mr. Will and his family. Direct their steps." He cleared his throat. "And send that storm back out to sea, so Adam—"

"Hold on." Adam pulled away. "What storm?"

"I'm sorry, Mr. Will." T Ralph looked him in the eye. "There's a hurricane. I thought you knew."

Adam reached for the television remote. "This thing isn't working"

T. Ralph took the remote. Two clicks and there it was, a swirl on the meteorologist's map, working its way north through the Caribbean. A storm named Chris.

"It will be okay, Mr. Will. God will take care of your family. We will pray."

"You pray, T…I have to keep my eyes on this…" He reached for his phone. "Pray that I make it home before it's too late."

"What's written all over my face?" Grace smiled, pretending to laugh off Abby's remark as she climbed the ladder to hang the last birthday banner. "Joy?"

"To be honest, don't see a lot of joy right now."

"Well, I'm pretty sure even you'd look like this if you'd been battling crepe paper and curly ribbon all day."

Under normal circumstances, Grace wouldn't behave this way. But since returning from Minnesota, she hadn't had one normal day. All week she'd been too overwhelmed to take time for devotions, too busy to listen to the news, or write in her journal. Thankfully Adam would be home in the morning, a full day before Sammy's party.

It wasn't until the last candy bouquet was centered on the kitchen counter that Abby announced she had to leave. Grace was grateful. She needed time alone to take care of last minute details. She needed time to pull herself out of the dark hole she'd allowed herself to fall into.

But Abby seemed to take forever, packing her bag slowly, filling it with plastic containers containing samples of the food they'd made for Sammy's party. On her way to the door Abby stopped. "So what did Adam say about the storm? Is that why he's coming home early?" She dropped two wrapped candies into her canvas bag. "You know, people at work are talking."

"He's worried." She opened the door for Abby. "But that's Adam. Nothing's going to happen."

It didn't matter that she stood there holding the door, Abby seemed reluctant to leave, turning around just before she made it outside. "Listen, I can't leave until I come out with it." She set her bag of leftovers on the hall table. "Your thoughts, that's what's written all over your face…all those should-be's."

"Not now, okay, Ab." When she stepped back inside, Abby followed.

Even though her voice was tender, Abby's words pierced like arrows. "You're thinking that you should be decorating for two birthdays. Am I right?"

"Uff-da." A rush of tears inflated the clump in the back of her throat. "I can't talk about this now. Can't I just enjoy Sammy's party?"

Abby kept talking. "You know what you need to do. I'm not kidding; you've got to tell him before someone else does." Abby rolled her eyes toward Derrick's apartment. "I just have a feeling."

Grace tensed the muscles on her face, until they were so tight not one tear could escape. "It's been hard…that's all. I'll be fine after Sammy's party."

"You'll be fine after you tell Adam." Abby dug through her purse. "Which reminds me, I have something for you." She moved further into the hall. "Want me to stay? I mean the girls are spending the night with Adam's folks, right?"

"Yes, but the party, and with Adam coming home in the morning, I've got a lot…" Once again, she opened the door for her friend. "I guess I'm just tired."

"Then take this." Abby placed a paper about the size and thickness of a business card in her hand. "I think you already know the quote, but

I made these…even stuck magnets on the backs." She gave her a quick hug. "Read it."

As soon as Abby left, Grace kept her promise. She sat on the porch bench and studied the card. In the center of a colorful border that looked like broken ceramic pieces, sixteen little words.

She read the card once. Twice, and then she wrapped her hand around it and walked under the birthday banners, past the candy bouquets, outside, all the way to the beach, letting the words sink deep into her bruised and broken soul.

It's amazing what God can do with a broken heart…when he gets all the pieces.

Would she ever be able to release that one remaining broken piece? Would she ever forgive herself?

In the middle of the questioning, her phone rang. It had to be Adam's tenth call that day. This time his voice came across almost panicky as he suggested she cancel Sammy's party.

"That's crazy," she told him as she walked toward the beach, "especially now that you're coming home."

"I don't care how crazy you think it sounds. There's a hurricane and it's predicted to move further north into the Gulf."

"Abby just left. She didn't seem worried." As she walked along the shore, she hugged the phone between her shoulder and ear, barely sensing the water lick her toes, scarcely able to focus on what Adam was saying. The truth was, she couldn't pull her heart away from Abby's card.

It's amazing, she repeated the promise to herself, *what God can do with a broken heart, when He gets all the pieces.*

"Grace, you're not listening." Adam's accusation pulled her back.

"I am, but I can't cancel Sammy's party, not on a two day notice. Uff-da…anyway, nothing's going to happen before you come home."

In the end, Adam seemed satisfied with her promise to keep an eye on the weather channel.

They'd no more than ended their conversation when Derrick walked up behind her. "Thirsty?" He opened a bottle of water and held it out to her.

The last thing she wanted was to encourage Derrick, so she just kept walking, kicking her toes through the water, and trying to ignore the inside urgings that insisted she run. They were as silly as the gut feeling she'd had when she returned from picking up the balloons and cake for Sammy's party. As she neared home she'd noticed the car was on empty; and she felt compelled to stop and get gas. But reason took over. The warning light had just come on, and she had plenty of gas to make it home and back to the station at a more convenient time. Even so, when she passed Island Phil's, she almost felt a gentle pull on the steering wheel.

Without looking at him, she told Derrick she wasn't thirsty. What if Adam called again? She couldn't tell him she was walking on the beach with Derrick, especially after he'd changed his mind and was coming home early and staying home long enough to get started on the adoption.

"Watch it." Derrick snatched her arm, pulling her to a quick stop and jerking Abby's card from her grasp. She tried to rescue it, grabbing at the swirl of water that had sucked the paper in, but it was too late. "You almost stepped on that stingray." Derrick pointed to a patch of sand. "Open your eyes, right there next to your left foot."

Except for a small bump in the sand the stingray was barely visible. A flash of gratitude allowed her to be drawn closer to Derrick. "Adam says there's a hurricane. Do you know anything about it? He's afraid it might turn this way."

Derrick didn't answer. He just shook his head and continued walking, so close that every once in a while his shoulder touched hers.

Despite the stingray, she shuffled deeper into the warm water. Derrick followed. "It's almost time for me to leave…you know…my boat's ready and—"

"Have you worked out the dates with Adam?" She waded deeper, using her toes to search for the card.

"Ya, it's all cool." He moved in front of her, blocking her way, looking into her eyes as he shared his plans. "I'm ready to leave anytime."

The sun was lower in the sky now, its afternoon rays dancing across the waves as far as she could see. It was the kind of afternoon she dreamed of sharing with Adam, but he was almost two thousand miles away, and Derrick was close, staring into her eyes just the way he used to do.

"How can that guy spend so much time away from you?" Gently, he touched her elbow.

Her stomach seemed to lift and spin. She couldn't stand still like this, face-to-face with Derrick. With each roll of the waves, she could feel more sand sucked out from under her feet. She wobbled, fighting to hold her balance. When Derrick cupped her elbow to keep her from falling, it seemed almost natural.

"I need to go in." She turned toward shore. As soon as she did, Derrick tightened his grip on her elbow, steadying her steps.

"Wish I'd wised up before it was too late. I want you to know I hate leaving you…I'll even miss the girls." He tilted his head and his voice cracked with tenderness. Both of them were fighting for balance now, their legs almost rubber against the waves. "You've taught me a lot." He wrapped his arm around her shoulders and gave her a soft hug. "About the Bible and stuff."

All she had to do was move away. But she didn't.

Derrick was leaving in a week. She'd never see him again. Maybe this was her only chance. Since she returned from Minnesota, he'd been so much kinder. If she didn't ask now…when?

"Are you ever lonely, Derrick?" Once they were out of the water, she stopped and turned to face him. "Ever think of her?"

"Her, Grace?" Derrick plunged his hands into his pockets and blew a laugh through his nostrils. Like that, all the nice disappeared. He walked away, but not too far before he turned. "I don't miss a half-kid I never knew. And I'm not going to ask God to forgive me for that."

When he clomped away, she ran after him. "My heart's seen her a hundred times." One way or the other, he had to know the truth. "She's not a half-kid; she's as total as you and me."

"There never was a she." He stopped at the foot of his stairs. "But you'll never understand, will you? You keep this stupid talk up; and you'll end up crazy…loonier than that old Fisher guy who goes to your church."

"He's not crazy. If you knew him—"

"Who's to say I don't, better than you and Adam and every other person on this god-forsaken island."

She felt dirty. Maybe it was because once again she had fallen into the trap of believing he had a spark of goodness in him. Maybe it was her wrap-around skirt, the hem heavy with salt water, or the things he was saying about old Fisher Johnson. She'd allowed him to get too close. "You listen to me, Derrick. I'm not crazy; and I won't forget." He didn't deserve to know the truth about their baby.

"Look." His voice turned almost gentle again. "I'm just afraid if you don't handle this right, the whole thing might blow up and you'll end up losing." For a second time that afternoon, he draped his arm around her shoulder; but this time he pulled her even closer.

She tried to wrench away. Instead of pumping blood, it seemed her heart pumped a thick pudding of regret and panic. Derrick rested his heavy chin on top of her head and breathed deep. "Play your cards right." The gentleness was gone, and each word sounded more threatening than the one before. "You've got a lot to gain here, Grace."

She backed away. "I thought there was hope. But there's none."

Five minutes later, when she was safe inside, her arms and legs still trembled. She sat alone in the bedroom, in front of the veranda doors, watching to make sure Derrick didn't come close.

As she sat there, the sky changed from blue to shades of orange and pink; unfolding a pastel path across the water and up the beach, until its orange and pink slung itself over the tree tops all the way to her lap.

It should have been magical.

But nothing would be magical ever again until Derrick was out of her life.

Derrick leaving…Adam coming home…the truth neither man knew. Long after the sun went down, those were the only things she could think about.

And in-between her thoughts, she did her best to push back the urge to get in the car and drive to the island gas station.

Chapter 36

"If you live anyplace within the cone of probability..." Grace turned the television volume louder. The meteorologist, a skinny blonde in a short gray skirt, stood in front of a map and brushed her hand across southern Florida. "Near the coast, especially the barrier islands, it's time to prepare. Bring in trash cans, tables, chairs, anything not bolted down. Gather your important papers and plan your evacuation." She cupped her hand around her ear and for a minute broke eye contact. "This just in..." The camera zoomed in. "Those of you living on the islands, they're requesting voluntary evacuation now."

"No." The box of tissue tumbled from her lap. "This isn't fair." Fear fueled the anger that had been smoldering all morning, ever since she answered the first phone call.

Abby had called first, even before Grace got out of bed, insisting she head up to Orlando with her. "I doubt they'd close the stores," she said, "unless there's a super good chance the hurricane's going to hit."

But she hadn't been ready to give up on Sammy's birthday, not even when the clown called and said he was leaving for North Carolina. "Don't hold your breath," he warned, "the juggler is already out of here."

Less than an hour later, the man with the bounce house and party supplies called. "Can't take the chance," he said. "An island is the last place I want to be if that thing hits. Last place you want to be too, Mrs. Will."

"What about...we signed a contract."

"Listen, lady, I'm telling you, whether or not there's popcorn and snow cones, the party's cancelled." He didn't even try to hide the mock in his voice. "Have you watched the weather this morning? No one cares about a kid's birthday, not with Hurricane Chris sitting out there."

The last call had been over an hour ago and here she was, still waving the remote in front of the television, still searching for someone who would tell her Hurricane Chris was not heading toward Tesoro Island.

She turned to a local station where a reporter stood in front of a resort on a neighboring island. Behind him, an elderly man walked his dog and a young couple strolled hand-in-hand, slouching every few minutes to pick up one of the shells that had washed up on the beach. "It's hard to believe landfall may occur anywhere between here and the central Gulf coast." The reporter walked a few steps to a poolside bar where vacationers had gathered to listen to the latest predictions. "So how do you feel having a hurricane interrupt your vacation?" He slid his microphone toward a man with a sun-red face.

The man held his drink high and clinked it against the cans of those standing around the bar. "Bring Hurricane Chris on." He chanted louder than his drinking buddies. "We can handle her."

"You know they're calling for voluntary evacuations? In as little as twenty-four hours, this bar might not even be here. When do you plan to leave?"

"Another." He pushed his empty can toward the bartender. "Staying right here. No reason to leave."

Grace walked to the French doors. Even if he was drunk, the guy was right. Nothing out there hinted at disaster. Just like every other day, morning glory vines decorated the path to the beach, weaving splashes of purple through sea grape vines and around the trunks of palm trees. Her eyes rested on the spot where she and Adam stood at sunset just months ago. She could still see him standing there in his white dinner jacket, tan and handsome enough to appear on the cover of *Gulf Coast* magazine—could still feel his hand wrap around hers and hear the sound of his voice as he spoke the vows that were meant to define their marriage, "From this day on, in all I do and say, I promise to love you and exalt our Savior's name…together, with you."

Together. That's the way she dreamed it would be. In the morning when she opened her eyes, he'd be the first person she'd see; and in the evening his head on the pillow next to hers would be the vision that ended her day. But that rarely happened. On top of everything, she'd made life miserable for Adam ever since he'd backed away from the appointment with the attorney. Sure she'd been disappointed, but she had no right to be impossible.

Her phone rang, and she ran to grab it off the kitchen counter, answering just before it went to voice mail. "Dear, we've been waiting for your call." Even though it was Adam's dad who phoned, she heard Marjory in the background, telling Gordon what to say. "We have to put our heads together and decide."

It didn't matter that she wasn't ready to put her head together with anyone; it was clear they expected her to give up and go along with their plans. She stepped outside and sat on the edge of the pool, dangling her feet in the clear blue water. "Decide?"

"When we're going to evacuate." She could hear Marjory's promptings. "Let me turn you over to Mother. You girls make the plans."

She leaned back, kicking her legs through the warm water as she waited for Marjory to make her way to the phone. The sun was already so intense that even with sunglasses she had to squint. Palm branches stretched silent against a perfect sky; and the birds were exactly where they should be, the little ones doing their silent morning strut up and down the shore, pecking through the sand while larger ones squawked and soared overhead. Every so often, like a handful of white confetti, they dropped into the water, fishing for breakfast. Everything was as it should be, maybe even better.

No wonder she doubted the predictions.

"Yes, dear." Marjory sounded short of breath. "Would you like to give Sammy the news? She's here. I can put her on. I just hope her little heart isn't broken."

"No." How dare Adam's mother take it upon herself to decide Sammy's party should be cancelled? She pulled her legs out of the water; and did her best to keep her voice pleasant. "Have you looked outside, Marjory? Uff-da, it's beautiful, really gorgeous. I have the cake and, even without a clown, we can have her party." She meandered inside, leaving a trail of wet footprints. The birthday banner, crepe paper and candy bar bouquets were still there; and so was Sammy's clown cake. In the frig, apple juice, enough for a dozen children, hot dogs, and the salads she and Abby had spent an entire day making. Marjory had no right doing this, not when she'd promised Sammy this would be her best birthday ever. She retraced her steps, swabbing her watery footprints with a paper towel. "It's her birthday...And Adam promised to surprise her...did you know he's coming home today?"

"You're watching the weather, aren't you, dear?" Marjory's voice turned secretive, barely above a whisper. "I doubt Adam will make it. Anyway, I want to leave early, before everyone's fighting to get off the island. Can you be ready by...say three or four?"

Just like Adam's mother, resentment flared inside her soul, *willing to sacrifice her own granddaughter's birthday so she doesn't have to fight traffic.*

Category Two, the words flashed across the bottom of the television screen. "Wind speeds around 100 miles-per-hour. Folks, even if it gets no stronger..." The camera zoomed closer to the meteorologist. "Hurricane Chris is strong enough to rip trees out of the ground, take roofs, and smash up mobile homes. And..." She stepped back and moved her hand across her blue map. "As it approaches, crossing the warm Gulf waters, it will gain strength, maybe to a category three...or four."

Still, she wouldn't give in, not to Adam's mother. She turned her back on the television. "Well, Marjory, I'm not exactly ready to tell Sammy. If you're anxious to leave, drop the girls off now. I don't want to hold you back."

"We wouldn't leave without—"

"Adam's coming home. And if we have to evacuate, we'll do so together."

As soon as the call was over she phoned Adam, hoping he would talk some sense into his parents. But that didn't happen. "There's one bridge; and Mom's right; before sunset it will be bumper-to-bumper. I want all of you out of there. I'll change flights and meet you in Atlanta."

She couldn't believe he was taking his mother's side. "What about Sammy's party? For all we know, the hurricane will head north."

"Grace, listen. You're not actually willing to take the chance, are you?" Adam's question held the force of the strongest storm.

"No, of course not. You know that." She opened the refrigerator and began stacking containers until there was just enough room for Sammy's cake. "I'll start packing the girls things."

"Yours too." She could hear his fingers move across his laptop. "This thing's getting stronger. I want all of you out of there."

"Adam, come home. I'll wait for you."

If Adam was so convinced the hurricane was heading their way, there was too much to do. She pulled the list through her mind. She had no choice about disappointing Sammy. But she would not disappoint Adam. Whatever it took, she'd make sure the house was safe. The outside furniture had to come in and Adam's computer and papers had to be saved. "Adam, what needs to go into the safe room? Oh, and where are the hurricane shutters?"

"It's been over thirty years since a hurricane came anywhere near the island. We don't have shutters. Have Derrick check the shed. There should be boards for all the windows; Dad had them cut a few years ago. He can put them over the windows. But, listen to me; I want you to leave with Mom and Dad." He swallowed loud. "You and the girls... nothing else matters."

"Uff-da, I'll be fine," she said. "Let me do this, Adam. I'm staying until you get here."

Before Adam could argue, she spotted Derrick driving the golf cart toward the shed at the back of the garage. Just yesterday after he showed up on the beach she'd pledged not to have anything more to do with him.

But now she had no choice.

"Derrick's back. He's plugging in the cart."

She moved the phone away from her face and stepped outside. "Derrick." She waved to get his attention. "I need your help."

"Knew it."

"Knew?" Grace opened the door for Derrick.

"Even with mean old Hurricane Chris..." He held up his fingers as if to place the words inside invisible quotation marks. "You wouldn't leave, not without me."

His words made her insides writhe. "I might leave with Adam's folks and the girls."

"Leave? Nobody's leaving." He opened the refrigerator. "I was just at the marina; and water's smooth as glass."

"Don't lie. Are you saying nobody is leaving, not even the dock master?"

"You got it." He popped open a can of soda. "So when does the kid's party begin?"

"It's not," she said.

"Now if that ain't...I'm biting my tongue on this one, Grace."

She slumped onto the edge of the sofa. "Adam and his parents cancelled the whole thing."

"Bunch of selfish..." He sat beside her. "Just tell them you're not leaving, not for a storm that's sitting out in the middle of nowhere."

She didn't know why; but she felt small next to him. And all of Adam's reasons to cancel Sammy's party and evacuate felt small too, small and unreasonable. What if Derrick was right? What if the storm never even came close to Tesoro? She would have cancelled the party for nothing.

A calmness crept across Derrick's face. "Listen," he said. "Mark my words; it's all going to fall apart long before it gets anywhere close to us."

Grace had no idea who to believe. But that didn't matter. She'd already promised Adam she'd take care of the house. It was bad enough she had to break her promise to Sammy; she wouldn't break the promise she'd made to Adam. But first, she dialed Adam's folks and asked to speak with Sammy.

"Hi, Sweetie." She stood in front of the windows with her eyes closed, hoping Sammy wouldn't hear the tears in her voice. "Are you having a fun time with Grandpa and Grandma?" Her head hurt and her legs felt shaky so she returned to the family room and dropped onto the sofa. If only she didn't need Derrick, if only he wasn't listening to every word. But she had to overlook all that. All that mattered was Sammy's little heart. She prayed it wouldn't be broken. "Listen, I just talked to

Daddy." She gazed up at the birthday banner. "And you're a big girl, right? I know you'll understand. Daddy says we need to have your party another day because there's a bad…it's a very bad storm…and…"

For the next five minutes, she tried to reason with Sammy. "I know, Sammy. I know. If I could, I'd send the storm far, far away." She saw Derrick roll his eyes as he flipped to the back page of a magazine. "Listen, Mommy is going to pack your things."

For reasons too sad to grasp, she dismantled the candy bouquet that sat in the center of the coffee table. "You and Kate get to go on another little trip with Grandpa and Grandma. It will be fun. I promise."

"Are you coming too?" Sammy sounded confused.

"Later…with Daddy. But right now Mommy has to stay here with Mr. Derrick. He's going to help me make the house safe…then tomorrow Daddy and I will drive up to Georgia so we can be with you. How does that sound?"

"But will I still have a party with my friends and a real clown?"

"I promise you will, Sammy…when we get home…after the storm."

"Will Daddy still come?" Sammy was crying now and Grace ached to hold her tight and tell her everything was going to be okay. "Mommy, maybe Jesus will send the storm away because I really hate storms."

"I hate storms too, Sammy. So you have to pray, okay? And I have to go upstairs and pack your suitcase."

As soon as she got off the phone, Derrick shot from the sofa and stomped into the kitchen. "No one bothered to ask me if I'm willing to hang around here to take care of Adam's house." He leaned against the counter, an unlit cigarette tight between his fingers. "What about my boat? Ever think I might want to ride this thing out with her?"

"Ride it out? I thought you said—"

He pushed himself away from the counter. "This whole thing just makes me barnacle-spitting-mad, that's all. Think, Grace; is that too much to ask?" He moved toward her. "Can't you see; Adam just expects us to swallow his barnacles. That ain't going to happen. Not anymore."

Her face burned and her head throbbed as a knowing grew inside her. Somehow she knew she couldn't say anything about his cigarette. Even if he lit it, she had to hide her disgust. Even if she disagreed, she had to pretend agreement. "You're right." The words tasted like poison;

but she said them again. "I know you're right. The trouble is, I'm stuck with all this work. Will you help me, please?" She stood at the bottom of the stairs, hanging on to the banister. "I have to pack the girls' bags and—"

"We're both getting a raw deal here. All that work you put into the kid's party, and on a whim they cancel, every one of them taking off on me and you."

"You're right. Uff-da, what do I know?" Her hands felt awkward, like she should be doing something with them, so she removed her barrette and combed her fingers through her hair. "Everyone is leaving...and I just need help."

"Not everyone's leaving." He moved closer. Then in the most soothing voice, he spoke the words she was desperate to hear. "There's not going to be a hurricane. Mark my words."

CHAPTER 37

Grace stood just inches from the car, dizzy with second thoughts as Adam's dad squeezed Kate and Sammy's suitcases into his over-packed trunk. Her inner voice, the one she always counted on, had vanished.

Maybe the hurricane would turn north, or fizzle out in the middle of the Gulf. Maybe it was headed straight for her and she should evacuate now, before it was too late.

Ridiculous, that's what she kept telling herself, *worse case, you and Adam will join the girls day after tomorrow.*

She had just given Kate and Sammy a final kiss, and was telling them to buckle up when Adam's mother stepped out of the car and pulled her into a hug that was longer and tighter than any she'd ever received from Marjory. "I wish you were coming with us." She removed her ladybug sunglasses and stared straight into her eyes. "It's not too late."

Grace glanced at the girls sitting in the back seat, only slightly aware of what was going on. There was no doubt in her mind, Marjory would give her life for Kate and Sammy. But now, for the first time ever she got the feeling that her mother-in-law cared about her. She felt the damp warmth of Marjory's hand wrap around hers, and the force of her gentle squeeze.

All she had to do was throw a few things into a bag. Maybe that was the smart thing to do. But what about the promises she'd made to Adam. The boards weren't up yet and…

Before she could make a decision, Gordon got behind the wheel and turned the key. Marjory released her hand and Grace backed away from the car, forcing a smile. "Drive careful" she said as she blew kisses toward Kate and Sammy. "See you in soon."

And then they drove away.

Less than an hour later she sat alone at the kitchen table, her phone trembling against her ear. "They're fixing to close the airport." Those were the first words Adam spoke.

"Adam, they can't do that. It's starting to rain, but—"

"They have." It was like Adam scraped the words off his tongue. "It really looks like Chris—"

"This can't be happening. How are you going to get home? Adam, you have to."

"I'll figure something out," he promised. "In the meantime, tell Derrick to get those boards up. I want the French doors covered first. That's where we're the most vulnerable."

It didn't matter that the doctor had warned her not to lift anything over ten pounds; for the rest of the afternoon she worked side-by-side with Derrick, moving the patio furniture into the family room, garage, and shed, covering every window and door with the heavy boards. Pain twisted and pulled its way across her shoulders, around and down her neck. It felt like electric shocks were traveling up and down her arm. Even though the doctor had said she no longer needed the neck brace, she thought about strapping it around her neck, just for added protection, but decided she didn't want to waste precious time. Her fingers prickled; her ankles and feet swelled. But she kept working, holding the boards as Derrick screwed them in.

She worked so she didn't have to think about what was coming.

Sometime late in the afternoon she realized there were no birds swooping into the Gulf. The usual mid-day drones of lawn mowers and boats were silent, fearfully silent.

She did her best to push the fear away by promising herself that after the boards were in place she'd feel safe. Instead, she felt as if she'd been thrown into the cavity of a dark and deep cave. Wherever she went, upstairs or down, stone silence surrounded her. Even with all the lights on, she'd never been in such cement-solid darkness.

When her body could take no more, she slumped onto the sofa and gathered her hair into a damp knot, clipping it off her neck. She sat motionless, too exhausted to protest when Derrick stood in the kitchen and lit his cigarette.

"You're looking pretty rough there, Grace." He pulled two bottles of water from the refrigerator and handed one to her. His face was as red and wet as a slice of watermelon. "I'm taking the golf cart down to the marina." It was as if he was talking to himself and she had to strain to make out even a few of his muttered words. "Before this thing hits…" He blew a nostril-full of smoke away from her and flicked his ashes into one of Sammy's party cups.

She'd seen him like this before, refusing to make eye contact, pacing and mumbling. It was how he'd reacted when she told him about their baby. But he'd found a way out.

And somehow she knew he'd find a way out for himself this time too, no matter what it took.

"You're coming with me." He reached down and pulled on her arm. "We'll be safer on the boat."

"Are you crazy?" She pulled away.

"I'm not the crazy one." His voice grew stronger. Again, he grabbed her arm, this time above her elbow, squeezing it tight to the bone. The pillow that had sheltered her lap rolled to the floor.

"Stop." She struggled to shut her ears to the words he spit at her.

"Sitting, trapped in a house like this, right on the beach, you got to be crazier than that husband of yours." He dropped her arm and walked away. "Better pray I come back for you, because I'm the only chance you got."

And then the door slammed.

She didn't know how to pray, that he stay away forever, or come back so she wouldn't be alone. How would she survive if she had to ride out the hurricane alone? How would she survive if he returned? It wasn't safe to put her life in Derrick's hands. But what other choice did she have?

After he left, she returned to the only place she felt safe—the sofa—curled up, and with her arms wrapped around her pillow, she pushed herself to focus on the television.

As one horrifying story after another filled the giant screen, she held the pillow tighter, enclosing her baby. Most shocking, was the story of a little six-year-old boy on an island to the south of Tesoro. The camera captured his grandparents standing in front of a pile of sea-soaked rubble. The grandma, her shoulder length gray hair wet around her sun-weathered face, clutched a tiny baseball cap. Sobs filled the air as she told how, just hours earlier, their grandson was alive, huddled between them under a mattress in the closet of their home. "Everything's gone." She buried her face in her husband's chest.

The grandfather wrapped one arm around his wife, and with the other, he wiped his crooked fingers across his face. "Our grandson…we call him our little Sunshine. I couldn't hold him. I tried." He raised his tear-red eyes to the sky. "Please…we have to find him."

Grace gasped. It could have been Kate or Sammy.

And now it could be her baby.

She longed to feel Adam's arms, or at least hear his voice. *The facts are clear,* that's what he'd say. *Nothing is going to happen.*

She pulled her phone from her pocket. "I can't do this without you," she said when Adam answered. "They're saying it's going to hit early tomorrow…and Derrick…I'm really terrified...there has to be a way..." Every swallowed tear was back, running down her cheeks and neck. "Adam, I shouldn't be here. Not alone."

"Where's Derrick?"

"Back at the marina." Another category five wave of fear swept over her. "He tried to get me out on his boat. I can't do this."

"I know, Sweetheart. I'm trying. Listen, this is what I have, might be the best I can do. I'm booked into Orlando." She could hear his fingers pound the keys of his computer as if they were pounding an old typewriter. "From there, even if I have to hitch-hike, I'll find a way to get to you."

And then there was silence.

"Grace, I just checked the weather site. I want y'all to listen." Adam's words came slow and deliberate, as if he were choosing each one individually. "Do not wait for me. Get off the island now."

"Now, Adam? I can't."

"You heard me," he insisted, "Now."

"Please." She hugged the sofa pillow tighter. "It's so dark in here. Adam, don't make this worse. Come home."

"Listen to me. Joel keeps a room at The Airport Inn. That's where I want you to go."

"Adam, I told you; I can't."

"Don't give me that. Grace, you—"

"But I can't." It felt like her heart was running wild and there was no way she'd ever be able to tame it. When she got up from the sofa, her legs were so wobbly that she gave in and let herself drop onto the kitchen floor. She leaned against the cupboard and hugged her knees, "The gas station is closed. It's too late. The car…I didn't stop for gas…I should have…I was in such a hurry to get things ready for Sammy's party that I didn't…I just didn't take time to buy gas."

At first she thought Adam was using God's name in a way she'd never heard him use it. But then she realized he was praying, praying with a passion that thundered his voice. "Jesus. Jesus Christ. Oh, my Jesus, help."

CHAPTER 38

Adam tucked the phone between his shoulder and ear, freeing his hands to pull the bottle of Tylenol from the outside pouch of his suitcase. Stress twisted his headache so tight that it felt like the top of his skull would have to blow off before he'd get any relief. But not once did he fall into the depths of panic. He rubbed the back of his neck and took a deep breath. There was only one explanation.

In the middle of a hurricane, God was quieting him with his love.

He'd already called for a taxi and now all he had to do was wait…and pray…and do his best to talk Grace through what was coming her way.

According to the latest update, the bridge off the island would close in fifteen minutes. From that point on, there'd be no police, no ambulance or emergency response teams, no help for anyone left stranded on the island.

Saving his wife was as impossible as sweeping sand off the beach.

Or stopping the growth of cancer cells.

"I'm heading for the airport now," he promised when Grace answered her phone. "I'll do my best to get to you before anything happens, but I don't know..." He moved the phone to his other ear, knowing full-well even if he'd already landed in Orlando, he'd never make it to Grace in time. He had to face the facts. Even with the earlier flight, he was powerless. Absolutely powerless.

In between sobs, Grace repeated the same things. She was sorry for not leaving with his parents, sorry for not filling the car with gas. "I should have…something told me—"

He raised his voice to stop her. "You didn't know. I didn't know," he said. "You just wanted to give Sammy a happy birthday."

Now was not the time to ask her why she'd left the car on empty. Still, how many times had he warned her that when you live on an island, you have to be prepared for the worse?

Be prepared. That's the way he'd been taught to live. He even owned an old generator for emergencies.

The generator. Why hadn't he thought of it sooner?

It might be Grace's one chance.

Even though it had been years since he'd even moved the generator from the back corner of the garage, at the beginning of each summer he had several containers of gasoline delivered, just in case.

"Hon, where's Derrick?"

"Derrick?" Her voice was softer now, almost defeated. "He came back a while ago, and he's in the family room."

"I need to talk to him now."

"He's sleeping. I can't..."

"I don't care." He looked at his watch. Thirteen minutes. That's all they had until the bridge closed.

For the first time since this whole thing started, he could feel hope growing inside him. What did he have, five, six gallons of fuel put aside? Whatever was there; it was more than enough to get Grace off the island.

Grace stood just feet from Derrick with the phone pressed against the side of her face. "Wake him." Urgency fueled Adam's words. "You've got twelve minutes until the bridge closes. Wake him now."

She had no choice; not only because Adam was insisting, but because Adam had a plan.

As far as she knew the only plan, to get her off the island.

"Derrick." Slowly, she moved her hand toward him, holding her breath as she tugged his shoulder. "Adam wants to talk with you."

Derrick shrugged her hand away, and when he did, every "what-if" of the last twenty-four hours flared.

What if she hadn't believed Derrick's promise that the hurricane was nothing more than a joke?

What if she'd left when Adam told her to?

She raised her voice. "Derrick, wake up. Adam has a plan."

An automatic string of forbidden words dirtied the air. "See me sleeping here?" He dropped his face into his hands and his feet to the floor. "What did I tell you?" He glared at her. "I got to get some rest. Besides, that guy never had an original plan in his life." He lay back down, turning his face toward the sofa cushions.

She didn't know what was making her sick, Derrick's grimy words or the approaching storm. All the way up to last night, she'd looked for signs of change in Derrick; and sometimes she thought she saw them. Sometimes she actually believed God was speaking to his heart. Maybe God was; but it didn't appear Derrick was listening.

At least not today.

"Derrick, stop. Please. Take the phone."

He swung his feet onto the coffee table before he took the phone and held it inches from his ear. It was as if he was trying to prove that whatever Adam had to say wasn't important. But that was okay, because what it did was allow her to hear most of what Adam was saying.

"Derrick, there's gas in the garage, enough to get Grace off the island...you too."

Derrick pulled a paper clip from his pocket and rolled his eyes toward the ceiling. "Five gallons...eleven minutes...Airport Inn..." She listened as the cracks in Adam's voice grew more frequent. If only she was brave enough to put her head next to Derrick's so she could hear every word.

"Ya, well..." Derrick stood. "Your plan just won't work," he said. "But I thank you for being concerned." He was looking at her now, a smile lifting the corners of his mouth. "Let's just say..." He spun his paper clip between his fingers. "Grace and me won't be leaving the island...not by car. And we won't be staying at some fancy hotel. With all I was doing for you, I figured the least you owed me was a little gas. Just used the last of it, matter of fact."

She paced to the other side of the room, trying to find an inch of space where she felt safe. Still, she could hear Adam's voice as over and over, he asked the same question. "What right...what right did you have to take that gas? She's my wife; what right? What right?"

"I'm here. You're not." Derrick's voice held no hint of emotion. "So I guess that gives me every right."

She knew better than to grab for the phone. One touch of Derrick's finger, that's all it would take and Adam would be gone. Maybe until after the storm.

Maybe forever.

She took a deep breath. "Derrick, please." Her face was wet and burning and her hand trembled. She didn't know where the words came from, but suddenly they were in her mind and on her tongue. "Derrick, if you want me to trust you, give me the phone."

"Don't you worry about her spending a little time on my boat, Mr. Will. Your wife trusts me." Grace's insides writhed. More than ever, she wanted to push him away. He moved closer, loosely wrapping his arm around her shoulder. "Be quick." He held the phone to her ear. "I got the golf cart all charged up. And it's just raring to go."

Adam looked at his watch. In three minutes the bridge would close.

Oh God, help me find the right words. Over and over Adam prayed old Fisher's prayer. *Oh, God, help. Oh, God, help.*

And God was answering. He knew because the things he was telling Grace were not coming from him. "Grace, move away from Derrick. You can do that."

Her whisper trembled. "I think he plans to ride the hurricane out on his boat. I can't, Adam." Her voice was wet with tears. He'd give anything if he could take her in his arms. But he couldn't; and for the first time since Beth's death, he had no choice. He had to believe, really believe, God had the power to rescue.

He wheeled his suitcase to the door of his hotel room. "Walk into the kitchen. Pour a glass of juice, something like that."

"This is my fault. I should have—"

"Are y'all far enough away from him? Can he—"

"No, I don't think so."

"You'll have to pretend." The elevator door opened and he pushed his suitcase in ahead of him. "Listen, you're right; he's going to try to get you on his boat. Let him think you're going along with him." The elevator jerked into motion, and he stood in front of the sealed door, watching the numbers light up—seven…six…five, praying the elevator would not stop before it reached the lobby. "Let him think you trust him; but listen to me. Do not trust him. Do you understand? Do not step foot on that man's boat. Where is he now?"

"Sofa, watching television."

"You can't worry about saving Derrick. Get the key for the safe room. You know where it is."

"Cookbook shelf."

If only he could hear her steps, anything that would tell him she was still okay. But all he heard was static. *Lord, please,* he prayed, *keep this line open.*

"I have the key."

"Hide it."

"My jacket…on the chair."

"Perfect. Zip the key in the pocket. First chance you get, lock yourself in. Do not come out until I get there. Tell me, Grace, tell me you'll do that."

When he saw the taxi turn into the parking lot, he stepped into the pick-up zone. Almost before the driver had a chance to bring the taxi to a complete stop, he opened the door. "Airport," he said as he tossed his suitcase on the seat. He buckled his seat belt, continuing his conversation with Grace as the taxi turned onto the highway. "I should make it to Orlando in four hours."

Even as he said the words, he knew four hours didn't mean a thing. After that, even in good driving conditions, he had almost four hours on the road. Any minute, the phone service could go down. In fact, it was a miracle that it hadn't. That's why he had to say something wise, something that would comfort her when there was no phone service.

It wasn't until the taxi came to a stop in front of the airport that the answer came. "Remember this, Honey." He had no doubt the words were God's gift to both of them. "You are in the Lord's grip." He wiped his face with the back of his hand. "Do you understand, not the hurricane's…not mine…not Derrick's. You are in God's grip."

CHAPTER 39

Grace slipped the phone into her pocket. Maybe Derrick wouldn't notice. Maybe, if she kept her eyes closed, she could block out the boarded up windows and doors, the absolute darkness and booms of destruction that had taken over her life.

And maybe she could believe what Adam said before the storm ended their call. *You're in God's grip, safe in God's grip.*

But Derrick's presence stabbed through her, more treacherous than the eye of any storm. She forced herself to look into the family room where he was still sprawled on the sofa, his eyes hidden behind sunglasses, his dirty feet pushing against the same pillows the girls rested their precious heads on.

She had a choice. She could take her chance and make a run for the safe room now, or she could play it safe, pretend cooperation, and kindness, and whatever it took. And while she was pretending, she'd keep her eyes open for a more perfect opportunity. She'd only get one chance to save herself and her baby. Beyond doubt, this was one of the most important decisions of her life.

"May I bring you something to eat?" She couldn't stop her voice from shaking.

"I'll take some of that salad and a piece of cake." Derrick pointed the remote at the television.

Even before she had time to push a serving spoon into the center of the salad, Derrick helped himself to Adam's place at the table, spreading his hurricane chart across one entire end, and setting the old lap-top, the one Adam had given her, on the chair next to him.

She wanted to ask what gave him the right to take things that did not belong to him, but she held her tongue as she spooned three heaping scoops of salad onto one of Sammy's clown plates and set it in front of him.

"I need to throw some towels in the washer before the electricity goes off." She forced herself to move slowly, as if this was just another day, instead of the only chance to save her life. She gathered a small armload of anything she could find—pot holders, towels, and dish cloths before taking a step backwards toward the laundry and safe room.

"You won't be doing laundry today, Grace." Derrick swiped his hand across the front of his shirt. "And you won't be saving that cake either. Might as well cut me a piece."

"I need to wash…" She squished the towels close to her chest.

"Don't give me that."

"I was thinking I'd save the cake for Sammy." Her head spun. Could he see right through her? "It's Sammy's…her birthday cake… and I don't want to cut into it." She tightened her throat to keep her voice from shaking. Out of all the birthday plans, Sammy's cake was all she had left.

"If it makes you happy," he said, "we'll pretend we're celebrating." He smiled and snapped the fingers on both his hands while he bounced his head to a beat only he could hear. "I'll even sing the birthday song if you want. Happy Birthday to…"

She hated his voice. It tugged and twisted her insides. How could she cut into Sammy's cake? She could still see her little face, how for over a month on every trip to the grocery, she'd run to the bakery and slowly turn the pages of the cake book, stopping at pictures of the princess and pony cakes, commenting on how pretty they were; but her first choice never changed. From the beginning, Sammy wanted a clown cake and circus party.

Never once, in all their planning, did she imagine Derrick eating Sammy's cake and Sammy far away in another state on her birthday. She pulled the cake from the refrigerator and held the knife over it. "Derrick, I can't." One right after another, her tears dropped on the clown's red frosting cheeks. "Please don't make me."

"What the..." In an instant, Derrick shot to his feet, grabbing the knife, slicing, swiping crumbs onto the floor. In one thrust the happy face was irretrievably disfigured. "It's a cake, Grace, a stupid cake." When he pushed a hunk onto his plate globs of frosting dropped to the floor.

Silently.

But they should have made the sound of a thousand explosions.

"Now, you can either eat a piece or throw the rest in the trash. We're out of here soon so I don't care."

She was certain the pain would never stop. Derrick growled, just like he used to, his face growing redder as he told her to get tough. She better stop caring about kids and stupid cakes. "Care about staying alive," he said. "When I say, we leave. There's nothing else we can do, got that?"

But Derrick was wrong. There was something she could do. She had the key. She had Adam's prayers and God's grip.

She had to believe nothing else was more important.

Would she ever see Kate and Sammy again, ever smell their strawberry shampoo or touch their sweet faces? Would she ever again hear them call her mommy, ever spend an evening waiting for Adam to walk through the door, or ever be taken into his arms? Was she going to make it out of this alive?

Grace had her doubts.

Derrick paced around the table, a lit cigarette snug between his lips, stopping every now and then to listen to the latest weather reports. "Those of you still on the islands...find a room in the center of your home...a bathroom or..."

She didn't need a meteorologist to tell her the outer bands of Hurricane Chris were already moving onto Tesoro. Like a hammer, rain beat the roof. Wind rammed and wrenched the boards they'd hammered over the doors and windows. The sounds grew louder, and she could feel the knots inside her head and stomach tighten. Pictures shook on the walls. Without warning the electricity cracked off, then silently back on. Through it all, not for one minute, did Derrick let her out of his sight. Not once did he give her enough of a break to grab her jacket and make a run for the safe room.

And with every minute that passed it became more and more difficult to picture herself in anyone's grip but Derrick's.

Derrick turned the television to its maximum volume, but the rain and roaring winds muted even that. Nothing seemed real. When he wasn't pacing, Derrick sat at the table, flipping through television channels.

She tried to force her thoughts to better places by imagining the feel of Adam's hand wrapped protectively around hers, his voice soothing her soul. *You're in God's grip...in God's grip...in God's grip.*

With the tips of her fingers, she held her eye lids shut. Her eyes burned from Derrick's smoke and her tears. She could no longer sense time. Where was Adam? How close to Orlando? How long until he started driving toward her? Was he praying? He had to be praying because like a giant snake, fear constricted her mind and soul until there was little breath left in her own prayers.

She had to make her move soon, so she sat at the table, across from Derrick. He'd taken over almost the entire table, the curled edges of his hurricane chart held down by the same red tackle box she'd found under his bed.

"You ready for the truth?" He marked his chart with a black marker from Sammy's art kit. "Someday you're going to thank me." Without warning, he dropped the marker and reached both hands across the table, touching the tips of her fingers.

She pulled away. "Your cigarette. Please, Derrick. The smoke isn't good for my baby."

Why hadn't she tried to escape sooner? She pulled her jacket from the back of the chair and slipped her arms into the sleeves. "I have to go to the bathroom."

"In a minute." He opened his tackle box. "I sent them, Grace, every page. It's over."

"My life over?" She raised her eyes to meet his. "You're doing your best, aren't you, Derrick?"

"Your scam of a marriage. It's for your own good," he said.

"You're wrong." Did he really think he had the power to keep her away from Adam? *In God's grip. I'm in God's grip.* "Adam's on his way." She pushed her chair away from the table.

"You still think so?"

Time was running out, and so was Derrick's patience. She could feel it. "I really need to get into the bathroom."

"Sit down, Grace." She had no other choice but to do as he ordered. When he reached inside the tackle box, the joy in his eyes, the way his shoulders lifted—she could tell it was more than a simple tackle box he was reaching into.

It was his treasure chest.

Like never before, she wanted to run; but she didn't. Instead, she got up slowly, watching as he pulled stacks of bills, held together with thick orange rubber bands, out of the box. "Got every penny Adam paid me, even that bonus for the painting. Should be more than enough to get us to Guyana."

"Guyana? I'll only slow you down." She zipped her jacket until it was snug, all the way to her throat. If only she could zip it higher. Somehow, she had to hide her terror, push it down so it couldn't reach her eyes. "Derrick, I have to go to…." She tried to back away, but he grabbed for her hand, pulling her back to him.

"All this time, all the money Adam paid me, I saved." He squeezed her hand between his. "For us."

All this time? What was he talking about? Guyana? She wasn't even sure where Guyana was. Like a fist out of nowhere, Derrick's words smacked her. How long had he planned to kidnap her? That's what this was. She yanked her hand out of his clutch.

"You're going to kidnap me, Derrick? You can't be serious."

She wanted to sanitize her hand, hold it under hot soapy water. She wanted to drop to the floor and curl into a ball. She wanted to run. There he sat with that full-of-himself-face. Was there any little corner of her life he hadn't tried to destroy?

She'd almost convinced herself that she'd lived through the worse. There was nothing left: but then she looked inside Derrick's box of treasures. "What…what are you doing with…?" Her lost journal…

Derrick had her lost journal. The money wasn't his treasure. Her journal was.

Fear and anger coiled themselves together, even tighter. It didn't make sense. Every inch of her body...her legs and arms and throat, all the way to her head...pulsed. "That is private. You can't just...Why is my journal in that box?"

He fanned the pages in front of her. "I'm not an evil man, Grace." He closed his eyes. "You got to remember how good it was for us. That's who I did this for—us. And I only copied some of your writings and sent them to—"

"Adam? You wouldn't." She reached for her journal, but Derrick was faster, sweeping it beyond her reach. "Why? I don't believe..."

"You will, next time you talk to him, but he may not want to talk to you. After he learns the truth, he won't want you. That's the kind of guy he is. But I will. Always."

While one storm pounded her home, and another her soul, in a voice that ignored it all, he forced her to sit next to him and listen as he read one entry after another, her private promises to God and herself to tell Adam—or not tell him depending on the date at the top of the page—about her first child, the baby that was Derrick's, the child that was Sammy's age, and should be sharing her bedroom, but wasn't.

Because of what she had done.

Every confession, every scrap of shame, every doubt, it was all there tucked inside Derrick's tackle box. Her ugly past had been e-mailed to Adam.

She no longer cared about the hurricane. Whether Chris hit or not, it didn't matter. Maybe Adam had already opened his e-mail. Maybe the truth had already made it into his heart.

There was only one thing she knew for sure.

Even if she got out of this alive, her marriage would not.

Shame held her head down. From the beginning, she'd lied to Adam. That's what the secret had been. A lie. She was not the person Adam thought she was, the person he'd fallen in love with. How was she going to live without his touch, his voice, his love? How could she live without Kate and Sammy? He'd probably never let her see them again, never give her a chance to tell them she was sorry and she loved them, loved them more than anything.

Even when Derrick called her name, she couldn't look him in the eye. "Grace, I'm talking here. You listening?"

"When?" She felt as if some force outside her body lifted her head and forced her to sit taller than she had all day. "When did you send them?" She placed her hands flat on the table, bracing herself against the truth. Before he could answer, fear dropped away leaving behind a rage like she'd never felt before. Pushing her chair back, she stood facing Derrick. "What have you done?" Her soul was ready to explode. "Who cares about a hurricane? I might as well be dead." She crisscrossed her arms against her stomach. And that's when she remembered.

Not every important thing was gone.

She held her hand there, flat against the tiny bulge. She had to think, had to listen. Surely God would direct her. Surely He would keep her safe in his grip. Not for her; she didn't expect him to do it for her.

For her baby.

CHAPTER 40

Time skulked, each minute felt like an hour. Grace had no idea why Derrick was waiting, not when he'd already made up his mind to ride out the hurricane on his boat. She kept her eyes closed. It was the only way she could hold onto the kind of hope she needed, hope that said someplace deep inside Derrick's gloomy soul there was a spark of common decency.

Just one spark that would let her baby live.

"Open your eyes." At first she thought Derrick was going to jump over the table.

Strong category three…wind-speeds 125…Chris beginning to wobble… uncertain landfall, the words scrolled across the television screen.

"You read that, didn't you, Grace?" There was celebration in Derrick's voice. "Chris is wobbling." His hand grasped her shoulder. "Get up."

Jesus, her heart and everything inside her cried, *my baby.*

She wanted to grab onto the tabletop and tell him she would never let go. So many plans had been born at this table—wedding plans—plans for a nursery—plans to finish the girls' quilts.

She'd planned; and she'd promised to tell Adam the truth.

Now all her plans were ugly broken pieces.

"How many times do I have to say it? The thing's wobbling." He stuffed his hurricane chart into the box. "This is our chance." He tapped the tip of a fresh cigarette on the table.

Without a word, Grace stood and moved toward the door.

"Take it." Derrick thrust a flashlight into her hand seconds after the lights and everything electric died.

"There's a battery lantern in there." She pointed her flashlight toward the safe room. "Let me get it."

"We don't have time for no lantern." For a second Derrick's light seemed to go out of control, sweeping first across the kitchen ceiling, then along the floor, where Sammy's cake soiled the tile. He reached for her arm, turning her, forcing her close to him.

"I can't walk fast, not in the dark." She grabbed for the countertop.

"You're going to." He wrapped his hand around her arm, digging his fingers painfully into her flesh as he dragged her into the old garage that was now nothing more than a storage shed. "You got the code; raise the door," he said.

The door moved slowly, and as it did, sheets of rain and swirling waves of palm branches and murky sea water swamped the floor, rising fast until the warm muck licked her ankles.

Derrick didn't seem to notice.

"Derrick, why are you doing this?" She stomped backwards, splashing brown water up her legs. "Please don't."

"This—all this—it's for your good."

"You can't protect me, not out here. We're standing in ocean water and God knows what else." She shined her light into the muck. "Maybe sewage. There could be snakes. You hate snakes." Never before had she felt more unprotected.

From that point on, Derrick's words sloshed together. "Do what I say…too much at stake…my boat." He tugged on her arm. "Forget Adam."

Forget Adam. The curse stung and ripped at her heart.

She fastened her feet to the floor and wrapped her arms around her stomach. "Uff-da, I can't. I just—"

"Ya, you can." He placed his hand in the center of her back and pushed her forward. With all the lawn furniture and the girls' toys taking refuge in the small space, there was no room to turn around, no place to hide, just a dark and dangerous path forcing Derrick's body against hers.

"I know storms," he said. "After we leave the marina, we'll head into the mangroves."

She raised the hood on her jacket. Pulling the strings tight, she knotted them under her chin. *Have you let go of me, God? I can't feel you.* She was a breath away from the door. *Let me feel you.* Already Hurricane Chris sounded and felt like she was standing under the power of a raging waterfall. Rain whipped her face, stealing her breath and her hope. *Please, God, please.*

At that moment, completely muted against the storm, she felt the pulsing vibrations of her phone. Pushing back from the door, she took the phone from her pocket and held it close to her face. "I'll do whatever you want." She turned to face Derrick. "Please."

Derrick's eyes looked wilder than they had all day, and she knew the only way he'd allow her to answer the phone would be if God suddenly made it impossible for him to refuse her request. "Thirty seconds." Derrick rolled his eyes. "Better show me some gratitude."

"Adam, I'm sorry." Her heart seemed to stop. This might be the last time she'd hear his voice. The last time he'd hear hers. "I should have told you everything. I should have left sooner."

"Listen." Adam's voice crackled and she knew that one way or the other, either by Derrick's hand or the storm's, it wouldn't be long before their connection would be broken. "Orlando..." It was the only word she heard. Static and the storm's roar exploded in her ear. And then there was silence. She slipped the phone back into her pocket, and once again Derrick didn't seem to notice or care.

"Now, Grace." He grabbed her shoulder. She had no choice but to move. Rain pelted her face and arms like an army of a thousand needles. She couldn't breathe, could barely see the golf cart's white roof. She felt Derrick's hands on her shoulders, pushing her against a wall of wind and into the cart, forcing her down against a cold, drenched seat until her feet came to rest on a floor puddled with sludge.

Chapter 41

Grace held her breath as Derrick pushed his body next to hers, grunting curses. He thrust his red treasure box into her lap, demanding she not let go, and fought to fit the key into the golf cart's ignition.

God, how can you let him do this? You promised, the words stood against her fear. *In your grip…I'm in your grip.*

Run…run…run. Now. She felt Derrick's rage mount as the key refused to fit into the ignition. *Run…run.* Her baby's life was at stake. She had no time, no other choice, no other way to save the life innocently growing inside her. For the first time since being forced into the golf cart, she took a breath. "No," she whispered. It was the only word she had. "No." When she spoke, a fresh boldness pushed her out of the golf cart. "No." This time the word came out louder and stronger. And then, without looking back, she pushed the box from her lap and ran.

One hope fueled her race. *My baby's life isn't over yet, because I'm running in the center of God's grip.*

"Hurricane Chris is no longer wobbling."

Adam shot to the edge of his chair. *Oh, God, please don't let this happen.*

In one heartbeat, the motel lobby grew silent as everyone—stranded Red Cross volunteers, Power Company employees from states as far north as Indiana, a group of young men dressed in matching Bible verse t-shirts—leaned anxiously toward the television.

From this point south, the interstate had already been closed. They were stranded together with their tablets and laptops, crumpled tracking charts and phones.

Despite all their modern electronics and old-fashion maps, they didn't have control. Not one of them could push a button and send Hurricane Chris back out to sea.

Adam brought his laptop closer and clicked on his mail, hoping for the miracle of a message from Grace. One-by-one, he scrolled through the list, but other than something from Derrick, and the usual notices from office stores and lumber yards, there was nothing.

"This video just in…" Adam's attention was drawn back to the television. "Chris has picked up strength and is once again heading toward land."

Derrick's e-mail would have to wait. He leaned toward the television, searching the screen for a landmark that would tell him Hurricane Chris was attacking some other island.

"Folks you're going to want to see this...Pirate Island." The words pushed him back against the chair. It couldn't be. Pirate Island was just a few miles away from Tesoro. God wouldn't do this.

He closed his eyes, allowing pictures of his beautiful wife to play across his mind. Grace walking barefoot along the beach, kicking her toes through the water, urging him to join her. He saw her hair, shining, blowing like a scarf of amber silk across the backdrop of a rich blue sky.

Yes, he saw her. But it was his own voice he heard.

Next time, Grace. I'll walk barefoot, next time. What was wrong with him? How many times had he said the same words?

And then he saw her in her honeymoon dress, dancing slow and close, her leg brushing against his. *Later, Grace. We'll finish the dance later. I promise.*

Adam opened his eyes just in time to see pieces of a roof peel away and take to the air. "Looks like it's going to be a direct hit on Pirate, next in Chris' path…little Tesoro Island…a strong category four…wind speeds exceeding one- hundred-fifty-miles-an-hour."

As reports came in, more stranded travelers squeezed into the lobby—an elderly man leaning on a walker, a woman holding a baby over her shoulder. *Our baby,* the realization shot through him. It wasn't just Grace. Their baby's life was at stake. How big? Just inches long, trusting his mommy to protect him. And Grace would. She was that kind of mother. He'd seen it with his own daughters. She'd never stand back and allow a child to be harmed.

He wouldn't allow himself to doubt, not now. Was Grace home or was she trapped on Derrick's boat? He had no idea where she was. But God did. And He would keep both Grace and their baby safe.

God had to because He was the only one who could.

Not once, as she jolted into the house, could Grace remember her feet touching the ground. In fact, she felt almost nothing except God's almighty hand.

Over… under…all around her. Protecting…gripping…pushing her safely forward.

Safely through.

But she also felt Derrick closing in, determined to pull her back. She wrapped her hand tight around the key. She was unsure where the thought came from; but as her flashlight lit the corner of the breakfast bar, when she was steps away from a straight run toward the safe room, she was impressed with a knowing that she must knock over the stools that sat at the bar.

"Ain't no use." Derrick came nearer; panting heavy as she grabbed the back of Kate's stool and pulled it down behind her with more strength than she knew she had. Barely slowing her pace, one after the other, she did the same to the remaining stools.

And as she did, Derrick breathed his curses.

At last her hand reached for the safe room door. *Open. Close. Lock.* She ran the life-saving instructions through her mind as she darted inside.

But then, just before the door slammed, Derrick's voice howled. And this time it was more than curses of anger.

It was shrieks of pain, so excruciating that it made her stop just short of locking the door.

"My leg." Derrick's voice exploded from the kitchen.

"Liar." She had no idea why she wasted her time. She wrapped her hand around the metal door.

"Your stupid stools…my leg's broken."

All she had to do was close the door, and she and her baby would be protected from the storm…protected from Derrick…but something inside pushed her to chance a look. She took a small step beyond the door and followed her light into the kitchen until its beam landed on the floor and Derrick, the victim of her pushed-over stools and the slippery birthday cake frosting.

"Thank God," he said.

"God?" The outer bands of the storm roared louder, sounding like a hundred jets taking off all at the same time. "Should have thought of God sooner." Keeping her distance, she aimed her flashlight and words straight at his bent leg. "Like before you destroyed my entire life."

"I didn't send your journal, Grace. I lied." He reached toward her. "I couldn't think of any other way…I swear."

The entire house shook as the roof and boarded windows fought back against the storm's terror. Every sensible thought insisted she lock herself in the safety of Adam's room. Still, she held the light steady, aiming it on Derrick's pain-twisted face as he struggled to push himself toward her.

"You can't leave me here." Fear spilled from his eyes.

"Too bad, Derrick." She turned her back on him. "You left yourself here. Me too." She never wanted to see him again. If there was ever someone who did not deserve saving, it was Derrick.

Just as she stepped back inside the safe room, another one of Derrick's agonizing pleas boomed through the air. "What about that Jesus of yours?" It was like he spit the words. "What makes the little Jesus girl better than everyone else?" Terror propelled his voice. "If you leave me here, you're no different."

Not different? How dare he? He'd seen a thousand ways she'd changed. And he hated every one. Certainly God didn't expect her to rescue Derrick. For the first time ever, being changed didn't feel much like a blessing.

It felt more like a burden.

"Take them." She threw her flashlight into his lap. "This is going to hurt, and I don't care." She grabbed him under his arms and pulled. Walking backwards as fast as she could, she dragged Derrick and his broken leg toward the safe room, leaving a trail of blood. The only words that could rise above Derrick's curses and the hurricane's fury were the words of her prayer.

"Lord Jesus, help."

CHAPTER 42

Adam didn't see the guy coming. Now here he was, a man who looked not much younger than his dad, standing on the opposite side of the coffee table.

"You mind?" The stranger settled into the chair across from Adam. "Gibbs." He stretched his hand across the table. "Friends call me Gabby. Gabby Gibbs. I'm with the electric crew from Ohio…caravan of six trucks. First time I've done anything like this." He aimed his weather-beaten finger toward the television. "Pretty bad, huh?"

Adam closed his laptop, sliding it closer to his planner and hurricane chart. Once again, Derrick's e-mail would have to wait.

"You look pretty shook." Gibbs placed his notebook on the table.

"Following the hurricane." Adam turned slightly, nodding toward the screen. He didn't want to be rude, but the last thing he wanted was to encourage conversation, especially with someone named Gabby.

He glued his attention to the lobby's big screen, hoping Gabby would take the hint. "With winds this powerful, we expect more structures to fail." The meteorologist's eyes followed footage of a roof soaring through the sky like a metal kite. "This is it. Our crew has taken cover. Hurricane Chris is about to make landfall on Tesoro."

Not since Beth's death had he felt so helpless. The exquisitely shaded road leading to his home was already gone, barricaded with heaps of debris, palm trees, yanked out of the ground like bunches of carrots; street signs, crushed like wadded sheets of tin foil. And its full-force hadn't even made it on shore.

Hide her. Oh, God. In Your hand, hide her.

If only he could hear just one more "uff-da". He pulled the phone from his pocket. He'd give anything to hear her voice, anything to be able to promise that from now on he'd be the husband she deserved.

But again, a recording told him to try his call later.

He was too numb to cry, too dead on the inside to feel sick as he watched reruns—early footage of islanders fleeing their homes, footage taken by photojournalists whose job it was to follow Hurricane Chris' path—blankets, pots and pans, sea-soaked mattresses, children's storybooks, their wet pages flapping in the wind—personal belongings that belonged safe inside homes.

"How could anyone survive something like that?" Gibb's voice cracked.

"At least they got everyone off the island, didn't they?" Someone leaned on the back of his chair. "Because if they didn't...I just hate to think...know what I mean?"

Adam wanted to push everyone away. All at once he could feel again, feel the fear boiling inside him. *Not Grace...please, Lord, please.*

"Anyone have someone down there?" When Gibbs spoke, the other voices grew silent.

Propriety forced him to look Gibbs in the eye. "My wife." His jaw tightened. "She's in the middle of it...alone with our security man." Everyone was looking at him, and he wondered if they could see inside. "Last time I spoke with her, he was trying to force her out on his boat. In the middle of...he's crazy." Adam couldn't stop his hands from shaking. "If she's not with him, she's alone on the island, probably the only one, except for those crazy weather people." He held his hands under his eyes, pushing back the pressure from too many unshed tears. "I can't lose her. If I don't get to her soon, I don't know..."

Not once did anyone interrupt. But when Adam was done talking, Gabby Gibbs waved his buddy over. "Pete, we got some heavy work to do here." Gabby's hand rested on his shoulder. "You're a believer in Jesus Christ, aren't you, Adam? I can see it." He squeezed his shoulder and Adam nodded. "You believe Jesus is able to take care of your wife better than you, better than anyone? That's what He's doing right now."

As Gabby and Pete prayed, the group grew. Two Red Cross workers pulled their chairs into the circle. A few minutes later the hotel clerk took a seat, then the kids from Orlando, and the man with a walker.

They prayed for Grace and the motel clerk's mother, for everyone in the path of Hurricane Chris. And as they prayed, peace grew inside his heart. It was a peace he could not understand.

But in the middle of the peace, as the most powerful prayers he'd ever heard filled the lobby, uninvited questions pulled at his mind. *What about Derrick? Have you prayed for his rescue?*

He did his best to convince himself the voice was nothing more than his own foolish thoughts. God didn't expect him to pray for Derrick. The man had stolen every drop of gasoline that could have gotten Grace off the island. Truthfully, it would be fine with him if Derrick ended up at the bottom of the Gulf, food for sharks. That's what he deserved.

"It's late." Gabby looked at his watch. "Anyone we still need to pray for?"

For as long as he could, Adam remained silent. But the words were in his throat, fighting to escape. "If y'all could pray for Derrick, the security man I spoke of. Pray that God will rescue him too." He closed his eyes and waited for Gabby or one of the others to pray.

"Adam, why don't you? Go ahead." Gabby gave his shoulder one more squeeze.

He didn't think he'd ever be ready, but the silence was uncomfortable; and he could only stare at his folded hands for so long. He had no choice. "Heavenly Father…" The words came out raspy. "I ask…we ask…that you keep Derrick safe." He cleared his throat and opened his eyes, peeking at the stranded travelers gathered around, their heads bowed and nodding in agreement.

"Yes, Lord." Gabby raised his empty hands, cupping them as if he was expecting God to fill them with a miracle.

"And, Lord, I release Derrick to you, to your justice. And because it's never too late, I release him to your mercy."

Chapter 43

Early in the morning, long before sunrise, the full force of Hurricane Chris crashed onto the island. Everything—the ceiling, walls, even the floor—quavered. Grace sat on a plastic stool, as close to the door, and as far away from Derrick as she could. Even with her arms wrapped tightly around the battery powered lantern, her body trembled. As far as she knew, she had two options for making it through without breaking apart.

She could close her eyes and pretend to be somewhere else, like the bowling alley with Kate and Sammy. That's what Hurricane Chris felt like—a hundred pound bowling ball thundering down a wood alley.

Straight toward her.

Or she could keep her eyes open; tell herself over and over the things Adam had told her—that she was safe in God's grip, and everything she needed to survive was here.

Everything was—all in properly marked bins on shelves attached to the room's high walls. Flashlights and a radio—the kind that require no batteries—her lantern and cases of bottled water, food, blankets, pillows, even a tablet of colored stationary and pens. That's the way Adam did things. He planned, and provided, and did everything right.

Everything except marry her.

She shielded her stomach with the palm of her hand. "I won't let anything happen to you, precious one." Her words were tender, filled with a hope that wobbled with each new punch and growl of the storm. "We're in God's grip…that's what your daddy promised."

The compulsion to protect this invisible life was far greater than the urge to protect her own. With each new rumble her shoulders hunched then lunged upward as fear collided with an inner hope that no matter how strong the hurricane grew—even if it became a monster category five—she and her baby would survive.

If only she had the same knowing about the rest of her life.

A life without Adam.

She tried to push the thoughts away. Only God knew what would happen in the days and years ahead. He would do what is right in His sight.

At the other end of the windowless room Derrick lay still and silent, his eyes staring blankly and his arms wrapped around the scrub bucket she'd given him in case he went through on his threat to "heave out his guts." His leg, splinted and stretched in front of him, was nothing short of a miracle. How many years ago had she learned how to splint a broken bone? Over the years she'd forgotten the unused information. But God brought it to mind, clear and fresh as the day she learned.

She still didn't know if she'd done the right thing when she dragged Derrick into the room. Just the thought of splinting his leg had chased her stomach into her throat. The very last thing she'd wanted to do was touch him.

Or give him reason to touch her.

But within minutes of closing the door, she set her revulsion aside. She pulled a piece of wood flooring, left over from Beth's kitchen remodel, from the stack of boards leaning against the back wall. Then she wrapped a faded child's comforter around the board and Derrick's leg, securing it with a couple of old belts from the bag of clothes she'd put aside for the Salvation Army.

Now here she was trapped in a tiny room with him, the hurricane raging all around her. *Was this room really safe? Did Hurricane Chris have to force to rip off the door?* Her thoughts rolled like waves on an angry sea. She felt hot and miserable. Her skin pulled, stretching until it seemed about ready to rip apart. She'd give anything for a way to elevate her feet. Already her ankles were puffed to almost twice their size. She moved the small battery powered fan closer, angling it up toward her face, reminding herself that pregnant women existed on the islands for hundreds, maybe even thousands of years without air conditioning.

If she was this miserable, what about Derrick with his broken leg?

Three small steps, that's all it took to get close enough to check on him. She pushed his fan closer, until the breeze moved his hair. And then she stood over him, shining the lantern on his face. Derrick's skin had returned to its normal color, and she was thankful he no longer complained of the pain.

"Do you need a drink?"

Derrick nodded and when she handed him a bottle of water, he asked her to move the bucket. "Jush make sure I can get to it." His words were mushy, as if his tongue had grown too big for his mouth. She wasn't sure if he sounded that way because of shock or the pills. Derrick pulled a plastic bag from his treasure box. It was more than half full of pills, white, green, all of them undoubtedly illegal. She wondered if he'd helped himself to Adam's leftover and forgotten panic prescription. It didn't matter. Anything that would quiet Derrick was fine with her, even if it was illegal.

He'd stopped talking about his boat. In fact, he didn't react to the storm, even when it seemed to explode on top of them.

She stepped back toward her stool, sat, and closed her eyes, imagining the boards she and Derrick had nailed into place. Surely, they'd been yanked away from the windows by now. She was certain she'd felt something big, like one of their palm trees, crash through the roof. Little doubt, it had come to rest in the middle of the family room.

By now, all their treasures had to be floating in sea water.

Adam would want her to prepare for when the hurricane ended. She once heard someone say that there were more deaths after a hurricane than during it. Drowning, they suggested, was the greatest danger. When the time came to open the door, she had to keep that in the front of her mind. She also needed to make a list of things to do to protect herself and her baby. If only she had her journal. Instead, she reached for a tablet. At the top of a page she wrote, *Things I Need for Survival.*

Think, she urged her mind to focus. *How will I know when it's safe to leave? What should I bring with me when the storm is over? Think.* But every time she started probing her mind, bits and pieces of Bible verses she'd memorized when she was a little girl fought their way to the front of her thoughts.

I will never leave you nor forsake you…

You are my hiding place…

Grace turned off the battery powered weather radio and listened.

Listened to a sudden crash of silence.

With all that was in her, she wanted to open the door. But she couldn't. Just because the hurricane had moved away didn't mean the danger had.

She stood and stretched, holding her watch close to the light. Three o'clock. While the hurricane still raged, she'd firmed up her decision to quietly return home to Minnesota. Her secret was out. What else could she do? The worst part was that the truth had not come from her. It had come from Derrick. But his truth wasn't really the truth. It was the lie she'd told him all those years ago, that she'd actually gone through with the abortion. Either way, her truth or Derrick's, adoption or abortion, Adam would never forgive her.

If it was just her, she'd leave before sunrise, before Adam had a chance to call or come looking for her. But it wasn't just her. She had to protect this baby. And the house could be flooded, filled with snakes and alligators, maybe even wild raccoons with their beady little night eyes.

"Bring that light over here." Derrick's hands shook as he fought to open his pill bag.

"It's over, Derrick. Listen." She shined the light on his pill bag. "Someone will come for us…probably not until after sunrise, but maybe you shouldn't take so many pills."

Her warning came too late.

She stood there, looking down at him, admitting to herself that Abby was right. From the beginning, Derrick had been the light stalker, playing his sick game. For some reason she wasn't angry. Not anymore. She actually pitied him more than she pitied herself because when it was time to leave the safe room, he'd leave with nothing.

She'd at least have her baby.

Where would she be this time tomorrow? Where would Adam be? And the girls?

She feared living the rest of her life without them. It wasn't money. Adam wasn't the kind of man who'd deny support to his own child. But this baby would never be as precious to him as Kate and Sammy.

She had no one to blame but herself.

With every minute that passed, the room grew smaller. She turned away from Derrick and shined her flashlight on the door. Oh how she wanted to run. Run forever. Run through the dark until her baby was born and she had someone to hold.

Someone to love.

Be still and know that I am God.

When Derrick's snoring interrupted her thoughts, she spoke over his racket. "Lord, you helped me through the hurricane. Help me now. How am I going to live without Adam? Without Kate and Sammy? Uff-da, Lord, I'm sorry." Her voice grew softer. "Forgive me for the secrets. Forgive me for my lies." She tore two sheets of paper towel from the roll on the bottom shelf. After wetting them with a few drops of her drinking water, she laid the towels over her eyes. "Lord, I know I was wrong not to trust Adam with the truth."

Grace, trust Me. Trust Me with all your heart. Don't rely on your own understanding. I will direct your path. Give me your broken pieces.

If she told anyone that while hiding from the hurricane, she had a conversation with God, they'd think she was delusional.

But she understood the truth.

What she didn't understand was why God would waste His time speaking to someone like her. She was the one responsible. Not Hurricane Chris. Not even Derrick and his e-mails. It was her foolishness, trying to hide the truth from Adam. "Oh, Lord Jesus, if only I could relive last year, I'd trust you." She reached for more paper towels and poured more drops of water over them. "I'd tell Adam the truth. Every single word."

Her feet and back hurt more now than ever. It didn't matter if she stood or sat, she couldn't get comfortable. But it was okay because God had given her one more chance to be a mom.

It was more than she deserved.

As the minutes ticked slowly forward, the radio static diminished enough for her to hear that Hurricane Chris was moving across the state, losing strength each mile it traveled. The updates were devastating. Tesoro and the surrounding islands had taken the brunt of the storm. Hospitals were full. Fatalities had reached six and were expected to go higher. All access to the islands had been cut off.

And would remain so for days.

Days? No, that's too long, God. I can't be stuck inside this room for days, not with Derrick.

Again, the words waved across her mind. *Daughter, trust Me. Trust Me with all your heart.*

CHAPTER 44

Surrounded by the dark humidity of early morning, Adam leaned against his rental car and stared at the palm trees that framed the motel's entrance. As if they were announcing a celebration, landscaping lights rose out of mulched earth, casting a festive red glare on tree trunks.

But today was not a day of celebration.

Before they'd called it a night, Gabby had insisted that he join the caravan when they headed south in the morning. He'd agreed, knowing it would be easier for him to get through any troubled areas if he were traveling in an official group. In little more than an hour the sun would rise. His goal had been to be half way home by sunrise. But that wasn't about to happen. Nothing depended on him. When he peered inside the lobby he saw Gabby and Pete, each with a cup of coffee, slowly making their way toward the front door. At first he was irritated by their unhurried pace; but by the time Gabby slapped the roof of his car, he was done being irritated. All he could be was grateful.

"Hang with us, Brother. Be making a pit stop about an hour out," Gabby said. "If you need to pull over before then, give a call." Gabby pulled himself into his truck and waved out his window, motioning for the lead driver to pull ahead.

At last he was heading home. If he had his way, he wouldn't be traveling toward the rear of a caravan; he'd be alone, passing every vehicle on the road.

But God had used Hurricane Chris to get tuff with him; and now, more than ever, he was aware of how much he needed people. His need went beyond Grace and his girls. He needed strangers like Gabby and Pete and the others in the caravan. He needed old friends like Fisher.

Where would he be without Fisher?

He could still feel the way his heart exploded when his phone rang around four that morning. "Your family make it off the island?" Fisher sounded no different than he did on the sunniest of days.

"No." He got up and stepped into the same clothes he'd worn the day before. "I mean, I don't know. Are you still on the island?"

"No, took the boat up river a couple days ago. Heading back that direction soon." "Fisher, I'm hoping Grace is in the safe room, but Derrick was trying to force her to ride out the hurricane on his boat."

"Ain't no way."

"Can you get to her? I'm leaving from here in a couple hours, but—"

"Not by car, you won't get on the island." Fisher's voice held no fear. "Bridge closed, roads blocked. No one's supposed to go near Tesoro, that's what the big shots are saying."

Fisher couldn't actually be going along with the restrictions. That wasn't like him. *Say something, Fisher. Tell me you'll find her. Tell me nothing will stop you.*

"But who listens to big shots?" Adam could almost see Fisher spitting a wad of tobacco over the side of his boat. "I'll swing by your house on my first run. Keep trying to call her. I hear every now-and-then a call gets through. If she's at the house, tell her to be on the beach by nine, no later. I won't be waiting, don't have time for no fooling around." Fisher's voice trailed off. "If she's there I'll drop her at Shepherd Beach on the mainland. It'll take you a little finagling through town, but you can come for her there."

Adam adjusted the rearview mirror. He still rebuked himself for not calling Fisher before the hurricane. It had been a while; but he used to swing by his property with the girls. The man was eccentric. Instead of a landscaping service, a family of goats took care of his lawn. It seemed he'd spent a lifetime making certain neither time nor money found their way down the mud road that led to his bay front property. To the discontent of zoning and tourism officials, peacocks and goats scuttled around the yard in total tropical freedom. Just like Fisher.

He had to admit, God sure had a sense of humor. In so many ways, he'd looked down on Fisher, always insisting Kate and Sammy wash their hands all the way up to their elbows after a visit. Now, this tobacco spitting man with dirt under his finger nails, and his stinky old fishing boat was the one God had chosen to rescue his wife.

At least he prayed that was God's plan.

When they turned on to the Interstate Adam fell into position behind Gabby. Ahead of them stretched a convoy of Red Cross vehicles and utility trucks, and behind two vans from the Atlanta church, each packed with emergency supplies and volunteers. Already traffic was heavy.

He gripped the wheel with his left hand and with the other; he reached for his phone. And then, before he tapped Grace's number, he prayed.

While the hurricane was exploding over the island, Grace had something to focus on. Now there was nothing. She pulled one of the boxes of Beth's belongings from the shelf and set it on the floor next to her, trying to make as little noise as possible. She didn't know how much longer she could stay trapped in the windowless room. All night she'd kept her movements to a minimum, not wanting to wake Derrick. It wasn't that she cared all that much about his comfort.

She cared about hers.

As long as Derrick slept, she wouldn't have to hear about his broken leg, or try to think up Bible verses that reminded her to treat her enemies with kindness. She wouldn't be harassed by thoughts that insisted she had to forgive him.

He lay sprawled on the floor, his mouth flapped open like some kind of hungry fish. She'd never heard anyone snore so loud; and she wished she could quiet him. But by now he'd taken enough pills to throw ten men into a deep sleep.

It's better than listening to him curse, she reminded herself as she slowly lifted the lid on the box sitting at her feet. Time didn't seem to be moving. She'd spent the night doing her best to make time move ahead. She'd struggled to pray, struggled to write her thoughts on the colored stationary stored in the room, but without her journal, her prayers and thoughts seemed feeble.

She pulled a tissue-wrapped coffee mug from the box, and ran her fingers over the words written around the rim.

World's Best Mommy.

How many times had Beth sat at the kitchen table sipping coffee or tea from this mug? One-by-one, she went through Beth's mementos, unwrapping and rewrapping each item, placing them back in the box just as they should be. When she was done with one box, she returned it to its place and opened another.

It was obvious that Adam had hired someone to pack Beth's things. Every box was the same, white plastic with a pale blue lid, professionally labeled and packed with reminders of Adam and Beth's life together.

She wondered if Adam would pack a box with memories of her. Wedding pictures, photos of their Minnesota vacation, of her with the girls?

What about their wedding rings?

She went through Beth's photos of backyard barbeques, vacations, and family celebrations. In another box she found the girls' baby books sealed in individual zipper bags. Two of the heavier bins held books—devotionals with dog-eared pages and margin notes, romances, workbooks about raising children and setting elegant tables.

There was a book about cancer.

They were the belongings of a godly woman, a woman who deserved to be Adam's wife and the girls' mommy.

A woman without broken pieces, at least none that Adam had ever spoken of.

But could that be true? Didn't everyone have broken pieces, times when they did things their way, instead of God's, decisions that led to broken hearts and sin? Still, she couldn't imagine Beth's life with even one broken piece.

After Grace returned the final white bin to the shelf, she wrapped her hand around the door knob. Maybe she could unlock the door and open it just a crack, wide enough to know if it was safe to leave.

Not yet. The warning came from deep within. She stepped back, keeping her eyes on the door. How would she know when it was safe to leave? When the time was right, would she be able to gather enough courage to open the door?

She absolutely had to because she couldn't be here when Adam came home.

Cautiously, she took hold of the only box she hadn't opened, not today and not that day that seemed a lifetime ago. With her arms wrapped around the hat-sized box, she scooted deeper into the corner. Painted with delicate pink and red roses, she'd been drawn to this box ever since the day she prayed over every inch of her new home.

She was too tired to fight against her thoughts so she rested her head on the box and ran its soft satin ribbon between her fingers. As she fought to stay focused, the idea crossed her mind that perhaps the box held Beth's cancer wig. Maybe that was why she hadn't been able to open the box. Or maybe it was because out of all Beth's boxes, this one was the only one labeled in Adam's handwriting. She moved her fingers across Adam's backhanded script. Whatever was tucked inside the box was precious to Adam.

More precious than a Mother's Day coffee mug.

More precious than a book of wedding photos.

If I don't open this now, she told herself, *I'll never have another chance.* She gave the box a gentle shake.

Whatever was inside thumped gently. What if she raised the lid and found Beth's jewelry box, and inside the jewelry box a velvet box with wedding rings? Could she force herself to read the words Adam inscribed on Beth's ring?

She had as much right to open the box as she had to be married to someone like Adam.

Maybe in time she'd learn to ignore the way she ached for him—for those moments when they came together so tight and close that she could feel the beat of his heart. She'd find a way to snuff out the aroma of his shampoo. She'd be strong enough to close the ears of her memory to the way his voice reached her soul.

If she heard Adam's voice, she'd run to him. And fall into his arms. Her heart could not take the rejection that would certainly follow.

And that was why she had to find a way to leave before Adam came for her.

And before leaving she had to write a letter, releasing him from loving her. She held her watch close to the lantern. It was past seven o'clock. If he was coming, Adam had to be on his way, driving closer and closer toward home. She set Beth's hatbox on the floor and reached for the stationary. She didn't know how to begin her letter. *My Dearest Adam.* Crumple…throw. Several times, she started over until the right word came.

Adam. Simply Adam.

For the first time in their marriage, she told Adam all the truth. *As much as I fought to be the wife and mother you deserve, I never measured up, not even one day.*

A tear dropped on the pale pink stationary, and it looked like the paper had been stained by a scarlet drop. *In my past there lives a secret. But it's not really in my past; it's with me every day, every time I look at Sammy. I promised God I would tell you. But something always came up, something I could use as an excuse for silence. In the end, I decided not to tell you. I decided to live a lie.*

Tears filled her throat and eyes until they created a fog so thick she could barely see. She held a paper towel under one eye and then the other until her vision was clear enough to go on. *At first I said no to what Derrick insisted I do back then. It was beyond my imagination to ever do something like that. But Derrick told me there was no other way, except the abortion. Adam, this is not my first baby. My first baby was Derrick's.*

She felt herself going back to that one dark day and those that followed. The sights, sounds, and feelings of being smothered by her own sin. *I'm so sorry, Adam. I went to the clinic. Signed in. I sat there, waiting for my name to be called. All the time I knew. I knew I couldn't go through with what I'd agreed to do.*

She remembered how later that day she drove back onto the island, tears blinding her vision. She walked to the end of the weathered pier where Derrick's boat was docked. She told him it was done. She had the abortion. It was as if his heart was as dead as a fish packed in ice. Not one tear. Not one word of regret. She left the island the next day, flew home to Minnesota. She moved into her parents' home along with Steve and Maya Swanson, a young missionary couple who were living there while raising money to return to Peru. When the time came to deliver her baby, Maya was there. And it was into Steve and Maya's arms, she released her baby daughter. She did not tell them the name she had given her daughter. They would give her another. She did not take a picture to carry with her. She wanted to forget, to pretend this part of her life never happened.

She dried her eyes and continued writing. *You and the girls deserve better. I am not turning my back on you. I'm not turning it on Kate and Sammy. I am releasing all of you to someone better. Just like I did with my baby.*

When she was done with her confession, she pleaded for the only thing she dare ask to take away from their marriage. *I don't want money or anything else,* she wrote. *Just another chance to be a mommy. I promise you this, I will never ever turn my back on this baby. I will give my life for her.*

Even though time was running out, she couldn't sign the letter. Not yet. Whatever she wrote would be her last words as Adam's wife. And they had to be perfect. They had to show the truth in her heart. She set his letter aside and tore two fresh pieces of pastel stationary from the tablet.

One for Kate. One for Sammy.

She told her precious girls she loved them and she would pray for them every day. The words sounded empty, easily blown away by time. *You might not understand this now,* she wrote, *but God will give you a better mommy.*

And then, before she sealed the girls' letters in their envelopes, she signed each one, *Because I Love You.*

That's when it came to her. The words she put at the end of the girls' letters were even more perfect for Adam's.

Once again she laid Adam's letter in her lap. *Because...* Her hand trembled. But she forced it to keep writing. *Because I love you...Grace.*

When she was done, she folded Adam's letter, making sure the corners lined up perfectly. It was all so final and more painful than she ever dreamed it would be.

All her energy was gone, and she felt as if her very soul had died. She closed her eyes. Now there was only one thing left to do.

Take the ring from her finger.

At first she held her ring tight. *I've lived through the worse,* she told herself as she pressed the ring to her lips. *It can't get any more painful.* She kissed the ring just once. Tears ran freely down her neck as she released her ring into the folds of the letter she'd written to Adam.

And then she sealed the envelope closed.

Because she loved him.

Chapter 45

Grace had convinced herself that writing the letters would be a good thing. Time would move faster; and once the letters were sealed inside their envelopes, she'd feel a sense of peace, or at least relief.

Instead, all she felt was empty.

She pressed her hands together. There was nothing she could do about it now. The letters were written, her ring sealed in the envelope with Adam's letter. Her entire life was zipped inside a quart size freezer bag.

Her watch said eight-fifteen. By now the sun was up, and the morning glories, if any had survived, were lining the path to the beach in full-blown purple.

Derrick groaned, drawing her attention to the far corner of the room. Without the help of his leg, he slowly pushed himself into a sitting position against the wall. "Get me something to eat," he said.

She pulled an apple from a bag on the shelf. "How are we going to get out of here?" She was surprised by how cold her voice sounded as she handed him a breakfast bar and fruit. "Have you given any thought to when we can open the door?"

"When your hero comes to rescue you," he said. "How am I supposed to know?"

She backed away. "Now would be a good time to come up with—"

"Does Adam even know you're here?"

There was nothing more he could do to her, so she admitted the truth. "I haven't talked to him, not yet, anyway." She held her phone next to her ear. "Still nothing."

"No signal…no Adam." Derrick reached his half-eaten breakfast bar toward her. "Get rid of it."

She pointed to the bucket. "Your arm's not broken."

Without saying another word, Derrick pitched his breakfast leftovers into the bucket. When he was done, he opened his bag of pills. "My last ones," he said before gulping them down.

For the first time since she dragged him into the safe room she saw fear in his eyes.

Waiting in quiet was more difficult than waiting in the storm. She dropped her head into her hands and closed her eyes. "Lord, all I know," she prayed, "is that some way I have to get off this island. Please, I really need to go home."

But how would she know when it was safe to leave? And was there even a way off the island?

Even Noah in the greatest flood of all time had a bird who helped him know when it was safe to leave the ark.

Maybe her answer was that close too.

It would be like God to put the answer within plain view; but she'd gone through every inch of the room, every corner, every box.

Except the box she'd been afraid to open.

What if her answer was inside that box? A safety check list…an official check-list describing when it would be safe to leave.

Once again, she reached for the flowered box. Once again, she set it on her lap.

This time she untied the ribbon.

As she did, an unexpected bud of hope pushed its way through the broken pieces of her soul. What if the contents of the box made all the bad go away? What if there was a way to start over as Adam's wife and Kate and Sammy's mommy? She'd give her life for just one more chance.

Hope gave her strength to lift the lid.

Terror closed her eyes.

She waited for what seemed like forever before she looked. When she did, there at the bottom of an otherwise empty box, was something she'd never imagined would be there.

A Bible.

Her hands shook as they took hold of the book. There was no doubt it was Beth's, the blue and white quilted cover stained with fluids of life…and death.

Her knees quivered, causing the box to tumble from her lap as she drew the Bible close. She held the book to her chest, and then she fanned its pages. Maybe God would transform a highlighted verse into her raven, telling her when it was safe to run.

Before she could read one word, four envelopes slipped from between the pages, floated, and landed silently in an almost perfect arch at her feet.

Her hand shot to her face. Could these be the letters Beth spoke of on the video, the letters she'd written just before she died? She bit down on her finger, bit hard until her teeth pinched the flesh where her ring should be. And then she gathered the envelopes, bringing them close, smelling the familiar lily of the valley aroma that had filled every room when she first met Adam.

One at a time, she read the first three envelopes. *Adam…Kate…Sammy,* each name perfectly centered. Each envelope sealed. She could understand the girls' envelopes. Maybe Adam was waiting until they were older before turning them over to Kate and Sammy. But his? Why hadn't Adam opened the envelope containing Beth's final letter to him? Would he do the same with her letters, hide them away in some secret box?

She held the envelopes only for a minute before unzipping the plastic bag containing the letters she had written. Carefully, she placed Beth's letters inside, on top of hers.

To hold them longer would be disrespectful.

Whether or not Adam had opened the envelopes, there was little doubt they were Beth's sacred last words to her family. Her blessings. Her hopes. Hopes that could never include someone like her.

When she pulled the last envelope from her lap unexpected tears clouded her eyes, making it almost impossible to focus. *For Adam's New*

Wife and the Girls' New Mommy. The room spun. *To me.* She gripped the envelope tight as the words shot through her heart. *From Beth, to me.* She forced herself to read the words again. *Adam's New Wife and the Girls' New Mommy.*

Then like a sledge hammer, truth struck. *Not good enough.* It struck again. *Never good enough.*

The letter was never intended for her. She could no longer dream, no longer pretend that something like this belonged to her. It did not, and so she released the final envelope into the plastic bag with the others.

Chapter 46

"Thank you, Jesus." Adam took his hand from the wheel and raised his fist in victory. "Oh, Jesus." He pressed the phone against his ear. "Let her be in the safe room."

It was close to nine, only minutes from Fisher's deadline.

Two rings. He felt the warmth of a tear roll down his face; and then another. As he brushed tears with the back of his hand, he felt the prickle of a chin and cheeks that needed to be shaved.

Three rings. He glanced at his speedometer. Not once had they even come close to driving the speed limit. Once again, he thought about breaking away from the caravan; but for all he knew, there were restricted areas ahead. If that were the case, he'd have to ditch the rental and go the rest of the way in Gabby's truck.

Quiet me, he prayed. *Lord, I really need you to quiet me with your love.*

Four rings. A radio reporter announced breaking news. National Guard troops had been called in to protect against looters. Until further notice, islanders would not be allowed to return to their own neighborhoods, or homes. He fought desperation by reminding himself of the miracle of a phone that was ringing. To think that he'd almost given up trying to reach her was almost too much to take in.

Five rings, maybe more. "Grace." He thumped the steering wheel. "Answer. Oh please, God, let her answer."

And she did.

Grace panicked. How could she talk to Adam? At first she'd held the phone tight, starring at a screen illuminated with the name she loved more than any other name in the world. Maybe, if she squeezed the phone tight enough, she could make him go away. She pictured his face turning red with anxiety, his eyes overflowing with fear. And she knew that no matter how much it would hurt to hear his voice, Adam had a right to know his baby had made it through the hurricane.

Even before she put the phone to her ear, Adam's voice spilled out. "Grace, are you there? Can you hear me?"

"Yes." If only she'd been strong enough to force herself to let the call go to voice mail. "I'm in the safe room. Our baby is fine."

"What about you?"

The connection was perfect, without static or any of those clicks.

"When can I leave? I need to—"

"Listen to me. I want you out of there now."

"Now?"

"Don't bother to take anything with you."

"Just get out of there. Fisher's waiting on the beach. You have to—"

Then, before she could ask if he'd read Derrick's e-mail—before he said the words she longed to hear—the line went dead.

Her heart not only felt broken; it felt crushed, as if all that was left were the powdery ashes of a life that barely grew beyond a dream. One more time, she looked at sleeping Derrick. *Stay here.* She wrote. *I'll send help.* She placed the note close to him and pulled her blue beach bag from its hook, stuffing the sealed bag of letters inside.

And then she opened the door.

"Mommy's fine," Adam said when Sammy answered his mother's phone. "I talked to her and she's fine. Fisher's fixin' to pick her up in his boat."

"Hip-hip-hooray." It took no imagination to see Sammy's little feet leave the ground as she spun in festive circles, her hair bouncing like strands of golden curly ribbon. "Daddy, I knew Jesus would keep Mommy safe because Kate and me prayed really hard. Grandpa and Grandma prayed too. And Grandma cried. But I told her—"

He swiped his hand across his eyes. "You told her not to cry. That's my little Sammy. You might be the shrimp in our family but you have faith about the size of a—"

"I got faith the size of a great big whale. Daddy, that's what you always say."

He talked to his mother next, and then Kate. Neither of the girls asked about their bedrooms or any of their treasured belongings. His mother didn't wonder out loud about china or silver or any of her belongings that had been passed down from his grandparents. He knew why.

Grace and their baby had survived. Nothing else mattered.

And the only question everyone wanted answered was when they'd all be together.

"Soon," that's what he promised Kate and Sammy each time they asked. "As soon as I can pick up Mommy."

When his Dad came on the line, he tried to turn his attention to more practical matters. "Don't know how bad it is," he said. "But I figure we won't be able to live in the house for a while. I'll need several leads on decent rentals on the mainland."

"What are you worrying about?" His dad's question shook him. "We've lived through a miracle." Quiet emotion filled his dad's words. "Where you'll live, that's something we can work out when everyone's together."

Right there in the front seat of his rental car, a warm feeling covered Adam's heart like a homemade quilt. Grace was safe. Their baby was safe. They had survived what newscasters were already calling the most deadly hurricane to hit the barrier islands in over a hundred years. His dad was right. Where they lived didn't matter.

Half an hour after talking to his family, the caravan pulled off the interstate one last time before reaching what was already referred to as "the disaster zone."

He shouldn't have been shocked. The line of cars and trucks curved around the station, all the way to the frontage road. He pulled in line, the front end of his car almost touching Gabby's bumper. There was no point keeping his car running. All around him people stood or paced alongside their cars with phones pressed tight against their ears while others desperately punched the keys. In between attempts to reach loved ones, travelers kept their eyes the prize—a spot next to the gas pump where they could fill their cars and containers.

Once again he tried to reach Grace. When his call didn't go through, he joined the group who had gathered next to Gabby's truck. Gabby was on the phone. But that didn't stop him from blurting out the news. "Grace made it." He looked into the faces of each of the men who had become his friends. "She's safe."

Someone slapped his back. A couple guys yelled, "Praise God." Their voices so loud that heads turned. The college kids hooted and bumped into each other in some kind of crazy dance.

Gabby's eyes filled with tears. "Hear that?" A deep smile spread across his face as he spoke into his phone. "Honey, tell your friends to keep the prayers coming. Pray that Adam and his wife will be together by tonight."

As soon as Gabby finished his call, he wrapped his arm around Adam's shoulder. "God's just being God," he said.

"But, Gabby, can you believe it?"

"Believe?" Gabby leaned against his truck. "Never doubted. Not for a minute." He pulled a wrinkled hankie from his back pocket and swiped it across his face. "How long ago did you talk to her?"

"A few minutes, then the phone went dead and I haven't been able to reestablish a connection. Old fisherman from our church is bringing her to the mainland."

When the vehicles ahead of them inched forward they returned to their own cars and trucks. Just before he got in his car, Gabby called back to him. "Before we leave, give me Grace's number. Two folks trying to get a hold of her is better than one."

"Fixing to write it down," he said as he tore a page out of his planner.

Chapter 47

Grace sunk her toes into the warm sludge. If only she was wearing boots instead of flimsy flip-flops. The gunk squished like greasy worms between her toes and under her heels. Insulation hung from the ceiling, its warm and putrid waste dripping on her head and down her neck. With each drop, she cringed, grabbing on to whatever was there, pushing forward while doing her best to be vigilant each time she dropped her foot. But she wasn't careful enough, because something sharp slashed between her toes. It was too late to step back; too late to stop the sudden stinging pain that ripped her foot.

Keep moving, she warned herself as she raised her foot to pull some of the larger glass splinters from between her toes. She had no choice but to force her foot back into the salty muck. *You can't stop now.* The small glass slivers would have to wait until she was safe onboard Fisher's boat. Tears blinded her eyes, as the foul water soaked her wound.

Just like she imagined, the hurricane had deposited a giant palm tree in the center of the family room, tilting it like a ramp to nowhere against the upstairs banister. She dropped to her knees and crawled under the tree. The crawl seemed to take forever, and she felt smothered as her shoulders and head scraped against the ragged trunk.

When at last she could raise her head, she took a deep breath, allowing familiar gasps of salty sea air to fill her lungs.

Once outside, she limped around broken furniture and empty garbage cans that had blown onto the patio from unknown places. Their pool was gone…filled with garbage, dead fish, palm branches. Beth's hammock, torn and muddied, hung from the branches of a tree.

She didn't have time to mourn any of it. The time for mourning would come once she was away from the island.

No turning back.

She paused for a moment at the edge of their yard where she heard the slow and now gentle waves, and searched for a way to the beach. The path was gone. Trees lay on their sides, their root structures creating barricades as tall as a home. For a minute she thought it was hopeless; and she considered going back. Maybe Fisher had already come and gone. But then she saw them. One tiny purple flower. And another. An entire vine of Morning Glories wrapped around the trunk of a fallen tree, giving her courage to move on.

All she could do was weave her way through the maze of branches and fallen trees. Debris scraped her legs and arms, but she kept moving. As soon as she reached the beach she saw Fisher's boat, bobbing up and down and Fisher standing, waving his arms for her to come.

For the first time in two days, a feeling of safety settled in her stomach.

She kicked her flip flops off and swished them in the brown water before dumping them into her bag. As she pushed herself into the dirty sea, broken shells and debris sliced into her already battered feet. She forced herself deeper, until she was up to her waist in water and filth. "Watch where you step," Fisher yelled. "Take her slow. I ain't going nowhere without ya."

When at last she was close enough, Fisher wrapped his crooked hand around her arm and helped her into his boat.

Adam opened the box he'd placed on the seat next to him, and pulled out a chocolate covered donut. He'd planned to use their stop for gas as an opportunity to buy supplies; but the shelves were stripped. No batteries, no water, bread, or sandwich meat. Finding two bottles of apple juice and a box of stale donuts was a miracle.

That's what he needed to concentrate on, the miracles. Traffic was moving at a fixed pace—no accidents or road blocks. That was a miracle.

A sense of hope assured him that Grace was safe in Fisher's boat, heading toward the mainland. She was alive; and he was almost home.

Almost together with Grace.

Seeing her, touching her soft skin, taking her into his arms and holding her there as long as she wanted to stay, that would be the greatest miracle of all.

He did his best to keep each miracle in the front of his mind. But Grace's phone hadn't worked since he told her that Fisher was on his way. And neither had Fisher's. If only he knew for sure that she'd had enough time to make it to his boat, it would be easier to concentrate on the miracles.

He brushed the donut crumbs from his slacks, and opened a bottle of apple juice, taking a swill of the warm liquid. Grace had already been through the worse; that's what he had to remember. The hurricane had passed. Today was a new day, one with a cloudless sky and just enough breeze to wave the overgrown grasses along the interstate.

Still, with every mile he traveled, conditions worsened. Mangled billboards and road signs were the first evidences of Hurricane Chris. By the time Gabby and the others in the caravan pulled away, leaving him to continue the last few miles alone, light poles and trees lay in jumbled heaps alongside the road.

But nothing could have prepared him for the devastation once he crossed the river. From that point on, every speed limit and exit sign was gone. Motels, restaurants, landmarks that identified one exit from another, had been demolished or blown away.

The donut and juice turned in his stomach; and he wished he hadn't eaten. He opened his window, but the air was too hot and heavy. His attention was drawn to a leather sofa and refrigerator that had come to rest in a narrow canal that ran alongside the highway. Roofless and windowless homes lined its banks. Where had their belongings landed? In the middle of the Gulf? In the center of the road? He had to prepare himself for the worse, so he tried to visualize his home. For the first time in his life the sun looked out of place in Florida. The state he'd always called home no longer looked like paradise.

It looked like a war zone.

And Grace was trapped in that zone. Trusting him to find his way to her.

CHAPTER 48

Grace barely had time to take her place before Fisher jerked his boat forward, maneuvering it away from Tesoro's coast. She didn't want to look back, but her heart insisted. No matter how much it hurt, she had to take one last look at everything that was.

From the safety of Fisher's boat, she had a full view. Everywhere she set her eyes it looked like scenes from one of those old gray science fiction movies her dad and brother used to watch, one with armies of sea monsters escaping from the depths of the sea, tromping and destroying everything in their path. Hurricane shutters swung from balconies like twisted tinfoil accordions. Rubble surrounded roofless homes. There was nothing to go back for.

"Your phone still work?" Fisher reached his phone toward her. "Use mine if you want to call Adam and let him know I got you."

"Mine's okay. She unlocked the double plastic bag she'd placed hers into. "Thank you, though.

She was still battling the urge to call Adam, just to let him know she'd made it off the island when Fisher pointed to a box sitting close to her feet. "Tweezers and antibiotics, bandages, and other stuff in there. Better take care of your foot."

She did as Fisher suggested, barely feeling the pain. *No turning back,* she reminded herself. *I'm doing what's best for everyone.*

For the next few minutes, except for the motor-buzz and sluggish smack of Fisher's boat as it slammed the waves, she and Fisher sat in silence.

How could she do this to Adam?

Her phone broke the silence.

"Ya going to answer it?"

She looked away. "Not now." Even with the motor humming along at slow speed, they had to shout to be heard.

She could not answer all the questions Adam must have for her, not now in front of Fisher, especially since she had to scream to be heard.

Besides, even if Adam was calling to say he'd pick her up, she wouldn't be waiting for him. It wasn't possible, any more than it was possible for her to be there while Adam rebuilt the house or when he explained to Kate and Sammy that she was never coming home.

Saddest of all, Adam wouldn't be with her when their baby was born.

Just feet from the mainland, Fisher slowed the boat. "Listen to me." He leaned toward her. "Don't know why you didn't answer that phone. Something's going on and all I got to say, if God's got anything to do with it, you'll be calling Adam pronto."

She didn't reply. Fisher couldn't understand. No one could. Instead she told him about Derrick's leg and that she didn't know why—especially since from the beginning he'd been up to no good, shining his flashlight into her window and going after her like a sick stalker—but after his leg broke she dragged him into the safe room. "He's still there," she said, "needing you, or someone to go back for him."

"I don't know anything about Derrick being no stalker," Fisher yelled over his shoulder. "You know, don't ya, I came by with a flashlight most nights you were alone." Fisher's voice was matter-of-fact. "Could be me that you saw."

"Fisher, you didn't..." She'd always thought of Fisher as being harmless. Quirky, yes, with his goats, and peacocks, and unkempt appearance. But he went to her church. He was in her Bible study group. He wasn't the kind of person who went around shinning lights into people's windows.

"Are you friends with Derrick?" She laid her hands flat across her lap. Her nails were filthy and broken. A band of white still marked where her ring had been.

"Didn't say he was my friend. Just keeping my eye on him and getting to know him some. Like I said, don't know nothing about no stalker." Fisher dropped a wad of tobacco into his mouth. "Did the same for Beth when Adam was out of town. Walked by at night, making sure everything was okay. Didn't tell no one, just did what neighbors do."

The words were barely out of his mouth when she remembered the first time Adam left. It was the day after they returned from their honeymoon. All of a sudden, the picture was fresh in her mind. Fisher walking with a sack of groceries. Adam stopping. Talking to him for less than a minute before he left for Minnesota.

If Fisher was telling the truth, then there never was a light stalker, only Fisher taking care of his neighbor. But that was only part of the truth. The good part. The rest of the truth stood in front of her like a wall of regret.

There never was a reason to hire Derrick. Never, not even for a second.

"Fisher." She leaned toward him. "You're a good friend. Thank you. But how did you know when Adam was gone?"

"Didn't always know, but it's a small island. News travels faster than them lizards." Fisher spewed his slug of tobacco-spit into the water. "Dock's gone. Going to have to wade in." He put his old fishing hat on the seat behind him. "You're choice, but I think you should give Adam a call once you make it to shore." He maneuvered his boat around the debris that littered the now shallow water.

Choice, the word caverned into her heart. If only she had known how one choice—the choice to let herself fall in love with a man she should have run from—had the power to change her life forever. There was a time she believed what Pastor Karl said about God forgiving her, but then Derrick came back into her life, and with him all the guilt and shame.

She still believed in God's forgiveness. But, as hard as she tried, she could not forgive herself. She was just too broken.

She sat with the phone in her lap. How much did Fisher know? There wasn't time to make him understand. Besides, how could he?

"I'm not sure if I can reach him."

"Phones are working, off and on."

"I'll try a little later."

For a moment Fisher was silent, and so was she. And then, just before he anchored the boat he said, "I want you to wait on the beach for Adam. You know, God wants you to wait."

How could he know what God wanted for her life? She barely knew. Still his words hung in her heart.

God wants you to wait.

Fisher lowered himself into waist deep water and held out his hand. "Can't stay and baby sit you." He looked back toward Tesoro. Then he took her bag and rested it on his shoulder while she lowered herself over the side of his boat.

She cringed as her legs disappeared into water filled with tobacco spit and grunge. If Fisher hadn't been there, pulling her forward through the muck, she would have jumped back into the boat.

"Tell Adam I'll be making runs all day." He set her bag on the beach. "That should do ya. If he wants to check on the house, have him meet me here. I can give him a lift. Only way he'll get to the island for days." Fisher waded back into the water.

She stood on the edge of the beach, secretly hoping her rescuer would stay just a little longer.

Turn back. Don't leave. She stopped the words before they could find their way to her tongue. *Tell me again why I should wait for Adam.*

"Fisher." She waved, calling his name until he turned around. "Don't forget Derrick." She waded into the water, up to her ankles. "I left something important on your boat." She cupped her hands around her mouth. "A plastic bag." Somehow she managed a grateful smile. "Give it to Adam, please. Thank you, Fisher. Thank you for everything."

For a moment she thought he might come back. But he didn't. He mashed a fresh slug of tobacco between his teeth. "Don't you leave. I got you this far, now you pray old Fisher's prayer," he said. "Hear me?"

"I will," she said as Fisher spun his boat back toward the island.

Chapter 49

Grace stood on the beach alone. Once Fisher was out of sight, she let her tears run. There was no reason not to. She turned toward the parking lot. Almost every foot of its surface had been taken over by fallen trees and sea-whipped boards from the old pier. She played Fisher's off-handed warning over in her mind. "Them hotel vans swing by every few hours," he'd said, "but don't go taking one because Adam's coming after you."

"Oh, Lord." She sat on the damp trunk of a fallen tree. Her eyes were weak from so many tears, her entire body exhausted with grief. "Lord, I'm done fighting. If you send the van before you send Adam, I'll take the van. But if Adam comes first, I'll know it's your will that I go with him, not forever—just until I can arrange a flight home."

The promise was barely off her lips, when her phone rang. She reached into her bag. Without thinking, she held the phone against her ear.

"Grace?"

Her heart leapt. Her cheeks and eyes burned from her salty tears. Reason told her to hang up.

Love told her to hang on to every word.

"You're safe. Thank Jesus, you're safe."

Her finger hovered trembling over the disconnect button, ready to push it without saying a word. But this might be the last time she'd hear his voice. Adam had a right to know his baby was safe on the mainland.

"Adam." She closed her eyes, waiting to hear her name just once more. No one ever spoke her name the way Adam did.

She was certain no one ever would.

Words stood on her tongue, words that would ruin her plan. *Adam, hurry.* She could almost see the sparks. *I can't live without you; I can't live without the girls. Not for another minute.*

"Grace, talk to me. Are you okay?"

"Yes. Where are you?"

"Just turning onto Beach Parkway. I'm almost there."

"Adam, please, you don't have to come. It's okay. Just let me go."

"Let you go? Where?"

She closed her eyes and forced herself to concentrate. *Remember,* the words drummed. *Adam and the girls deserve better...better than you.*

Could it be that Adam didn't yet know the truth? If Adam had read Derrick's e-mail, he'd beg her to leave. It didn't matter. Soon he'd know everything. And then he'd not only understand.

He'd be grateful she made it so easy for him.

"I'm coming for you, Grace." Over and over, he kept telling her about his plan to pick her up. "I've booked a room at the Airport Inn. In the morning I'll go with Fisher to check the house; and then we'll drive up to the girls. They can't wait to see you."

Adam had everything perfectly planned. But plans didn't always work; Adam knew that. He'd planned to grow old with Beth. She died. He planned to never fall in love again. He did. And he planned to enjoy the type of marriage and family that only someone better could give him.

"Just crossed Coconut Lane. "I won't be long. Did I tell you that we have a room at the Airport Inn?"

The words were barely out of his mouth when a van pulled into the parking lot, its four-way flashers blinking as it moved cautiously toward her. There was only one thing this could mean. God had answered her prayer. He'd made the van show up at this very moment. It was his way of telling her she was doing the right thing. As the van approached, she waved.

"Adam, I'm sorry." It was all she had time to say.

CHAPTER 50

Grace strained to make out the lettering on the side of the mud-caked van. She didn't care about a fancy motel; all she needed was a clean place to fall asleep.

She assured herself that once she was safe inside the van the pull toward Adam would lessen and she'd be on the way to her new life. But when the van came close enough to read the lettering, she dropped her bag to the ground. *Airport Inn.* It couldn't be. When the driver opened his door she took a step back. "I'll wait."

"Nothing to wait for." The driver walked around the front of the van. "Every hotel's filled up. Last pick-up, far as I know." He opened the door and stood back. "You're Mrs. Will?"

In that instant she knew the truth. Even before he called her, Adam had phoned the hotel to make back-up arrangements in case he couldn't get to her. Once again, Adam had taken care of every detail. One way or the other, whether in a hotel room or his car, she would have to face him. Adam would show up before the day was over; she was sure of that. What she wasn't sure of was whether she would be strong enough. She could almost see him standing before her, so close and so disgusted with the person he had married.

For now she had no choice. She climbed into the van, taking her place in the front passenger seat. Behind her a lady cooed over a tiny white dog as if it were her baby.

Grace looked straight ahead. Would she end up like that, with no one to care for but a dog? No, she'd have her child. A child she would love. One who would love her back, just the way Kate and Sammy had.

As the van struggled to make its way toward the hotel, she couldn't believe what had become of the city. People, dressed in as little as decency allowed, sat in lawn chairs in front of homes that looked as if they should be condemned, too exhausted and shocked to move anything more than a paper fan over their sweaty bodies. On the corners armed military directed traffic. Stores were already boarded up; streets blocked by piles of debris; traffic lights and trees down; almost everything destroyed.

After an hour of maneuvering through back streets, the driver pulled the van in front of the Airport Inn. "Safe and sound," he said as he held out his hand to the lady with the dog. "Just go to the front desk. They'll take care of everything."

Once again, she wanted to run. But she had nowhere to go. She was hot and thirsty. She needed a shower.

"May I help you?" The lady behind the desk broke into her thoughts.

"Yes." She pulled her purse from the bag. "Reservation for Will."

"Have your key right here." With a sympathetic smile, the lady slid a plastic card toward her. "Already taken care of."

Grace didn't have the strength to argue. Whatever the cost, she'd repay Adam once she made it to Minnesota. "Is your gift shop open? I didn't pack anything and—"

"It's closed, but I can take you in there. Pick out what you need and I'll put it on the card."

She went through the shop quickly, grabbing only necessities—toothpaste, bandages and antibiotic wipes for her foot, a pink Florida tank top, like the ones tourists wear, and a pair of white cotton slacks. When she was done signing for her purchase, she walked down the hall to her room. Within an hour, she was able to reach the airline.

In two days, first flight out, she'd be going home to Minnesota.

It was precisely what she had planned. It was the best—no, the only—thing to do. Once the reservation was made, she had nothing to distract her. She'd lived through Hurricane Chris and she had no desire to see footage of it played and replayed on every television network. She parted the drapes; gazing out at what little was left of the parking lot. Downed trees, twisted pool chairs, even an up-side-down boat and smashed trailer, littered the lot, leaving little room for cars.

If only she knew what kind of car Adam was driving. He could pull up any minute. How would she handle seeing him? She'd been so confident leaving would be easier than this.

Using toiletries the motel provided, she showered and washed her hair. For the first time since she left the island, her mind was clear enough to feel the pulsing pain of her slashed and tattered feet. By the time she pulled back the bedspread and slipped between the sheets, she could barely keep her eyes open. The sheets felt cool and smelled fresh. It seemed like forever since she'd smelled something so wonderful, forever since she'd slept.

For a moment her mind drifted back to all that had happened; and she knew her escape from Tesoro was nothing short of a miracle. "Oh, Lord." Her eyes were open, fixed on the rotation of the ceiling fan. "I really messed things up, thinking old Fisher was some kind of stalker, ending up with Derrick under my feet, keeping my past a secret from Adam. Forgive me. Help Adam and the girls know how much I love them. Give Adam a better wife and the girls a better mommy, one that will love them more than I ever could."

On the slight chance Grace might still be where Fisher had left her, Adam drove to the beach, but like Grace had warned, she wasn't anywhere in sight. All he could do was pray that the van had picked her up.

Something inside urged him to stay, so he parked the car and walked toward the shoreline, calling her name. There was no response.

He stood close to the water, allowing the mucky waves to lap at his feet as he stared across the bay to a patch of green that was home. The lighthouse still stood, and for him, it was a sign of hope.

Almost the only sign.

Something was wrong with Grace, something even worse than facing a hurricane.

His mind couldn't stay on course. The hurricane might be over, but he had an unexplainable feeling worse was nipping at his heels. It was more significant than the attorney appointment or that momentary hesitation he'd had about coming home for Sammy's birthday. It had nothing to do with what might have happened to his house or property. All that could be replaced.

But he could never replace Grace.

Why, Lord, why do I have this feeling? The prayer raced through his heart. *You have to know because you know everything. Show me, God. Show me what's going on with my wife.*

When his prayer was done and he was ready to leave, he spotted Fisher anchoring his boat a few feet from shore. He waded toward him, waving his arms to get Fisher's attention.

"Not trying to tell you what to do," Fisher said as he made it onto the beach. "But if she's not here, you better be going after her. Something's not right."

"I'm fixing to," he said. "Pick me up here in the morning?"

"Be here around nine." Just before Fisher turned to leave, he placed a sealed plastic bag in his hand. "Wish I could have talked some sense into your wife," he said.

Adam didn't ask any questions. Somehow he knew the answer was in the plastic bag old Fisher had given him. Even though all it contained was a packet of envelopes, it felt heavy, as if it contained every piece of his future.

One more thing he knew, he had to open the bag before he went to Grace. His stomach still felt sick. If only he could go back, he'd change so many things. He sat in the car and pulled the envelopes out of the bag.

There were seven. He returned the girls' letters to the bag. They each had two, one from Beth and one from Grace. He should have given them Beth's letters long ago, but every time he was fixing to turn them over, he told himself they were still too young. He was more confused than before. Why would Grace write letters to the girls? It didn't make sense, not when she was a day or two away from seeing them.

For the first time since burying the letters and Bible in the hat box, Beth's letter was in his hands. He wanted to open it, but he would have to wait. Stress and fear, hope and hopelessness, the silence and darkness had taken its toll. Now was not the time for Beth's words. Besides, he already had a good idea what she'd written.

The same words she'd spoken shortly before her death.

He placed her letter back in the plastic bag along with the girls', promising himself that he'd read it as soon as life calmed down. Then, once again, he closed his eyes.

There was only one letter left, written in Grace's script, tiny and almost perfect. He opened the envelope and reached inside where his fingers wrapped around a ring.

Grace's ring.

Why would she do this?

He found his answer in the words of her letter.

Derrick's child. His stomach wrenched. She'd given birth to Derick's child. He thought he was too tired for emotions. He was wrong. He thought the struggle to make it home was the most agony he had to go through, but that struggle didn't even come close.

Grace was leaving. Why hadn't she been able to trust him? He hated the truth, hated it with a passion that tore him to shreds, but didn't she trust his love for her? God had forgiven her. He would too.

How could a man turn his back on his own child? How could he force someone he loves to get rid of her baby? A man, a real man, couldn't.

Was this why Grace loved Kate and Sammy the way she did? Were they simply substitutes for the child she gave away? He had to stop the questions that flooded his mind. If he didn't, there wouldn't be any room for forgiveness.

Or love.

"Quiet me, Lord," he prayed. "Just quiet my mind with your love."

He wished he didn't have to drive. Even after his prayer, he felt as if his hurricane was just beginning as he maneuvered toward the Airport Inn. Grace had been rescued. He was grateful for that. But now his marriage and his family needed rescuing. Somehow she had to see the truth. They would work this out. Her past didn't matter. It didn't change his love for her. He did his best to hang on, but the hurricane inside him raged, crushing every dream for his future.

A future he couldn't live without Grace.

The closer he got to Grace, the more he thought about Beth's letter. If only he'd read it before he tried to build his new life with Grace, maybe then he would have been a better husband, one who did not spend so much time living in the past. If he hadn't held part of himself back, it would have been easier for Grace to tell him the truth before Derrick ever walked into their lives.

He pulled into the hotel parking lot. All he could do now was pray it wasn't too late to rescue his marriage.

Chapter 51

Even though Grace knew she'd have to face Adam at least one more time, his tender presence overwhelmed her. She remained still, with all but her face buried under the covers.

Despite her decision to leave, she still longed for him. But more than that, she loved him. She also loved Kate and Sammy. The days she'd been accepted as their mommy would forever be the most treasured moments of her life. If only she hadn't been so stupid, she could have made the days last forever. But love was why she had to let Kate and Sammy go. They deserved someone better—someone more like Beth.

So did Adam.

He stood alongside the bed, touching her shoulder, asking her to wake up. She could smell his minty gum and hear the sadness in his voice. By now Adam knew all her ugliness. He knew she'd done something that would forever mark her as unworthy of the love he and his daughters had given her.

"Please talk to me." Gently, he placed his hand on her back. "Grace, I need you to talk to me."

She sat on the edge of the bed. "Don't turn on the light," she said. "I don't want you to look at me."

Adam did as she asked. When he sat next to her, it was all she could do not to drop her head on his shoulder. In the dim evening light, she could see that his slacks were wrinkled, and she wondered if he'd slept in them all night. His shoes were caked in sludge. "Did you get Derrick's e-mail? Adam, I promise I never had the abortion. He wanted me to, but I couldn't. I just couldn't, and I never told him because he didn't deserve to know his child is alive."

"I could care less about Derrick's e-mail, but I read your letter," he said as he squeezed her hands between his. "Now, I'm fixing to pound some sense into your pretty head."

"Nothing can change what I did. Not even you."

"All I care to change is your mind."

"Please don't." She pulled her hands free. "I've already decided; I'm going home. It's best for everyone."

When Adam placed a hand on each of her shoulders, she could almost feel her will melting. He turned her to face him. "Please, Grace."

It would be so easy to give in.

And so selfish.

This was no different than when her parents and brother died. She remembered sitting in her pastor's office, sobbing, telling him how she couldn't imagine life without her mom and dad, without her brother Grady. She longed for them. Who was going to walk her down the aisle on her wedding day? Who was going to teach her the secrets of caring for a baby? No one could make her laugh the way Grady had. She longed for them. And she was sure she'd give anything to get them back.

Pastor had tried to comfort her with Scripture, but grief pushed comfort away. Just before he prayed, her pastor came out from behind his desk, sat in the chair next to hers, scooting it closer until he could place his hand on her shoulder. "My dear," he said, "you are so young, and I understand how much you miss your family. But tell me this, believing what you believe about heaven, would you really want them to come back here?"

Longing screamed, "Yes."

Love whispered, "No."

Just like now.

"I don't think I can do this." Why couldn't he see he deserved so much more? "Please, Adam. You've got to know I'm the wrong person for you."

"Why didn't you read your letter, Grace?" Adam pulled Beth's envelope from the plastic bag she'd given to Fisher. "It's addressed to you." When she refused to take hold of it he placed it in her lap.

She wanted to swat it away. "It's not for me."

"It is." Adam wouldn't give up until she took the envelope in her hand.

The letter felt out of place in her grasp, like a piece of stolen candy. What could Beth possibly say to someone like her?

"Read it," he said. "You owe us that much."

"I can't be so close to you, Adam, not when…" Adam was right, she did owe him this, so she moved to a chair in the corner of the room and switched on the lamp. As gently as she could, she opened the envelope addressed to *Adam's New Wife and the Girls' New Mommy.*

"Before you read Beth's letter, you have to know one thing."

"I know, Adam. I know how much I've hurt you, how much I've hurt the girls. You don't need to tell me."

"I do," he said. "Before you read Beth's letter, you need to hear the truth." When he took the letter she'd written from his pocket, she wondered if he was going to read every word and try to make her explain everything she'd done. Even from across the room, Adam could see right through her. She felt low and filthy. Whatever Adam had to say, whatever words Beth's letter contained, couldn't change a thing.

"Your past does not define you." Adam leaned forward, waving the letter she'd written as he spoke.

"Then what does?"

"Jesus. Jesus Christ defines you." He tore her letter into pieces. "He defines you as a new creation." Adam tossed the scraps into the trash can. "Now read the letter that truly matters."

At first she couldn't look at Beth's letter. It was all she could do to hold it in her hand. *I don't even know your name, but for some crazy reason, I feel as if I know you.* The first few words were almost too much to believe. *Perhaps you are a friend. Maybe we know each other from our church or club.*

"Adam, have you read this?" She looked across the room to where Adam sat on the edge of the bed, his hands folded, his head bowed as if he was praying.

"No." When he looked at her, she saw sadness in his eyes like she'd never seen before, not even when he talked about Beth. "It's your letter, Grace, not mine." Again, he folded his hands.

She had no other choice but to continue. *When I learned about my cancer and that it was triple negative, I was so frightened. Not of the surgery or treatments. I would have done anything to survive for my family. Then when the doctors told me that things had gone too far and, except for a miracle, I was not going to survive, an unexplainable peace actually washed over me.*

I am not afraid to die. I am ready for heaven. Ready to meet my Jesus, face to face. So ready to fall into his arms.

Grace reached for the box of tissues. "This is what I mean, Adam. She was so much more than I could ever hope to be. You've got to see that."

Adam shook his head. "I don't," he said, "and neither does God."

This time she didn't argue. *The agony for me was the realization that I soon will leave Adam and the girls. At first, I didn't want anyone else to be Adam's wife. I didn't want anyone else to be my daughters' mommy. That was my job and I was certain no one could love them the way I do.*

"I can't do this, Adam." She placed the letter in her lap.

Adam walked toward her. "May I?" He took the papers from her and sat on the floor facing her.

"Then I read the book of Job." His voice cracked as he read. "Amazing what comfort that book gives me!"

When Adam placed his hand on her knee, she didn't pull away. "The next words are written with red ink," he said without looking up. "I know that my Redeemer lives, and that in the end he will stand upon the earth." Adam's words were garbled with tears. He cleared his throat. "I will see God; I myself will see him with my own eyes."

She handed Adam the box of tissues. "Adam, you shouldn't have to—"

"I want to. Grace, listen to this." He got on his knees beside her and held the letter so they both could see. "I now know one thing for certain. God never takes away unless He replaces with better."

A deep sob, one that sounded as if it had escaped from the deepest place in Adam's soul, filled the room. She could feel herself breaking. When Adam read the words a second time she felt every bit of resolve crumble. "God never takes away unless He replaces it with better."

Adam cleared his throat as he laid the letter aside. "Oh, Grace, I'm so sorry. In the beginning, I didn't treat you like I should have."

For the first time that day, she did something she thought she'd never do again. She looked into Adam's eyes. "I'm sorry. You deserved my trust."

"For too long I was afraid, Grace. Afraid of moving out of the past, the way Beth wanted me to. If only I could go back and make it right for you."

"We can't go back, can we? No matter how much we long to." As she spoke, hope began to rise. She wondered if it was possible Adam believed what Beth had written. If he believed, could she?

Adam's eyes returned to Beth's letter. "This is the promise that has given me the most comfort," Adam breathed deep. "If God takes me to heaven, he will give Adam a better wife. He will give Kate and Sammy a better mommy."

She brushed her hand along the side of Adam's whiskery face, allowing his tears to soak into her skin like the sweetest perfume. "Adam, don't; it's too difficult."

The letter quivered in his hands. "I'm fixing to finish."

"Let me." Adam didn't try to hold on when she took the paper from his hands. "Just give me a minute." She took a long and deep breath. "If you are reading this, you are the better wife and the better Mommy."

Adam's eyes were still on the letter. Now that her secret was out, could he possibly believe what it said? Could she?

Adam took the paper from her hands and continued reading. "I thank you for loving Adam and the girls. Never question yourself."

They were both weeping now. She didn't pull away when Adam took her hand in his. "God has chosen you to love my family," together they read the last few words. "He has chosen you to teach them, love them, and hold them in your arms."

When they had no tears left, Adam stood and gently pulled her to her feet. "I should have told you," she said "but I felt so guilty, so certain you wouldn't want me if you knew I had given away my own child." They moved to the bed and sat close, holding hands. She still couldn't allow herself to rest her head on his shoulder, even after she saw that he hadn't removed his wedding ring.

"Did you ask God to forgive you—not for giving up your baby for adoption because you've got to know that was an act of love—but for stepping outside of his will with Derrick?"

She couldn't look at him. "Yes."

"Did he forgive you?"

"Of course."

"Grace." He cupped her chin and turned her face to his. "Then, how dare you refuse to forgive yourself."

His question cut deep into all the broken pieces of her heart. "Adam, I just need some time alone."

"You're not still fixing to leave?"

"I don't know. Adam, do you understand? I almost aborted my baby. When I was too chicken to go through with doing that, I gave her away." Even when she felt her nails dig into her palms, she didn't release her clench. "How can you trust me?" She searched his eyes, looking for disgust or pity, anything that would tell her his love had changed.

But all she saw was what had been there before.

"I just need to talk to God. Alone," she said.

After Adam left, she fell to her knees alongside the bed. She had no idea what she would say. The only words going through her mind were the words to Fisher's prayer. "Oh, God, help."

Outside the room, children ran down the hall, pushing each other against the walls, laughing and shouting. For a minute she was distracted, but then it was if a gentle presence drew her back urging her to proclaim, "Lord, forgive me for all the lies and not trusting your love, not trusting Adam's. I was wrong." She held her clenched hands in front of her. "Oh, God, help."

And God did.

Slowly, her fists relaxed until her hands rested palms up on the bed. "I forgive myself for every single thing you have already forgiven. I forgive Derrick." Without thinking, she raised her hands. "I release all my broken pieces, even my first child, to you."

When she was done, she stayed on her knees. Quiet.

Allowing God to have His way in her heart.

When Adam returned he carried a bag. “Burgers, it was all I could find,” he said. “Some restaurant down the road is grilling them out in their parking lot and giving them away. They said with no freezer, they might as well bless the community.”

She took the burger bag from him and set it on the night stand. “Adam, I never stopped loving you.” Her voice trembled as she stood facing her husband. “Are you sure you still want me?”

Without speaking, he drew her close. They stood in each other’s arms, face to face, their foreheads touching. Then, before he released her, Adam whispered two words. “Forever. Together.”

“I’ve made arrangements with Fisher,” Adam said when they got out of bed the next morning. “He’s taking me out to the house today. Do you feel up to making the trip?”

“I don’t think I want to go back this soon,” she said. “Besides, I want to call the girls.” She imagined the girls’ sweet faces. Serious Kate with her beautiful long hair, and Sammy with her dancing eyes. She couldn’t believe how close she’d come to walking away from them.

With Adam and Fisher on the island checking out the damage done to their home, the afternoon seemed to crawl. She thought about the days ahead, where they would live and where the girls would go to school. If only she could make the transitions easier for them. She knew there had to be a way.

When Adam returned from Tesoro, they began planning for the uncertain days ahead. As they tossed around their ideas, an idea crept into her mind, one she doubted Adam would agree to.

“Minnesota, Adam.” The words were out before she could stop them. “While we rebuild the Tesoro house, why don’t we move to Minnesota?”

“I don’t know.”

“My house, it’s empty. The girls have to change schools anyway. They can attend up there. Sammy’s always wanted to see snow and Kate loves the backyard apple trees.”

“You’d like to move back?”

"So much of your work is there. It will be good for us to be together more."

"It won't work, Grace." She was so distracted with trying to think of a way to make him see things her way that she didn't notice when Adam reached into his pocket. "Not until I do this." He took her hand in his and slipped her ring back on her finger.

Where it belonged.

Printed in the United States
By Bookmasters